THE MIDDLE DAUGHTER

Also by Chika Unigwe:

THE MIDDLE DAUGHTER

DAUGHTER

— A NOVEL —

CHIKA UNIGWE

DZANC
BOOKS

DZANC BOOKS

2580 Craig Rd.
Ann Arbor, MI 48103
www.dzancbooks.org

Library of Congress Cataloging-in-Publication Data Available Upon Request

ISBN: 9781950539468
First US edition: April 2023
Cover by Matthew Revert
Typeset in Bembo MT Pro by Palimpsest Book Production Ltd
Used with permission from Canongate Books Ltd.

Printed in the United States of America

10   9   8   7   6   5   4   3   2   1

For my goddaughters:
Maaika Okeke, Cindy Okeke,
Zite Unigwe, Gabriella Gideon-Nwogu,
Inne Vandenhoudt and 'Baby' Owolabi.

May this world never stifle your dreams.

'Earth opened to me down to deepest dark,
And floating through its underwater channels
I raised my head as if to turn my eyes
Toward stars almost forgotten to my sight . . .'

— from Book V, Ovid's *The Metamorphoses*,
translated by Horace Gregory

PART ONE

The Present, 2014

Udodi, the Chorus

When Komosu, the beloved,
Wife of the great god Chukwu
Went into his ime obi and opened that door they say
    she shouldn't have
Komosu was struck dead by light –

Oke odachi dalu, uwa welu waa
And the world came into being
Chukwu cried to lose his heart, his right hand, his breath

Idemili the divine, the strong, daughter of Chukwu and
    Komosu,
Worthy offspring of gods,
Consoled with the bag
Chukwu slung around her neck to heal the world
Of the ills that escaped from akpa afi
Hidden in that room that should have stayed closed

And so the world came
And so evil came
And so beauty came

And so life is . . .

3

Nani

I fear the man who is my husband.

The mattress heaves every time I turn, unable to sleep. The darkness outside is absolute, as if someone has upended a bottle of ink. A blackness that swallows up light. The room is cool and quiet. Sleep should come easy, swift in its suddenness, but I am fiddling with my phone, knowing that even though my mother can help me now, I will not call her. Too much has happened. If only I could call Doda. When I think of Doda, my father, this is the memory that comes to the fore: Doda sitting at the edge of his bed, my two sisters and me huddled joyfully together in it, his voice washing over us as he tells us a folktale. He smells of Lux soap and Marlboros. In this memory I am nearly eight. Ugo is six. Udodi is twelve. It is the first day of the long vacation and we are already predictably bored. Our mother is somewhere in the house but it is Doda that we seek out. It was always Doda. It was with him that I felt the safest. Even now, when he's no longer here, I will not go to Mother.

I also remember Uncle Ade, Doda's friend, visiting. It is the Friday that Udodi won her school's spelling bee competition and Mother's voice is girlish and happy as she announces this to the guest. 'My daughter is the smartest girl in her school! She's going to be a lawyer!'

'Too much book is not good for girls ooo,' Uncle Ade says with a little laugh.

'There's nothing like too much book,' Doda says. 'My children will have as much education as there is to be had!'

'You want your daughters to school themselves out of marriage? Who too much book help?' Uncle Ade asks, his voice moist with the laughter that is already spilling out.

'Marriage isn't more important than education,' Doda says, and Uncle Ade bursts into full, raucous laughter now.

'Let me hear you say that again when your three girls are old maids!'

'God forbid,' Mother says. 'My girls will marry and marry well!'

'It wouldn't matter to me if they never did. Their Aunty Enuka's perfectly happy without a husband,' Doda says to Mother, pinching my cheek playfully. I am ten years old. Too young to be thinking about marriage. Old enough for the conversation to make me uncomfortable. But I knew then as I know now that Doda meant it. If he were alive, Ephraim would never have happened.

I did not like Uncle Ade. Mother used to say that he carried himself with the smugness of a man with many sons.

'Why?' Udodi asked once. 'What's the big deal about sons?'

'There are people still . . .' Mother said, and paused to remind Aunty, our maid, to freeze some of the guavas she had plucked from the back yard that afternoon. 'There

6

are people who think sons are more important than daughters. Thank God your Doda isn't like that. Not the sort to kick his wife out for giving him only girls!'

Three girls. Udodi was the beginning, I was the middle, Ugo the conclusion. 'You are my short story,' Doda said all the time. The perfect short story. But perfection never lasts, a sleight of hand and everything splinters, your whole life is upended. And then one day you are in someone else's house wondering whether you will ever see your own three children again. My heart's tightness chokes out the rest of my thoughts.

The Past

Udodi, the Chorus

K'anyi tinyelu isi n'Uke n'Uga, anyi na-ayo ka isi kaa ahu.

As we enter this world we beg of the gods: may our heads achieve maturity.

Imagine this: three girls. A father. A mother. The house smells of loving. And living.

Smells of good-timing and a knowing that life is sweet. Until it doesn't. A collision of two worlds. Below, a distant thunder that throws up an explosion. That begins to rock the world above. Torpedoing the house. The three girls. The father. The mother. Starting with this: at school in America. Homesickness is malaria coating my tongue. Gritty dryness in my eyes. Bitterness on my tongue has been there since my finals began and the countdown to the holidays and therefore to Enugu started. Homesickness is crossing out the days on a calendar until the reunion: Father, Mother, three sisters together at last.

'But first *Friends*, yeah?' Bethany, roommate, asks.

'Yeah!' Back to the sylphlike Bethany, witness to my American life. Nights stretched by Vivarin to fit in studies. Who knew one pill could pack so much caffeine?

The universe aligned itself to my favour. The final

episode of *Friends* (Fuck! Yeah!) on NBC hours after my final paper, a party on Sunday, a Zambian student whose parties are legendary, a few days cavorting around Atlanta without the burden of exams and school. Glorious shopping for my sisters, fulfilling wishes of a pair of shoes, a tank top at a time. No one returns empty-handed. And that long flight to Lagos, and then home to Number 47 where I staked my claim the day we moved in, not even ten yet, held my two sisters by the hand and apparently announced, 'My house!'

Imagine this: lying in the back yard of Number 47, stretched out on blankets, looking ragingly magnificent like the wealthy on vacation. Once, I showed Bethany photos of Ugo and Nani leaning on the gate. Doda and Mother lounging at home, the chandelier above them, delicate, like pearls hanging.

'This is Africa?' Bethany asked. 'Are your folks like, what, royalty? Your house is like fuck! A fucking mansion!' Bethany, from Dallas, Georgia.

'America so big, city names are replicated?' I asked.

'America so lacking in imagination?' I asked.

'Fuck off, Yudo' – Bethany, who never gets my name right.

'It's *OOHDOUGH*, Bethany, not *Yudo!*'

'You should call her *Batanie*,' Nani to me when I complained. Mispronounce her name too!

Nani, who doodled all over a classmate's exercise book. Elementary 5. Her best friend, Mbanugo, said her room, of which she was proud, was the size of his closet. The next day at school Nani smuggled out Mbanugo's maths exercise book, hid in the bathroom and went to work: circles and mad swirls where neatness had reigned, chaos

12

where once peace had been, and got him in trouble with Mrs Ifeacho, the teacher. Nani told me. She told me everything. I knew her better than everyone else who thought her Nani the Quiet. Nani the Patron Saint of the Amenable. Nani to be covered in cotton wool and kept safe. Doda and Mother did not know when Nani ran away from home to punish them for missing her dance recital. She was eleven and deeply hurt. She got as far as the front gate and turned back, binning the soggy sandwiches she had made.

'I didn't know where to run to, Udo!' Of course she did not. Three girls raised in a city but not street smart. Nani, hard at the edges, hardness so well concealed in the soft folds of her body she forgot sometimes that it belonged to her. Ife anyi na-ayo bu ka isi kaa ahu . . .

Nani

On a Sunday morning, a week before Udodi was expected, the phone rang at three a.m. Nobody called before dawn unless it was bad news. If it was happy news, they would wait for a respectable time before calling. People, it seemed, could keep a lid on good news but sad news bubbled impatiently and demanded immediate release. Udodi, six hours behind in Atlanta, knew to time her calls well. She would call in the middle of the day, or in the evening when everyone was home. So when the phone rang, drilling its way into my dream, I knew it was bad news. The insistent ringing woke up the whole house and somehow all four of us – Ugo, Doda, Mother and I – left our beds and made for the sitting room where the phone was, opening and shutting our doors almost in sync as if we had rehearsed it, rubbing our eyes into various stages of wakefulness. We all must have reached the phone at the same time but it was Mother whose hand reached out and picked it up. I muttered a prayer under my breath, warding off whatever bad news was trying to find its way into the house.

'Hello? Hello?' Mother sounded agitated, as if ready to quarrel with whomever was calling. 'Who's this? What? Who are you? Tell me. Who are you? Eh? Who?'

Mother's tone was similar to the one she used when she got the bill for the disco lights Ugo and I had ordered just the day before. *What's this nonsense? Did you girls buy out an entire store? Tell me.* We had spent the weeks leading up to Udodi's return planning a surprise welcome home party. We missed Udodi. Her leaving tilted something in the balance of our world and Ugo and I could not wait to have her back for the holidays. I gathered stories for her which I couldn't share with Ugo or our parents: the boy in my class, Ebubedike, whom I had kissed and asked to be my boyfriend. How I took flowers and cake from the house to him. It was only to Udodi I could confess that Ebubedike and I were already planning on attending the same university in the US, on marrying after gradu-ation and on having two children. I had invited him to the party.

Father – whom we all called Doda because, for some reason, that was what Udodi had called him from the moment she could speak – and Mother had agreed to let us have whatever we wanted. A proper DJ, not the police band that played at our Christmas party, belting out one old people's tune after another. There would be canopies wearing necklaces of disco lights in the front yard; tables with gold-coloured tablecloths; long buffet tables with meat and fish and rice and spring rolls; jugs of orange juice and apple juice and Chapman. And in the back yard, a bouncy castle and a popcorn machine. 'This bash will be the talk of the estate,' Ugo told everyone she invited. 'Make sure you don't miss it ooo!'

I did not have to wait for my mother to scream and shout for Doda, flinging the phone away from her, 'Come and take the phone, I don't know what this person is saying about our daughter,' to know that Udodi had died. But it was I who got to the phone before him. Listening, yet completely unable to process what the voice at the other end was saying. Comprehension would come later when I replayed it in my head. Udodi's roommate had called with the impossible news of her death. She was American, this roommate, and had not prepared our parents for the shock the way people did when they brought news of a calamity as huge, as irreversible, as death. She had not asked for friends to sit with the deceased's parents. She had not broken the news to them in thoughtful, padded, manageable chunks. She had not asked if they were fine, had not said that Udodi was 'not very well'. She had just, wham!, given it to them and then repeated the same news to whomever was on the phone: 'I'm sorry Udodi died in a car crash tonight.' Sorry! Like she could have done anything to help it. I gave the phone to Doda, who had been standing beside me all along.

'Hello? Yes.'

He was not shouting. He had his civil servant voice. Polite. Low. Calm. Even under pressure, he never cracked.

'Yes. This is he. I am her father.' Then he kept repeating 'Are you sure? Are you sure?' into the phone, as if he were talking to a child uncertain of their facts. And then he said 'Well . . . well . . . Thanks for letting us know' in a firm voice like he was closing a business deal. But his shoulders sagged as if someone had dropped a huge, invisible weight on them, suddenly and without warning.

When he hung up, his motions slow and careful, Mother shouted, 'What are you thanking her for? What? Thank you for what, eh? What does she know?'

Mother would not take Bethany's word for it. She asked Doda to call the consulate in Atlanta. Mr Aliyu, the vice-consul, was their friend. If anything had happened to Udodi, Mr Aliyu would know. The embassy would be closed, Doda said. 'So call him at home,' Mother said. She stood beside Doda as he dialled. 'Put it on speaker,' she ordered.

The vice-consul picked up almost immediately, as if he was sitting by the phone.

'We heard something,' Doda said. 'Udo's roommate called with some disturbing news.'

Mr Aliyu let out a growl. He was so sorry. The girl should never have called. There are procedures but he wanted them to hear of Udodi's death from someone they knew, in person. He'd been trying to get a mutual friend of theirs who lived in Enugu to come and deliver the news. He was sorry. He was still apologising when Mother's *Nooo* drowned out his voice. And then she was a hurricane whirling in the sitting room, destroying vases and picture frames and upturning side tables and pushing our father, until she wound down and threw herself on the floor and began to wail, shouting, 'I am finished! I am finished! Take my life now. I am finished! Uwa m agwugo!' She pounded the floor. 'What am I still doing alive? Take me, God. Take me, God, and bring Udodi back!'

Dead. Deader. Deadest. I thought of the game we played as children, Udodi, Ugo and me. Three of us lying as still as could be in the middle of the parlour. Whoever stirred first was dead. The longest to stay still was deadest. Our resurrection was always sure and swift. I wanted this to be a game.

The maid, Mmeri, whom Udodi, Ugo and I called Aunty because she was older than we were, also came out of her room and threw herself on the floor, shouting out too that her life was finished, repeating the words as if she were a parrot. Mother stopped rolling and shouting so that all we heard was Aunty's voice, 'I am finished. Take me now. Take me! Uwa m agwugo.'

Mother screamed at Aunty to get up and go back to her room. 'Udodi a buro nwa gi! How dare you say your life is finished? What do you know about losing a child? Is she yours? How dare you?'

Aunty scrambled up and, still sobbing, only this time less loudly than before, wiping her eyes with the sleeves of her blouse, made her way back to her room, picking her way as if she could no longer see and the floor was landmined. If Aunty had had the courage, she would have told Mother that, yes, Udodi was her daughter too, as were Ugo and me. Aunty had known us since we were little. She had come to live with us when Udodi was ten years old. I was almost six. Ugo was four. She had seen us grow, and in a way she considered us if not her own children – she could not have been older than fifteen when she joined our family – then her little sisters. Her grief at Udodi's death, regardless of what Mother said, was real. Mother and Doda were always out working, so Aunty had spent more time with us than either of our parents did. She could have reminded Mother that when Udodi's first period came she had gone to Aunty because she, Mother, was not home. Aunty had given her her first sanitary towel. But Aunty did not say any of these things.

When we were kids vacations had been for long trips and local outings. Udodi, Ugo and I with matching hairstyles piled into Doda's 504 station wagon, coolboxes with drinks and food in the back of the car, Mother beside Doda in front. Once, when I was ten, we drove all the way from Enugu to Calabar, to Obudu Cattle Ranch, but the holiday was ruined because I became sick almost as soon as we arrived, and Doda said nobody could have fun with me in a clinic. Ugo had been upset with me, as if I had deliberately chosen to ruin a vacation that I too had been looking forward to. I had felt the beginning of a fever in the morning before we left but I was worried that if I told, Doda and Mother would cancel the trip. And so in the car, even though all I wanted to do was close my eyes and give in to the illness and have my parents fuss over me, I opened my mouth and sang along every time Mother raised a song. And I tried to eat when, two hours into the trip, Doda stopped so we could have the lunch of rice and chicken Aunty had packed for us. But four hours was long, and by the time we arrived at the resort my body could no longer hide my illness. Lying in the clinic, I had not felt sorry for myself. I had been sorry, rather, for spoiling the vacation for everyone else. When I tried to apologise to the family Doda told me, 'It's not your fault you got ill.' Mother said, 'Child, you really must stop saying you're sorry for things that you cannot help. Concentrate on getting well.'

Doda and Mother didn't see Udodi's corpse, prevented by a tradition that says a child that precedes a parent in death has sinned against the earth. Doda suggested sending a family member to handle Udodi's cremation and bring back the ashes. Mother scoffed at the idea. Did Doda really think his brothers were up to the task? Let Enuka do it, Mother said. Aunty Enuka was Mother's best friend and Udodi's godmother. 'Closer than a sister' was how Mother described her. Besides, Aunty Enuka was an American citizen. She wouldn't have to navigate the hoops the American embassy made Nigerians jump through before granting them visas.

'Let her go and bring back our Udo,' Mother said.

Aunty Enuka worked for herself, she could take the time off. No, she didn't mind going, she was honoured to have been asked. It was no trouble, no trouble at all. 'In and out, just like that,' she said, snapping her fingers. She was happy to be helping out in some form.

On the Friday after Udodi died Aunty Enuka returned from Atlanta. She, who did not care for tradition, had pictures of Udodi's corpse in case my parents changed their mind.

'She was so beautiful,' she told us, her voice breaking.

The accident hadn't ruined Udodi's body even though it had mangled her car. The damage was mostly inside. Internal bleeding. They suspected Udodi had fallen asleep and veered off the road into a tree. The ashes wouldn't be ready for another week or so but Aunty Enuka had to return to Nigeria to take care of some urgent business. She was lucky, she said, to have such a quick turnaround: Udodi cremated within days of her death. The crematorium could have Udodi's remains solidified into Parting Stones, 'a collection of smooth pebbles you could keep around the house'. Mother and Doda didn't have to decide now but it was something to think about. Or they could have the ashes turned into a diamond. People did that these days. Mother told Aunty Enuka to stop, she didn't want to hear any more. She wanted her daughter back. Not her ashes. Not some stones.

'Please take the booklet with you,' Mother said.

On the same day Aunty Enuka had returned with a catalogue from a funeral home of urns, keepsakes and jewellery, a gaily decorated truck arrived at the house loaded with the canopies and the tables we had ordered for the party Ugo and I had so meticulously planned in a different lifetime.

Mother saw it first and ran out barefoot, yelling 'Go away! Puo! Puo!'

Doda, Ugo and I ran to drag Mother inside but all our grief combined piled onto Mother and it pulled her down, and so we huddled in the middle of the courtyard, the sun flogging us with its merciless heat, sobbing into each other's arms while Aunty made sure the driver was paid the balance we still owed so that he could leave.

Udodi's death was the beginning of the raging storm but at that moment we thought that the worst had already happened, and that life would now treat us with more kindness.

Nani

After Udodi died, things fell apart. Everything took longer to do; it was as if my body moved in slow motion. I conserved my breath by hardly speaking to anyone. Not even to Ebubedike. Doda slouched, carrying his grief on his shoulders. Mother's was in her eyes, in the way they settled on you without seeing you. Ugo cried so much it seemed as if she would never stop. Grief never ends but it loses its rawness. With time, Doda did not slouch quite as much. Mother's eyes lost their mistiness. Ugo stopped crying.

I threw myself into my studies. 'You need to go out more, Nani,' Doda said when I passed up on a picnic with Ugo and some friends of hers to study for a science test. Udodi had been dead many months then.

'Ugo and her friends are too loud,' I said. 'All they do is just sit in someone's back yard and play loud music and eat sandwiches.'

'But you like music,' Doda countered.

'Not as loud as Ugo does,' I said.

Later that day Doda came to sit beside me outside the gate. He snipped off a rose from the rose bush and gave it to me without saying anything. He knew it was not just the music or its loudness that kept me indoors with my books. When Ugo and her friends went to some charity golf event with one of the estate's parents, and Doda asked why I didn't join them, I said I had a headache. When he asked why my friends no longer came round as often as they did before I said they were all busy, or ill, or had grandparents visiting. I didn't tell him that I had dropped almost all of my friends. Or that they had dropped me because I dragged around with me a thick quilt of darkness that sucked out all light. During recess I disappeared into the school library so that I did not have to sit outside with them, hearing the absence where Udodi's name should be. At the beginning, right after Udodi died, before the silence, there had been an awkwardness between them and me. Whenever I mentioned Udodi's name they went quiet or looked away. It was as if, at fourteen, I had no right to bring death into our midst.

After a while something folded inside me and made me seek my own company more and more. I didn't tell Doda any of this but he sensed something in a way Mother did not. Mother was too busy-busy with her job at the hospital, with her friends, with her meetings, with getting on with life, to notice. Mother and Ugo were alike in that way. They always had things to do, people to see, social circles to be the centre of. Doda was like me. We kept few friends. We went to parties but we didn't seek those gatherings out on a weekly basis.

But now, even Doda was concerned about me. He started taking me out on what he called our dates. Sometimes Ugo came along. Sometimes both Mother and Ugo joined us. Mostly it was just Doda and me. Every weekend we went for dinner. Genesis on Zik Avenue. Hotel Presidential in Independence Layout. Dannic Hotels in New Haven. Doda drove me (and whoever was with us) around Enugu trying out meat pies and Chapman and fried rice. We were an unusual sight: a father and his young daughter in restaurants full of young couples from the university campus or hordes of young men out for some beer. I learned more about Doda on these outings than I did at home.

'You know, I was going to be a writer,' he said once over our fried rice and beef at Genesis. 'I wrote an entire novel!'

'What happened in it?'

'The novel?' He looked up from his plate and I saw a smile come over his face. 'I'm not sure I should tell you. It wasn't any good.' He waved his fork in the air as he spoke.

'But you have to, Doda! Please?'

'Not even your mother knows about this!'

'Please, Doda?'

He put his fork down. 'Well, it was about a man who lost a bet with a friend and spent a year naked. I told you it wasn't any good!' He hurried over his words.

I started laughing. A nervous chuckle because, as funny as it was, as close as we were, we were not a family that said words like 'naked' in each other's presence. 'Naked', like 'sex', belonged on TV or in books. I wanted to ask Doda how someone could live naked for a year. How did his character survive it? Did he never go out? I asked, 'Why?' I meant why did Doda write a book about a man who lived naked for a year but he thought I meant why did his character keep his word.

'Integrity. Your word must be your bond, you know. Integrity. I think I was exploring how far someone could go to maintain their honour without compromising that same honour.'

Mother always said that Doda was a man of integrity. 'Your father would rather chop off his arm than cheat!' she once said.

Had Doda not died, Mother would never have set up the clinic. If Mother had never set up that clinic . . . But that was still in the future, the clinic and the babies, and as I sat with Doda in the air-conditioned coolness of Genesis there was nothing to suggest that two years later he would be dead.

One day, two years after Udodi died, Doda called us – Ugo and me – to the sitting room and, with Mother beside him sniffling into a handkerchief, told us he had some bad news. I swallowed the panic rising in me and sat. Ugo settled herself next to me. He had been feeling unwell, Doda said. Ugo and I looked at each other. Our father looked healthy. He got tired a bit more easily, took more naps, but apart from that he was fine.

'I have pancreatic cancer,' he said.

I knew of only two people who had had cancer: a classmate's grandmother and a former commissioner of the state. They hadn't survived it.

'Are you crying, Nani? I'm a strong man. I'm not going anywhere yet,' Doda said, his civil servant's voice never cracking.

I imagined him in boxing gloves, knocking cancer out, stuffing sand into cancer's mouth the way the boys who won wrestling bouts did to their opponents. I believed him. He looked strong enough to defeat any opponent. Despite myself, the image made me smile.

At the beginning he had tried to be the same old Doda, tending to his rose bush, telling us stories, joining us for dinner and asking about our school work. Then he started to lose weight and spent a lot of time in his room. We tiptoed around the house so we did not disturb him. His cheeks became sunken, so much so that his teeth suddenly seemed too big for his mouth. His hair thinned and his eyes dimmed. His trousers sagged around his waist. The last two months of his life, two months after his diagnosis, he went into a hospice. By then, the man who was called Ukwu Iroko by his closest friends because he was as sturdy, as solid as the trunk of the tree was now like a dry twig, something that could easily be snapped in two. Ugo and I cried every time we saw him. Maybe he had a talk with Mother but she said Ugo and I couldn't visit him in the hospice. 'Stay home, do your homework, see your friends, umu m.'

The next day, when Mother got ready to go, I walked with her to the car. 'I want to come. I want to see Doda.'

Ugo waved us off. 'Give Doda my love,' she said, crying.

Every day Mother went, I went too. I took him flowers I picked myself from our yard. I sat on his bed and held his thin hands, rubbing my thumb against his. Doda slept a lot. But even when he wasn't sleeping he said very little. 'Look after your mother and your sister,' he told me once, his voice small and hoarse. When, in his last week, he was no longer conscious, and he produced trickles of urine as dark as tea into the bag hooked onto him, and he moaned in pain when any part of his body was moved for a wash, and seeing him like that was like being stung by dozens of bees, I still went. I brought fresh flowers and binned the old. Mother sobbed and talked and told him jokes and laughed. She scolded him for wanting to die. She commanded him to get up and walk. I was sure that she was already descending into madness and that his death would bring it to its culmination.

The day he died, we were not there. We arrived only minutes late. Mother said Doda wouldn't have wanted any of his children to hear him take his last breath but that was scant comfort. She had a wild look in her eyes. But I was the one that ran mad.

Nani

Those were the days of melancholia. The house at Number 47, once bloated with laughter and songs and colours so bright they made the eyes hurt, now smelled overwhelmingly of heartache. When moments of happiness came there was always the undertow of joylessness. Even when Aunty made her famous jollof rice, grief intermingled with the spices so that the aroma of the food did not come wholly through.

One day, after Doda had been dead for a few months, Mother watched me drag the tines of my fork across the rice. 'Are you sick? Do you want to eat something else?'

I shook my head, no.

Mother sighed. 'You're wasting away. Do you want to leave me too? Eh? Have I not suffered enough?'

In the days after Doda's death, Mother had Aunty make Udodi and me our favourite dishes: plantain and eggs, jollof rice and chicken, okra soup and eba. Ugo had been lured back eventually into finding her appetite but mine stubbornly stayed away. All food tasted like cardboard. Doda used to say that the difference between joy and happiness was that the former was a state of mind while the latter was a temporary emotion. He had tried to explain it to me like this: 'When people say you can't buy happiness, what they mean is that you can't buy joy. You could be sad because you're poor and can't afford new clothes for your children and be joyful. And you could have millions of naira and no worries and have no joy. It doesn't mean you're not happy. You have moments of happiness because you can afford to buy things that make you happy.'

I had not understood it until now. On the walls hung relics of the past: family portraits of all five of us smiling, the ill fortune that would take first Udodi and then Doda still far away in a future none of us could have imagined. In one of the pictures I was between Doda's legs. I had a couple of teeth missing but my smile was wide and unabashed. If I thought hard enough, I could feel the warmth of my father's kiss on my forehead, I could hear his voice telling me not to mind my sister, Udodi: a witch hadn't stolen my teeth to buy akara. 'Your teeth have gone to make way for stronger teeth. It happens to everyone. It even happened to me!' I had believed Doda, of course I had. Believed that every loss came with a commensurate gain. Things died so they could return. When I scraped a knee playing oga with friends from school, he told me the old skin would give way to better skin when it healed. When the nail on my thumb peeled off from getting jammed in a door, I could bear the pain because Doda told me that its replacement would be stronger. Age and life would teach me that not all losses were compensated with gains. After my elder sister's death I thought that death would not touch us again. Lightning does not strike twice. The worst that could happen had happened.

There were enough people, billions of them, that Death could choose to lodge with. Yet, it had returned to Number 47. Set its sights on Doda and spirited him away. Fatherless and less one sister, I thought that I had learned life's lesson: happiness would always be elusive, something passing.

As weeks became months and my school work suffered, Mother's patience with me began to run thin. 'We all lost him,' she said, 'but life goes on. Do you know how many people are betting on me to fail? A widow with two girls? They are waiting for me to give up, for my daughters to fall pregnant, for us all to completely break.' The 'they' she referred to were some of Doda's male relatives who felt cheated by modernity and Mother's strength, both of which prevented them from inheriting their 'brother's' property.

A few days after Doda died his eldest sibling came from the village to 'see how my brother's family is doing'. When Mother told him he was not welcome to sleep over (Doda and the brother had not been at all close) he held his red chieftaincy cap between his hands and reminded my mother that in the old days he would have inherited her, married her and taken over all of Doda's responsibilities and everything else that belonged to him. Mother had swept him out of the house with a broom and the worst insult she could have hurled at him. 'Ngwa, out of my house! Out! Out!' she shrieked as she walked behind him, running the broom against the back of his trousers. 'It's not only me you'll inherit, you will also inherit my dead ancestors! Stupid man. Onye oshi!'

About a fortnight after Doda died, Ugo came to my room at night with two frozen tea bags. She plopped herself onto my bed. The mattress shook with her movement. She held the tea bags out like an offering. 'You should put these on your eyes tonight and leave them on until you wake up in the morning.'

Ugo wasn't allowed to wear makeup but she did anyway, applying pink lipstick in the car during the week, swearing it was lip gloss when her teacher asked, and adding eyeshadow and mascara at the weekend when Mother was out. She would usually scrub her face clean before Mother returned but that night I could still spy the green covering her eyelids.

'Why?' I didn't take the bags from her. I pulled the blanket up to my chin. I was freezing but I didn't want to switch off my air conditioner. The hum of it was comforting in an odd way.

'To get rid of the bags under your eyes, duh! Have you seen how puffy they are?'

She flung the bags at me. I threw them back at her.

'I just lost my father, you think I care how my eyes look?' I rolled away from her and turned my face to the wall.

'And I didn't lose him too, abi?' She was shouting. 'You act as if Doda belonged to only you. We lost him too!'

'Then act like it. You and Mother should act like it!'

I sprang up from my bed and stood facing her, all the anger I had been holding in since Doda died geysering out. I wanted the heat of my words to scald her. After Udodi died we all moved through life with identical heaviness, we had cried in each other's arms, but with Doda I seemed to be the only one still crying. Something was broken in me that remained intact in Mother and Ugo. 'You never loved Doda! You and Mother!'

31

Even to my own ears, my voice sounded strangely harsh. Ugo pushed me. I fell back on the bed, got up and threw a wild punch which caught her on the shoulder. Ugo hit me back and we were soon kicking and punching and rolling on the floor, trying to draw blood. Aunty heard the commotion and came into the room to separate us. She would not tell Mother, she said, if we promised her, *right this very minute*, that it would never happen again.

'You should be looking out for each other, not fighting! How do you think your father would feel looking down at you now? Or your sister? Ah! Do not let the Devil bring the spirit of division into this family . . .'

And on and on and on until she dissolved into a sobbing heap on the floor of my room, holding Ugo and me in a tight hug. The fight loosened something in me. Or maybe it loosened something in the way I looked at Mother and Ugo. After Ugo and I made up, first hugging each other awkwardly because Aunty ordered us to, *right this very minute*, and then much later, days later, when we began talking to each other again after I apologised for throwing the first punch, she told me that she sometimes heard Doda's voice.

'It doesn't feel to me like he's gone, Nani.'

'If he isn't gone, then where is he?'

I knew then that Ugo would never understand how I felt. How could she, convinced as she was that Doda was gone but *not* gone? There were days I wished I could regain my balance and be more like Mother and Ugo, walk with the lightness of foot that they did, eat Aunty's food without tasting something else underneath it, be with my friends and rock the world with our laughter. Resume life from where it stopped when death came calling, stop the world from going dizzy. Return to who I was before Ephraim barged in and tripped up my life.

Ugo

The day Ugo and Mother leave for America all Ugo
thinks about is that they are leaving Nani behind in
Enugu. *Live in America without Nani? Haba! What's left
of our family then?* Not even the thought of a home with
a swimming pool – which Mother promises they'll get
in the States – is enough to lift her mood. Long before
they arrive at their Atlanta suburb with massive homes
and huge back yards with swimming pools which stay
open all year round, where women have narrow waists
and strong legs, the men are broad-shouldered, and the
children all play sports, Ugo dreamed of a house with
a swimming pool. Aunty Enuka has a pool at her house,
which Ugo and her sisters have always admired, but
when Udodi went off to senior secondary school and
one of her new friends, whose father was a lawyer,
announced in class that they were having a rooftop pool
installed, a home with a rooftop pool became for a
while the sisters' dream too. 'Our own pool, on the
rooftop!' They had had to – as a unit – tell Doda and
Mother that that was the only thing they wanted for
Christmas.

'Doda and Mother will never agree,' Nani said, even

before Udodi had finished speaking, cutting into the rising excitement of Udodi's dream.

'But let's ask them first,' Udodi said. 'How can you just sit here and say they'd say no, if we don't ask?'

'What's the point?' Nani asked, rolling over on her stomach on the rug in the parlour, a teen magazine spread out in front of her.

'Haba! Will we not begin first by asking?' Ugo said, unwilling to let go of the image of towering over Enugu while she swam. 'Ours would be the only house on the estate with such a pool,' she said. At nine, it seemed important to her that Number 47 distinguish itself from the other houses on Umuomam Estate.

'But there's no point in asking if we know what the response would be,' Nani said.

'But we don't know . . .' Udodi said. 'We don't know that they'd say no.'

She snatched the magazine Nani was reading. Nani sat up.

'Remember how we begged for a pool like Aunty Enuka's? They said no to us then.'

'So?' Udodi asked. 'That was a long time ago. Do you live in their heads to know that they will say no again now? Are you a mind-reader?'

Later that evening Nani stood behind the door of their parents' room while Udodi and Ugo begged in the same identical tone. 'Please! Please! We'll be able to see the stars when we swim.' They heard her snicker when Mother said, 'What silly idea have you planted in your sister's head, Udodi?' Back then, Ugo believed, just like Udodi, that their parents could have been swayed if there had been three of them pleading, instead of two.

'This is all your fault,' Udodi sniped at Nani. 'Don't touch any of my things ever again!'

For days the other two wouldn't speak to Nani, and Udodi refused to let her borrow any of the teen magazines she had in abundance in her room.

At fifteen, Udodi had long given up dolls but she began to spend a lot of time with Ugo and her own dolls, dragging Ugo to the parlour to play where Nani could see and hear them. When Nani went out in the yard Udodi would decide that she and Ugo had to be there too. 'Let's have a picnic! Bring your dolls!' Ugo was in heaven. Usually it was Udodi and Nani whispering and giggling about *things* they told Ugo that she was 'too young to understand'.

When Nani reported her sisters to Doda, and he assured them that even if they had brought down heaven and earth, not just Nani, they still wouldn't have got the pool, they did not stop blaming her. Years later, when Nani left, Ugo blamed her for breaking up what was left of their family. Even after Ugo went to see her, even as she prayed that Ephraim would be punished by an eternal cycle of hot diarrhoea that scalded his buttocks, when the words Nani didn't say boomed in Ugo's head and told her the truth that Nani would not voice, Ugo squashed the voice and held on to her blame of Nani.

Nani

2007 was my year of firsts. First birthday without Doda. First Christmas without Doda. First school vacation without Doda. First real argument with Mother. It was also the beginning of the end of the life I had imagined I would have.

It started when the teacher Mother registered me with for SAT prep came to the house only a week and a half into our arrangement. Miss Oyibo, her hair extensions so long they reached her buttocks. I did not like her. The first day I turned up in her class she complained that my skirt was too short. 'Showing your body like a small ashawo. We can even see your nyash! You are here to study. Do not come to my class again like this.'

The next day I wore another mini skirt, surprising myself with my small act of rebellion. Maybe it was the weather. Reckless in how it withheld the rain even though it was the middle of the rainy season, creating sweat puddles behind knees and across foreheads. There was nothing normal about it. And now that recklessness had infected me too. Miss Oyibo sent me out of the class. For a week, I let Mother's driver drop me off but I never entered the SAT prep class again. I had decided by then that I wasn't going to America. I wasn't going to take the SAT. I just had to find a way to break the news to Mother. She and Doda had always wanted us to make use of the privilege we had to be born in America.

'You girls won't need visa. Nothing!' Doda used to say. 'Just finish your SS3, take your exams and go be great in America.'

I spent my days walking the streets of Chime Avenue, where the lessons took place. When I got tired of walking I went into supermarkets and spent the pocket money Mother gave me on soft drinks and cake and chinchin. I didn't think Miss Oyibo cared whether or not I turned up. My mother had paid in full for the lessons after all, and Miss Oyibo had other students. I didn't expect her to turn up to see Mother. After Miss Oyibo left Mother stormed into my room. She yanked me from the bed.

'So, Madam thinks she can go up and down Enugu disgracing this family, okwa ya?'

'I didn't disgrace anyone,' I mumbled, already thinking that it wasn't a good idea to talk back to Mother.

'I si gini?' Mother's voice was loud and incredulous. I was not the child to confront her. The middle daughter, always willing to please. But the wildness that had infected me tied knots in my ear and spilled words from my mouth.

'I don't want the lessons, I don't want the stupid SAT, I don't want to go to America!'

I had never told my mother this. I wasn't even sure until I said it that I really didn't want to go. Udodi had gone to America and died. Her body hadn't even been repatriated. I would have liked to see her. I would have liked to say goodbye. Those ashes Aunty Enuka eventually brought back were not the sister I loved. Udodi and I had expected to be together in Atlanta at the same time while she did her postgrad, going to the same school, sharing a room. We had these dreams. I was going to live with my sister again. What was the point of going to America if Udodi wasn't there?'

'I'm not going to America,' I said. I was shouting so that I did not cry. I wanted my mother to hold me in her arms and ask me why so that I could tell her everything. Doda would have asked. If Doda had lived, I may have found the courage to follow the path cleared for me.

'There's nothing I won't hear in this house!' Mother clapped her hands to emphasise the surprise of it. 'And you don't take the SAT, what then? You think I'll let a child of mine stay home and useless themselves? Let you lie in bed all day like a pregnant woman while your mates are doing big things in America? God forbid!'

She pushed me down into the bed. I sprang up and stood facing her, saying nothing. I saw something gather in her eyes. I was not sure if it was fear or concern but she walked out of the room. The knots in my neck untied themselves.

Mother never brought up SAT prep again. She spent a lot of time at her clinic or with the pregnant women who came to see her. When she was home Number 47 seemed too small for us. June stretched out languorously, like an obese pet. Ugo spent days visiting friends and flouting Mother's rules by going to parties on the estate without asking for permission. There was no one I wanted to visit. Almost all of my friends had left the city for the holidays: Enang and her family to Russia to visit her babushka, Ify and hers to Obosi to spend three weeks in her village, where her father was being made a chief,

Cordelia and hers abroad, to somewhere she was vague about.

'I am sure they are spending summer in Kenya,' Ugo laughed. 'If Cordelia was in real abroad, she would have said.'

Aunty must have noticed my listlessness. She sent me outside one day to gather some roses from the rose bush outside the gate. Usually Aziz the gateman was in charge of that, and roses were best cut in the early morning, as Aunty knew, but I could not say no to her.

'Don't come in here until you have enough for the vase on the dining table!'

She handed me a bag with the gardening gloves and secateurs she used when she cut the flowers herself, along with a small bucket of water, and sent me into the heat.

The roses bloomed a beautiful, healthy red. We called them Doda's roses because, when we were young, whenever any of us was having a bad day – a fight with a best friend, some illness – Doda would give us a rose and say it was his heart. For a long time I imagined Doda's heart beating red and rose-shaped inside him.

I started from the front as Doda taught me, snipping fast and dropping the cut flowers into the bucket of water. I was almost done when a voice said, 'Assemble the ones that are not *compretery* open. Those stay magnificent an extended time.'

I looked up to see a dark, older man clutching a Bible in one hand and a bottle of water in the other. He was maybe in his late twenties. His accent wasn't Nigerian but it wasn't one that I could immediately place. Dusty shoes, a shirt that looked like it might have once been white but was now the shade of an egg shell, an unfashionable haircut; with his careful but ridiculously grandiose grammar, this man was out of place in our neighbourhood.

I carried the bucket with the roses and started walking towards the front of the gate. I was raised not to speak to strangers.

'Please. Just a moment. Spare me a minute, please. I won't detain you long.'

He substituted 'R' for 'L' so that his 'please' and 'long' came out as 'prease' and 'rong'. *Compretery.* I held my laughter in. He gestured towards the bench beside the rose bush. His shirt had sweat rings under the arms. I shrugged. I did not care whether or not he sat. When we had visitors their drivers used the seat.

'Just a minute of your time, please.'

He plopped down on the bench under the shade of a guava tree and patted the area beside him. I stood. Aziz, who had been sitting inside the little room annexed to the gate and watching from the small window which looked onto the street, came out to ask if everything was fine, was this stranger disturbing me? He had a truncheon which he tapped against his leg while he asked, his eyes on the man.

'I'm fine, Aziz.' He was a conscientious worker, Aziz, but I resented that he treated me like a child. I could look after myself. Doda was gone. I hardly saw Mother. So what if I broke their rule and spoke to a stranger?

I gave Aziz the bucket of roses to take in to Aunty. Besides, this man intrigued me. He knew about roses, like Doda. I had forgotten that curiosity killed the cat.

'What's amiss with your security man? He thinks if he looks at me long enough, I will disappear?' He slipped off his shoes and sighed. 'He thinks he's a big man? All these people, once they have baton and gun, they think they are God. He who abides in me is bigger than he who is in him!' He twisted the cover of the bottle and took a long swig of water. 'Accept my gratitude for letting me sit. God bless you. My name is Ephraim.'

'Nanichimdum. Nani for short. The gateman was only doing his job.'

I thought his outburst as exaggerated as his language. He was lucky. Cordelia's gateman carried a dagger and once stabbed a young man he found loitering outside the gate. Poor Ezilo, that was the young man's name, had met Cordelia at a party at Nike Lake the Saturday before but had not had a chance to speak to her. He had got her address and, perhaps intimidated by the high walls around their house and the huge poster of a bulldog hanging on the gate warning 'INTRUDERS ARE EATEN ALIVE. ENTER AT YOUR OWN PERIL', had not walked up immediately to ring the bell but wandered around outside. If Aziz had been anything like Cordelia's gateman, this Ephraim would not still be standing. Or maybe he would. He did not look like a man who could be cowed by anyone.

I shook the hand he proffered. He smelled of damp clothes.

I'd expected a roughness to his palms when we shook hands, a texture that would have suited the rest of him, but the hand I shook was soft, baby-buttocks soft, like someone who moisturised daily.

'I have brought you good news. Do you know Jesus, the Son of God?' He patted the Bible in his lap.

An itinerant preacher. Doda wouldn't have approved.

'If they spend all day preaching, when do they have time to be productive, eh?' he would ask every time we saw one in the city.

Do you know Jesus, the Son of God? Even though I suspected he was asking a question, there was no inflection in his voice to suggest this. It was as if he had taken one look at me, taken in the magnificence of the house, and decided that I was too close in proximity to wealth, too comfortably ensconced in it to possibly know Jesus.

'Do I know Jesus?' I repeated to myself. I, like my sisters, was raised Christian, and like them I had been a regular church-goer before the tragedy that crushed our family and our faith.

'Yes.'

'Have you accepted Him as your Lord and personal saviour?'

Ephraim, not waiting for my answer, began to preach, his voice rising and falling, full of crescendos and filled with paced pauses, as if someone, a conductor perhaps, were directing his performance. I wasn't really paying attention but I was sucked in by his gumption. I sat, all the time aware of Aziz's gaze on me. If Aziz had the bravado to, I was sure he would have asked me to go inside, scolded me for talking to this man who had no business on our estate. I'd already embarrassed him by sending him back inside earlier. The worst Aziz could do was report me to Mother but I doubted he would. Security men were known for minding their business. They never quite became the family, no matter how long they stayed, that loyal domestic help like Aunty did. I also guessed that there was something about Ephraim that intimidated Aziz.

Ephraim preached into my silence. Blah. Blah. Blah. Big word. Big word. As he spoke he gestured wildly with his hands, pounded the air with the force of his conviction and thumped his Bible. He was starting to bore me but when he asked if he could stop by the next day I said yes. Mother had been complaining about me, how disappointed she was that I wouldn't follow the path carved out for me. Let me give her something to really complain about.

When Ephraim returned the next day he brought me a gift of boiled groundnuts, which I shared with Ugo even though she laughed at me and called him my boyfriend. He returned every day that week, his Bible under his arm, and always he brought me a gift. Offerings of fruit that amused me for their peculiarity but touched me for his thoughtfulness. Oranges. Bananas. Once a soursop. Sometimes he didn't open the Bible, just talked to me. I got used to him. His verbosity. His gifts. If anyone had asked me then, I would have said we were friends. It was an odd friendship but it was budding nevertheless. One day he asked why there was so much movement in our house, women coming and going. Pregnant or with new babies. Couples in fancy cars. 'Do you perchance have a place of worship inside there?'

I laughed. 'Church? No.' I shook my head. 'My mother is a nurse. They are her patients. She has her own clinic.'

The idea of turning our parlour or the back yard into a church like some of these new pastors did while they grew their congregation and saved money to rent or build a proper church elsewhere would have amused Mother.

'I see,' he said, but there was something in the way he

said it, in the way his sharp eyes cut at me, that disturbed me, so I went on.

'The women come to her, begging her to admit them to her clinic. And she takes them all in. Even those who can't pay!' Doda would have been proud of her. She was giving poor people private clinic treatment. I told her this once and she gave me a coy smile that was not like her. 'Her clinic is doing very well,' I said. Whatever had happened between Mother and me, I was proud of her.

'So have you made up your mind about America?' Ephraim asked, changing the subject. In my blossoming friendship with Ephraim, I had told him about the SAT I wasn't going to take. 'You should go. It's an exquisite opportunity.'

'I am afraid. What if I go and die like my sister?'

'Why would you?'

'My sister, my father, dead. I am scared. What if someone else dies while I am abroad?'

Where I could not talk to Mother or to Ugo about my fears, I found an ear in Ephraim. He asked questions and held my hands in his soft ones so that I found it easy to ignore the way he spoke and the way he smelled, and talk to him.

I told him things I could not tell anyone else. I told him of Udodi's death. I told him of Doda's death exactly a year ago. I told him about myself, about Mother and that we called her Superstar because she was, well . . . a superstar; she moved mountains. Even Doda had often referred to her this way, telling us, 'You might not know it but your mother is a superstar!' so that we imagined her in sequins and thigh-high boots and mini skirts like

Tina Turner, who was the superstar we liked most, an image we found so incredulous it made us laugh.

At other times I sat and Ephraim towered over me, gesticulating wildly as he preached and prayed, calling himself 'a robot in God's hands'. After praying, he would tell me that the 'spirit' touched him. And when the 'spirit' touched him it meant that God wanted him to help, so did I have anything bothering me I wanted to lay bare? Spurred on by his insistent questioning and this 'spirit' which touched him, I told him things. I told him how Udodi's death had made me lose faith. How it drilled a hole in my stomach and let the faith out of me. I told him of how we stopped going to church after Udodi died. Even Mother who used to carry church on her head no longer went. She no longer woke up the family early on Sunday morning to get dressed quick-quick or we'd be late for Mass, threatening that if we made her late we would see pepper. When the president of the Catholic Women's Guild of our parish came to the house and asked her why she no longer came to Mass, she gave the woman a tight smile and said, 'Uka di n'obi. Church is inside me. That's enough.'

I told him how I dreamed of my dead sister every night. 'I see her careening off the road, screaming my name, and I am always too late to help.' I told him things I had not been able to share with anyone in my family. They – Ugo and Mother – did not talk about Udodi or even Doda.

'They should talk about him. Jesus wants us to talk about those who are resting in the bosom of the Lord.'

His words comforted me. I looked forward to his visits. Where my friends had treated my grief as if it was something contagious, Ephraim understood.

'When my own father demised, I did not bathe, I did not eat. For months. They took me to the hospital and forced food into my mouth. I was walking around like a mad man,' he said.

Ephraim

Everything in Heaven and on Earth is ordained. There is no barricade elevated enough, no barbed wire sharp enough to keep God's word from manifesting. Nani does not know this but our meeting is not ordinary happenstance. From the premier day when the compass of the Lord directed my trajectory to her and her beauty consumed me like a huge conflagration, I settled the matter within me that my wandering eyes would cease to cast themselves upon others. Nani's beauty is coruscating like the morning sun, succulent like a ripe tomato. She is more beautiful than the roses in her garden. Her lips are like those of a siren. When she opens her mouth I want to fall inside it and construct an abode for myself. Mon Dieu! I cannot respire.

My beloved maman says that I was blessed with three things: a sugar eye, big hands and copious brains. My maman is right. I am an admirer of beauty. But a man who does not possess riches cannot get a girl like this who lives in a big edifice, a girl with skin like fresh fruit you want to bite, a fleshy banana you cannot wait to peel. If a man has no earthly papa with connections, his big hands will have plenty trouble making money and his copious brains will not be of service to him except to be a repository for all the words in existence. If you have no earthly papa at all to leave you even the coat your maman says he adorned himself in on a quotidian basis like a sapeur, a diamond like Nani will survey you like a rag that someone has employed to mop vomit off the floor, or chewing gum that is stuck on the bottom of her Sunday shoes.

How to win over a woman like her? Her ilk envisage that they are gods and people like me are but fallen angels not worthy of their beating hearts. I am sufficiently versed in the mocking ways of the rich: Frieda, back in my country, whose papa lived in an edifice as big as the Cathédrale Notre-Dame-des-Victoires de Yaoundé, laughed at me when I confessed my love for her; Delphine, whose maman's house my maman cleaned, interrogated the state of my sanity when I asked her to be my petite amie. And the worst of them all: a girl who came with her maman to buy manioc from my maman, a sellam-buyam trader at the market, declared that I had the effluvium of cassava. She, whose vocabulary in French is minute. If not for the crinkum-crankum of my life, I can asservate that I, Ephraim, would have been a doctor or a politician living a life of Byzantine luxury too. Did not my English teacher in école secondaire lament when my papa died and my trajectory of education was perforce amputated? When I speak in French and in English, do I not bamboozle my audience with the sizableness of my vocabulary?

How will you acquire her? the voice of doubt whispers to me. I barricade it with alacrity. Everything in life is ordained, and Nani is the female specie set aside for me.

I am not a sentimental namby-pamby but I have never desired any woman like I do this very rare flower of the desert. I shall remain assiduous until I have conquered her and we have made our connubial vows. So help me God of Abraham and Moses and the burning bush. Au nom du Pere, du Fils et du Saint-Esprit, Amen!

Udodi, the Chorus

Ula ge-eju onye nwulu anwu afo.
But the dead do not sleep,
The dead do not rest
Death does not stultify

I went to the rat that files the teeth
He sharpened my lower teeth but not the
    upper
The upper ones are spirit teeth, eze ndi
    mmuo
The rat told me to follow backroads:
Avoid the front ones, those belong to the
    spirits

This is true:

Youth is wasted on the young
life on the living,
sight on the seeing
the knowledge the dead have, on the dead.

What use is Power if mute it must remain?

If it did, we could get some respite:
from the torture of seeing both the present and the
    future,
not be tormented by all the I-wish-I-coulds.

I wish I could return. If I could leave, break through
    the surface for one more year. One more month.
    One more day. One more hour. One more minute:
I'd splay my palms on Mother's heart and, like a dibia,
    show her the future.

Where one falls is where their chi pushed them down
I'd make friends with their guardian spirits
guide my sisters away from harm:

take Nani by the hand and shout into her ears all the
    things that I have seen. I'd tell her do not. Do not.
    Do not. Force her to listen to me.
I'd hold Nani and say sister of my heart, my flesh, my
    blood, do not. I'd soften her sharp edges and
    sharpen her soft ones.

Give her the tools she needs to survive without being
    scarred much
(No one escapes life without a little scarring)

I can do nothing but watch as the unravelling begins,
    as the flowers that once flourished wither
and a drought visits her world and drags her into the
    darkness below.

The Past

The past was once both
the present and the future

— Ayanachi Ogu

Ugo

After Doda dies, Mother quits her nursing job and goes into private business. She sets up a maternity clinic. She just calls us into the parlour and sits us down as if we were adults and says, 'I enjoy being a midwife but I am done with government work. The pay is rubbish, the clinic is understaffed, equipment as old as Methuselah.' She hisses. 'We lost a twenty-five-week-old baby. Twenty-five weeks should be able to survive but we don't have the equipment to help pre-term babies in that nonsense hospital!'

She'd always complained about the poor facilities at the government hospital to Doda but he would tell her that it needed good nurses. 'The poor who can't pay deserve good service too, don't they, my superstar?'

'Don't I deserve good pay too? A buro m mmadu? Abi, I should stay there and be doing monkey dey work, baboon dey chop?'

Doda would remind her that, between them, they made enough already. And Doda's printing press was doing good business, making the family a lot of money. 'We are not suffering. You can afford to work there, give your services to the poor.' While Doda lived, she acquiesced. Now, with him gone, she does not have to please him.

'Are you going to work at a private clinic?' Ugo asks while picking fluff off her sweater. She wants Mother to get to the point. In her arguments with Doda, Mother would talk about the private hospitals headhunting her. Ugo doesn't really care what Mother does as long as they stay on the estate and she can go to college in America in the future. She doesn't understand why Nani isn't as excited to be going to America soon as she ought to be. Why Nani shuts down every time Ugo says, 'Ah! Soon you'll be an Americana.' Were she in Nani's shoes, she would already be packed and gone. Once, she told Nani that and Nani began to say something but then Ugo's friend, Mefo aka Radio Without Battery, came. So Ugo abandoned her conversation with her sister to hang out with her friend. When Ugo tried to revive the conversation Nani asked her to forget it.

'No. I'm going to open my own clinic,' Mother says.

What? Ugo's hand freezes. She and Nani look at each other and begin to shriek in amazement. This is the most exciting news ever. Ugo pictures herself saying, when asked at school what her mother did, 'Oh, she owns a clinic', quite nonchalantly, as if owning a clinic was on a par with owning a house or a car. That'll show Ifedi, who could not stop talking about her mother's nursery school, which, by the way, Ugo has heard is near Amechi Awkunanaw, the closest one could get to being in a village while still claiming to be in Enugu. She finds Ifedi insufferable. 'Haba!' she complained once to Nani. 'That Ifedi is soooo full of herself. Every day "my mother's school, my mother's school". She won't let us hear word.' She imagines swanning into school and casually saying, 'Oh, my mother's just set up a clinic.'

She scuttles close to Mother. 'Where will your clinic be? On the estate?' She imagines a clinic on the estate!

'No. There are plots for sale at Independence Layout extension, so if there's anything affordable and big enough there, I'll take it. Your Doda and I saved up quite a bit of money over the years, and that, added to what I made from selling the printing business, should give me enough to set this up.' The business was their Doda's passion. Their mother has never cared much for it.

Within six months Mother not only buys the land, she also builds what she calls her 'dream clinic'. Even for Mother, it is an incredible feat to pull off, Aunty Enuka says. Mother says the only difference between an empty plot and a mansion is money and not time. 'Contractors can work miracles when there's enough kudi to act as incentive,' she says.

Nani and Ugo dress in identical dresses with splashes of vibrant yellow and green for the ribbon-cutting ceremony. A representative from the Ministry of Health, a thin man in a safari suit and a red cap, gives a lengthy speech about service and commitment and good citizenship. While cameras click and flash, he is handed a pair of scissors with which to cut the ribbon tied around the front gate. He is applauded as if he has performed a magic trick, and Mother, radiant in a dress that billows out at the waist, says how much it means for her to be able to 'give back to society in this way' and how sad she is that her husband is not alive to celebrate with her but she knows that he is 'with us all today in spirit. Please eat and be merry.' She spreads her hands, as if they were angel wings, in the direction of the tent where six uniformed young men stand behind a table lined with food, waiting to serve. Ugo beams as her mother leads the way, walking daintily, carefully in those heels which bring her to Nani's five-foot-seven height. Ugo is so proud of her.

The two girls walk the grounds, too full of happiness to eat, admiring the buildings, Nani stopping every other minute to run her hands over the flowers that bloom all over the compound. The clinic, despite the intense colouring of the buildings (fuchsia and red like plastic Lego houses) reminds Ugo of the convent she and her sisters went to with their mother years ago, before Mother lost her faith, for a few days of retreat. Ugo hated it because they had to be mostly silent for the two days they were there. When she complained, Mother told them it was good to practise silence, to learn at a young age to meditate, to leave the chaos and the noise behind 'and listen to the stillness within'. Later, in America, Ugo will think of this silence often, surrounded as she would be by silence, a neighbourhood in meditation. Nothing but the noise of dogs barking, no neighbours coming to the door, no loud parties to celebrate a new job, a new baby, a new car. Nothing at all like Enugu. She will decide that she doesn't like silence. Like the convent, Mother's clinic is a row of bungalows, each with a neatly manicured lawn. There is a high fence for privacy and a gate with 'Rejoice Maternity Clinic' inscribed on top of it in huge letters. Beside the gate is a billboard with the name of the clinic painted above four smiling, pregnant women. The way they smile, they might have been advertising toothpaste.

Rejoice Maternity grows so much that within a year Mother has become one of the richest women in Enugu. She starts talking of expanding, setting up in other cities, employing more doctors, 'All these young graduates who can't get a job even with their medical degrees!'

The house is always overrun with people. Graduates with their diplomas in manila envelopes looking for work as nurses, as assistant nurses, as doctors; pregnant women who come for advice and friends of friends of friends asking for favours, bringing tales of children whom they can no longer afford to keep at school without assistance. Mother tries to help them all. A job here. A job there. A maternity bed in her clinic here. A scholarship there. *Haba! Mother sha is a saint. Period.* Number 47 begins to appear to Ugo like an extension of the clinic. The house is besieged almost on a daily basis by mostly young women, some of whom are visibly pregnant and for whom Ugo and Nani have to leave the sitting room so that they can chat with Mother. Sometimes her nurses accompany the women to the house. Mother begins parking her cars outside, even her beloved Mercedes-Benz. The garage is turned into a storeroom where boxes of infant formula, BournVita and tins of milk and custard are stacked. A big truck brings a new delivery every month and the gateman offloads the cartons, singing as he does so because usually Mother lets him keep a carton of tinned milk, two big tins of BournVita and a tin of custard for his family. Ugo loves that her mother is generous in that way. She smiles each time the gateman tells her, 'Your mama na good woman. God go bless am well-well. I never work for any person wey get big heart like your mama heart. Her heart big like ocean!' Mother is Ugo's role model; the kind of person Ugo wants to be.

The food is for the clinic's patients. 'Pregnant women

need to eat well and many of those who come to me cannot afford to do so,' Mother says when Ugo asks her.

One of the young women who comes to see Mother spends almost three months at the house, occupying the guest room. She is quiet and doesn't look much older than Ugo. She is skinny with a protruding lump taking over her body. Ugo and Nani become used to smelling the Dettol with which she cleans everything: her body, the bathroom, the floor of the guest room.

'Haba! She cleans and cleans. And she looks like she has kwashiorkor,' Ugo tells Mother.

Nani asks why a girl so young is pregnant. Mother says the girl was 'taken advantage of by an older man' but cannot tell her family of the pregnancy until she has had the baby.

'Where is her family?' Ugo asks.

'Owerri,' Mother says.

The girl ran away from home to the man responsible once she realised she was pregnant but he just gave her some money and put her on a bus to make the three-hour trip to Enugu to find the woman he'd heard could help her.

'My fame is spreading!' Mother looks so pleased with herself as she says it, the delight beaming off her face as if it has been slathered in coconut oil.

'Why did you agree to take care of her?' Ugo asks. She is so in awe of her mother, of how wealthy she is, of how giving she is. *True-true, Mother is a superstar sha ooo.*

'She has nowhere else to go,' Mother says in a way that suggests she doesn't want to discuss this further, as if her generosity embarrasses her.

For days, Ugo speaks of nothing but Mother's

munificence. The clinics she will build, the holidays she will be able to send them on. Later, in a future Ugo cannot yet see, she and Mother will leave for the US. There will be no new clinics. And she and Nani will not speak for many years.

Ephraim

Why is it that those who are in possession of backsides lack the knowledge of how to sit? Nani has the fortuitous fate of relocating to the Canaan of our times, and she is demurring to move like a car with a broken exhaust because her sister demised, and her father too. She thinks she has suffered. What a paucity of knowledge! She does not know what it is like for the universe to feed you suffering, to hold you in its malodorous, gargantuan, gigantic underarm and slowly strangulate you. Or how it is for boys bigger than you to strike you on the head and call you names because your maman sells manioc in the market and cleans houses of des femmes riches who give her their discarded clothes. Or to have one beignet, two beignets for your afternoon repast because your maman's manioc isn't selling well. Or to grow in a place where you are planted like a seed in sandy ground just waiting for the rains to flood you away.

The spirit is working in me. I shall be condemned no more to exist as I have. I luxuriate in fantasies of this Nani and of the two of us in God's own America. I sleep and I dream of my odyssey that began on a truck to

Nigeria, le geant de l'Afrique, to work as a carpenter, an electrician, a painter until the spirit spoke to me and instructed me to join a new church, terminating in doxology.

Nani

I looked forward to Ephraim's visits. Ugo teased me about him, calling him my boyfriend even though she knew that there could be nothing between us. Oil and water.

'It's a challenge to keep a straight face when he speaks,' I told Ugo. 'I just want to beg him to stop.'

My mockery of his pretentious language notwithstanding, I think she knew that I liked him. It wasn't romantic, I could never be attracted to him, but I enjoyed his company. He reminded me of Doda in his knowledge of roses. Every day he came he taught me a bit more about them. Even things Doda hadn't known to teach me, like using banana peels to keep them blooming. 'You chop up the peels and entomb them under the leaves. Maintain a distance from the stem.' And crushing egg shells and scattering them on the soil around the roses. The roses bloomed. How had he learned all of this? I asked once. He said it was a gift from God.

One day, maybe a few weeks after he asked if there was a church in our house, Ephraim came visiting. He had an unusual sneer on his face. He had a bag of fruit for me but he didn't give it to me immediately like he usually did. Instead, he asked for the name of Mother's clinic.

'Rejoice. It's on Independence Layout extension,' I said.

I did not wonder why he was curious. A part of me wanted him even to go and see it. The next day when he came he said, 'Nani, I found out something about this clinic of your materfamilias.' He thrust a bag towards me. The peculiar scent of kerosene mango escaped from it.

'Thanks,' I said. Kerosene mangoes were my favourite. I was touched he had remembered. 'Materfamilias?'

'Nani, your mother has a baby factory. That clinic? It's a baby factory.' He sat down and began shaking his legs as if he had all the words in there and needed to shake them free.

'What?' I said, laughing. 'She manufactures babies?'

Why couldn't he just speak like normal people did? I was sitting beside him. He held my hand and turned to face me.

'Nani, the pregnant women? She sells their babies. They don't have to pay her because she makes money off them.' Something cold slithered down my back. I shook off his hand. 'The babies go to wealthy people, your mother takes a titanic cut and gives the mothers a bit of money.'

'Shut up!' My voice trilled. 'Shut up!'

'You think she's Mother Teresa? You don't believe me, query her.'

He was shouting too. Aziz came out of the guard house. 'Miss?' I waved him back inside.

'You have no right to talk about my mother like that. You don't know her!' I shouted at him. I threw the bag of mangoes at his feet. 'You are evil! Go! And stop already with all the rubbish grammar. Go!'

I screamed. Aziz ran out of the guard house again, his truncheon at the ready. Ephraim took one look at him, turned and fled.

'Ugo! Ugo!' I shrieked Ugo's name as I ran up the stairs to her room. Ugo was in bed, wearing headphones, her iPod on her belly. Her eyes were closed and she was swaying her head to music. She did not notice me until I removed the earphones.

'What . . . ?' She stopped as she noticed the look on my face.

'I heard.'

'Heard what?'

I couldn't say it. It suddenly seemed too ridiculous to me. It couldn't be true.

'What?' Ugo looked at me, her head bent to one side.

'I heard that mother sells . . . sells babies. That's how she makes her money.'

'Heard? From?'

'Ephraim.'

'Him!' Ugo made a face. 'Why would she? And how would he know?'

'The cars, Ugo. All those cars.'

It was as if the scales fell from my eyes. Many of the pregnant women, some of them teenagers, came to see Mother without their parents. When they left, the cars – usually expensive ones – came to pick up the babies, and sometimes the mothers, who looked awkward sitting in them as if they were not used to such luxury, even though Mother said those cars belonged to the women's husbands or their parents.

'We'll ask her. We'll ask her, Nani. Although I wouldn't believe everything I heard.'

And that was what we did. We sat down with Mother after dinner and Ugo asked her.

'It is not trading in babies like you would trade in peppers or tomatoes,' Mother said, sounding amused. 'What I provide is a service. I place babies in good homes. The correct term is "placement". Why the long face, Nani?'

'Nothing.'

'I am providing a useful service. The people who come to me, both the "givers" and the "takers", leave satisfied. What am I doing wrong? Kedu ife m mmelu di njo? What I run is more than a clinic,' she said. 'It's more like a luxury hostel. And what I provide is a service without which many of these women would be having botched abortions or throwing away their babies!' She said it with the insouciance and self-possessed aplomb of a woman who did not doubt that she was saving the world.

She took Ugo and me on a tour the next day. I went because, despite everything, a part of me still wanted a mother I could respect.

The clinic was like something from another world. Every room had an electric bed with easy-to-use hand control. 'High tech!' Mother said. 'You girls should try it out!' Ugo lay on one, laughing excitedly, pushing buttons. In the lounge three pregnant women sat watching something loud and dramatic on TV. When we entered they stood up and greeted Mother.

'Good morning, Mummy!'

Mother ran her hands over the stomach of one. 'And?' she asked. 'How's the little one doing? Still giving you trouble?'

'No, Mummy,' the woman said, smiling shyly. She had a tooth missing.

'Won't be long now, and you'll be free,' Mother said. 'And then you can go fix that tooth!'

The woman smiled again, this time tentatively, a smile that was not quite a smile. I looked away. Nurses in smart uniforms walked along the corridor, popping their heads in to greet Mother. From one of the rooms we heard a shriek and the healthy cry of a newborn baby. Mother flashed a wide smile and asked us to wait in the car, strutted off towards the direction of the cry. I heard Ephraim's voice tell me my mother sold babies.

'How much for that one?' I said to Mother's receding back.

'She could have opened an orphanage. Given those kids a home. She doesn't have to sell them!' I said to Ugo as we sat in the car waiting for Mother. Ugo hummed something but I could see that she had decided to take Mother's side.

Yet, on the first of October 2008, I spent the day picturing in my mind's eye Mother and Ugo in Abuja, both of them in clothes made of identical wax print, Mother's silver afro a halo around her head, and her smiling benevolently for the cameras as she was decorated with a medal by President Yar'Adua. Underneath all that bitterness, all that disapproval of my mother, all of my wanting to get back at her, I would wonder if she and Ugo thought of me at all.

Ephraim

Fortune guided my steps to a dialogue between two of my church sisters. In the way of women, they spoke loudly and so I heard about the neighbour of one of them, a Jezebel who lay with another man and got pregnant. Fearful of being kicked out like an empty bucket by her dead husband's family, she surrendered the fruit of her sin to Rejoice Maternity. There is only one Rejoice Maternity in the entirety of this Enugu. Nani, you can turn your nose up until it touches the skies, your mother and my maman are both sellam-buyam merchants.

Nani

How could Mother have thought that what she was doing was right? Doda would never have stood for it. Doda, who would rather be held up by the police checking his car papers than bribe his way out. It annoyed Mother, that habit of his, his refusal to let money work for him in a place where everything was for sale. Mother's clinic was a betrayal of everything Doda stood for. This was her spitting on his grave. The anger and hurt bubbled together inside me so that I could not look at or think of Mother without imagining ways in which I could hurt her. Every meal I ate, knowing how it was paid for, choked me. It made me complicit. I hated Mother for making me an unwilling accomplice to her evil.

Ephraim stayed away for a few days. I missed having someone to whom I could complain about Mother and Ugo. Had my friends been around, I couldn't have told them about the baby factory. Every afternoon, I waited for Aziz to come to the door to say Ephraim was at the gate. The day he finally came I skipped to the gate, my mouth full of words, sad and angry and bitter.

'Your materfamilias, you must learn to forgive her,'

Ephraim said. 'She loves you, she is only doing this for love. She is not a saint but she is still your mother.'

'I don't think I'll ever forgive her,' I sulked, biting into the roast corn and ube Ephraim had brought. I could not shake off the memory, vivid and startling, of the faces of some of the young mothers – the crescents under their eyes a testament to the tears they had shed – as they were being driven off, their babies already belonging to someone else.

'The Bible says forgive. The Bible says honour thy father and thy mother.' He began to thumb through his Bible to find the right passage. 'Forgiveness is very important,' he said. 'We have a vigil at church tomorrow, to pray for the ability to forgive. You should endeavour to come.'

'I can't . . .' I began to say and then thought: why not? I did not want to forgive Mother but I would feel better if I got my revenge somewhat by breaking one of her biggest rules and at the same time repaying Ephraim. We were never to stay out past midnight. Even Ugo, who broke the rule of attending night parties without Mother's permission, always returned by midnight. Mother was away at a conference in Onitsha until the beginning of next week, Aziz would be easy to bribe, Aunty would never get me in trouble, and should Mother return from her conference before I did, of which the chance was slim, Ugo would cover for me. I had done her enough favours.

'Although if I were staying up all night, it'd be for a party, not a vigil!'

I crumpled two N50 notes into Aziz's fist, a bribe so that he would not lock the gate until I was home. Ephraim cut off a rose from the bush outside our house, pricking his thumb.

'For you,' he said. 'Put it in your hair.' I stuck the flower into a braid.

We took a taxi to the vigil ground, an open pavilion with a corrugated roof opposite the Apostolic Church of Jesus and His Twelve Disciples Keeping Us Safe in the Ark. It was the size of two football fields and it was packed. Strings of light bulbs hung from the ceiling, shining bright like miniature suns. I was so delighted that I had come, so glad to be part of this swaying, dancing, praying group where I could forget Mother, that I did not notice time speeding by. By the time I looked at my watch, wondering if it was not yet time to go, it was two-thirty in the morning. Too late for me to go home, as the guards who guarded the estate were not bribable in the same way our personal guard was. No one could get them, except in an emergency, to open the gates once they were locked at two a.m. They were paid too well by the estate community to risk losing the security of a job that was theirs until they were too old to be useful, just for a handful of notes from kids who wanted to stay out past their bedtime. They thought us too indulged, thought us the pampered children of wealthy parents and enjoyed nothing better than to shout 'Go back to where you are coming from' to any one of us who begged to be let in once they had locked up.

'What do I do now?' I asked Ephraim.

'What you can't do is return to your abode. If the gate's locked, it is locked. Nothing to do about that,' he said matter-of-factly.

'What do I do then, eh?' My right knee itched. The

joy I had felt earlier, singing and praying, was already deflating, and in its place was anger at myself and a horrible dread in the pit of my stomach. All the sweet euphoria of rebellion was gone.

'You can seek shelter in my humble edifice. First thing in the morning you get a taxi back to your estate.'

'No!' I had never slept in a man's house. If Mother found out, she would kill me. She was out of town but was due to return in the morning, on time for work. I could not sleep out. I would not, could not, spend the night away from home without permission, and certainly, definitely, not in a man's house. It did not matter how bad my relationship with Mother was, she was still my parent. Ephraim, even though he was my friend, even though we had become closer since he exposed Mother to me, and even though Aziz no longer thought I needed protection from him, was still a stranger. I had never been to his house. He had never been inside mine. All our meetings happened outside, on the bench by the gate, within the protective, albeit disapproving, gaze of Aziz. Ephraim did not fit the profile of someone who would be friends with any of the children who lived on the estate. He was noticeably older than I was, poorer than anyone who wasn't a domestic help on Umuomam Estate, and he might have carried an air of desperation around him that Aziz noticed but I, back then, had failed to.

'What do you want to do? If you're desirous of it, I can get a taxi to chauffeur us back to your estate.'

'No. They won't let us in. The rules are very strict. We had a few robberies in the past and since then everyone knows to be in on time or stay out. I can't go back there, not now.' I had told him this already. I scratched behind my knee.

'So you have to come back to my house.' He sounded impatient. His sentences no longer as long-winded as they often were.

'But . . .' I knew I was being silly because I had no other choice than to follow him. Besides, what harm was there in that? What was I so scared of? Nothing. He was a man of God, a friend who had never given me cause to doubt him.

As this now became my only clear option, I began to persuade myself it would be fine. Why should I stick to the rules of a woman who sold babies? I would certainly be safer in Ephraim's house than I would be on the streets of Enugu at that time of the morning. My palms began to itch and I blew into them to keep from scratching them. I prayed that Mother would not return before I did.

'But what? Are you afraid of me? Nani?' He sounded hurt and I quickly placated him.

Of course I was not, I said. 'But if my mother comes home before me tomorrow, I am in deep trouble.' I gave him an encouraging grin. I did not want to imagine how I might be punished. Mother did not beat us – the punishment of choice for many parents of my friends – but she was adept at punishing in other ways which hurt more. Pocket money was withheld. Outings were cancelled. Once, when I stayed out beyond my curfew, she made me do all the housework for two weeks. The only thing I didn't do was cook because I had never learned how.

'We better leave now or we won't get a taxi even to my house.' Ephraim's voice was urgent, reminding me that there were worse options than his house.

He had a point. I did not want to sleep in an open field either. That was where the real danger was. There was no reason for this fear settling itself into the middle of my stomach.

I followed Ephraim, allowing him to hold my hand as we squeezed through the crowd, everyone hurrying off to get home and get some sleep. I tripped once and he drew me up, his fingers closing tighter around my wrist. We moved with the surging crowd and I breathed a sigh when we finally exited the park and got on the road. There were no street lights, and the darkness would have scared me had I not been with Ephraim, who was humming a song about Jesus being his friend, 'a friend who will never, never leave me'. I walked quickly to keep up, singing bits of the song with him. I never let go of his hand while he tried to get us a taxi with a driver willing to go all the way from Okpara Avenue to Obiagu where he lived.

'All these drivers are thieves!' Ephraim said as one driver after the other either quoted him what he considered an astronomical sum, or flat out refused to drive to that part of town so late at night. One driver said, 'If my tires are slashed while I am dropping you off, and my earnings stolen, will you replace them?'

I wished I had brought my own money. I would have offered to pay what Ephraim said were the exorbitant fares some of the drivers were charging. I had changed handbags just before I went out to meet Ephraim and forgot to transfer my wallet from one to the other. I realised too late, on the way to the vigil, that I did not have my wallet. Ephraim had told me not to worry. He had enough money to cover our fare both ways, he said with an air of benevolence. And so not having my wallet had only been a small inconvenience.

'You would think I was asking them to drive us to Aaamerica!' He dragged out America like a song. 'Is it not human beings who domicile in Obiagu? Is it not in this same city? Why are they all acting as if we are armed robbers and undesirable elements there?'

Undesirable elements! The term would have made me laugh but I was too nervous to laugh, eager to leave and be safe under a roof. It did not even matter any more that it would be Ephraim's.

Finally price and fortune collided, and Ephraim dragged me, relieved, beside him into a taxi which smelt of cigarette ash. Ephraim settled comfortably in, and when the car had driven a short distance he asked the driver, 'You smoke?'

'Yes.'

'It's not good for you. The Bible says that a man's body is his temple and he must keep it crean.'

'Crean. Crean,' the man mocked. 'What are you? A god? I am my own god. Don't disturb me with your Bible. And mind ya own business! If you do not, I will drop you and your woman off here and you can walk the rest of the way to Obiagu!' He gesticulated wildly with one hand, the bracelets on his wrist jangling. 'If it is preaching you want to preach, let me warn you, not in my car. Carry that preaching and park it outside, if you don't want me to just drop you people off here. Nonsense! A man can't have peace in his own cab?'

I felt Ephraim stiffen, felt him fight to hold his tongue in check, and when we got to Obiagu and he paid the driver he let out the fury that he had kept in, calling on a thousand demons to attack 'that son of the Devil who calls himself a god'.

I had thought it out of order for Ephraim to lecture a grown man in his own car. I had only known Ephraim a few weeks but I knew him enough by now to realise that it would have made very little difference to him if I had objected. Ephraim saw it as his duty to 'bring the good news to everyone' and he would have felt it a dereliction of duty, an offence punishable by hellfire, to have kept silent. Ephraim's Christianity believed in either the ultimate reward, which is Heaven, or the ultimate punishment, which is Hell. 'None of that Purgatory you Catholics do,' he said once. People were bound for one of two extremes.

I stood beside him while he continued to rant, his anger gathering momentum, making it impossible for me to say a word. This overblown anger rattled me, on top of everything else. It made me jumpy. I wanted to go in, get away from the dark. I knew of this neighbourhood, had driven here with Aunty and the driver to go to the market, but I had never been into any of the houses. I knew people lived here, obviously, but I had never thought of them. Not in the way I thought of those who lived in GRA or on our estate. None of my friends lived in this part of town, and from what I heard from the driver and Aunty it was the centre of crime.

I was frightened and could not stop my heart beating hard as we stood in front of Ephraim's, a long, narrow building with two steps leading into an open courtyard, while he continued to curse a man who no longer heard him. I expected to be accosted by armed robbers, to be lifted up and carried away by an abductor who would send a note to Mother asking for a ransom. When I came shopping with Aunty here she often warned me to hang on to my bag, to be on the lookout for anyone who might come close enough to snatch it from me. Aunty told me once of a woman whose gold necklace was yanked off her neck. 'Which stupid person wears gold to the market?' Aunty said, before going on to relate how the thief was caught, stripped and burned by a mob of irate traders. I remembered that story now and imagined I could smell burning flesh. Fear must have seeped out of me and hit Ephraim, for he turned to me and said impatiently, 'This place is as safe as your area. Whatever you've heard, it's not true. The only difference between the populace here and where you live is money. And before God, money is nothing. Rien!'

He started walking towards the house. His flat was off the courtyard. He fished out the keys from his pocket and opened the door into a small, stifling parlour. He flicked on a switch. The light from the bulb bathed the room in a dull glow. There were framed images of Jesus and the chief pastor of the Apostolic Church of Jesus and His Twelve Disciples Keeping Us Safe in the Ark along the walls. A fridge was plugged in beside a red velveteen-upholstered sofa with a plastic jacket still covering it. Opposite the sofa was a wooden table on which a TV stood and beside the TV was a vase with plastic flowers. It was difficult to breathe in that room but I was too relieved to be safe out of the darkness to care.

However, the relief was only a small consolation. I wondered where I would sleep. Where was the bathroom? Against the wall was a dining table cluttered with food flasks and tins of evaporated milk and a kerosene lantern.

Underneath the table, I discovered later, were cartons of noodles. I wondered how anyone could live here and not feel imprisoned. A door led from the parlour into a bedroom. I did not see a bathroom. All I wanted to do was to lie down and wait for morning so I could go back home to the trusted cosiness of Number 47.

Ephraim said I could have the bedroom and he would sleep in his parlour. The bedroom was small, the size of my bathroom at home, and that bathroom was half the size of my mother's, which I envied. There was hardly any room for me to move in it. In a corner of the room was a bed with a mattress so thin it might have been a mat. The mattress was covered in a sheet that had once been white. I thought I spied splatters of blood, probably from mosquitoes, on it. It did not look very clean. There was no way I could sleep on this. I thought longingly of my own bed with sheets that smelt of fabric softener. The room was hot and I could smell my own sweat. I needed a bath! How did anyone survive without air conditioning in this heat? I felt slight pity for Ephraim. I had never been in any home where poverty revealed itself with such frankness. There was no attempt to camouflage it with fancy-looking bits and pieces. My network of friends was limited to people on my estate, in homes comparable to mine. We all had gatemen who lived in the Boys' Quarters – BQs, small buildings beside or behind the main house – but nobody from the main house ever went into the BQs. Aziz and Sani, the other gateman who relieved him, had rooms in the BQs they could use. Aunty had a room there too but I had never been inside any of them. My friends would be horrified if I told them I spent a night in a house like Ephraim's. They would not believe me.

A house with no AC. The windows, small and wooden, whatever colour they had been originally long chipped off. In a corner of the room was a bucket of water, and I could not imagine why anyone would store water in buckets or in a room. Did he not have running water?

'It's hot,' I said. I opened the wooden window. It did nothing to alleviate the heat.

'It will cool down. It is this hot because I left the window closed the entirety of the day. Mosquitoes. But you'll be safe beneath the mosquito net,' Ephraim said. I had not even noticed the net rolled up above the bed, bits of it mended with patches of cloth. 'I wish you a restful repose.'

'Okay. Thank you.'

I tried not to let my discomfort show. I tried to think more grateful thoughts. What did it matter that the house looked rundown? And everything was worn out and dirty? Ephraim had saved me from sleeping in the open. I lifted my wrist to my nose as if to wipe it but, really, I wanted to smell something familiar, my perfume, something better-smelling than the dank and suffocating stench of the room. On the floor, by the door of the room, was a mosquito coil and I asked Ephraim now if he could light it, hoping that the smell of the coil would overpower the other mustiness. There was a cupboard beside the bed, and from there he brought out a matchbox and a multi-coloured wrapper.

'Sorry, I have no nightgown to lend you.' He laughed at his own joke and I smiled at his attempted humour. He lit the coil, slid his hand in his pocket and brought out a key. 'Barricade the door. I will knock at five if I don't see you, so you can get a taxi on time before your materfamilias finds out. You will be fine. Goodnight. Don't forget to pray.' He closed the window. 'We don't want mosquitoes to use you and do party!'

He laughed. I felt obliged to laugh back.

'Goodnight, Nani.'

'Goodnight. Don't let the bed bugs bite.'

'Bed bugs? I don't have bed bugs.' He sounded embarrassed.

'No. I didn't mean that. Never mind. Goodnight.'

I locked the door, removed the key from the lock and undressed. I was grateful for his thoughtfulness. I tied the wrapper under my arms and sat on the bed praying that the hours would fly by. The tip of the coil glowed red and, just like I had hoped, its smoky incense smell took over from the unpleasant odour of the room but the smoke stung my eyes so I closed them.

I must have, despite my aversion, fallen asleep because when I heard Ephraim at the door I sat up. Could it already be five?

'I'm coming,' I shouted, to let him know I was getting up, getting dressed and coming out.

The room was dark but slants of light were already creeping in through the shutters. I had just managed to only half sit up before Ephraim came into the room wearing nothing but a pair of white boxers, so incredibly white they glowed in the darkness.

'Ephraim? How?' I sat up properly now, surreptitiously tying the knot of my wrapper tighter, trying not to stare at his boxers, at his penis standing erect. I wondered why he had not covered it up. If he hadn't noticed, I wasn't going to embarrass him by pointing it out.

'Spare key.' There was something excitable about his voice.

83

'Okay. But please can you go so I can dress? I am not dressed yet. Thank you for coming to get me.' The sleep was clearing quickly from my eyes. His voice made me anxious.

It scared me that he had a spare key to the room, and that he had let himself in without my consent. Unless . . . unless he had knocked and I had not answered? After all I had been sleeping. But why would he come in in his underwear? And why had he not left so I could dress?

I held the wrapper tighter around me. I tried not to panic, and said again, 'Thank you. Now please, let me dress up, or we'll be late and I'll be in serious trouble with Mother if we are.'

He moved closer into the room. 'It's not yet time to go. We have time. Don't worry. I'll have you back before your mother misses you.' He was now right next to me. Something was not right. I sprang from the bed.

'Why . . .?'

Before I could get the question out, Ephraim lunged at me from where he stood in one swift, liquid movement. With one hand he covered my mouth and with the other he began to fight me for my sparse covering. I sank my teeth into the fleshy part of his palm. He pushed me down on the bed and pinned me down with his body. Somewhere inside of me I thought I was dreaming still. I tried to push him away but he was a cat and he clawed me. And he was a mountain on top of me. And he was a rock crushing me. And he took. And he took. And he took. And he took. He let out an almighty shudder, collapsed on top of me and began to caterwaul. I heard him from far away.

'It's the Devil, Nani. It's the Devil. Please forgive me.'

The mountain rolled off me but my bones were pulverised and I could not gather the ashes of my bones and make them whole again.

'Please forgive me. I am sorry. It's the Devil. The Devil pushed me. God! What have I done? Won't you say a thing? Please say something.'

My body dissolved and split in two: one far away watching the scene, the other me lying there, dead. Deader. Deadest. The 'me' that was far away alternated between telling the 'me' lying in the bed that nothing had happened – that it was just a bad dream; that Ephraim was a Christian and would never do anything to hurt me; that the pain between my legs was not really there, it was a phantom pain and once I got up it would be gone – to telling me to get up, go home, report him to Mother; that Ephraim had done something bad and needed to be punished for it, must not be allowed to get away with it. Although this voice asking me to make sure he was punished was clear and loud, I remembered Chinelo and knew even then that I would tell no one of what Ephraim had done. When Chinelo from the estate was raped in a male student's room Mother said she asked for it. Doda had said that had she been his child he would have killed the boys responsible for raping her (*I would have cut off their balls!*). Growing up in Number 47, we learned that 'rape' was a heavy word. It was a sharp, black word that darkened rooms and sucked the air out of everything. It landed with a loud thud in the room every time it was dropped, and was therefore a word which must be hidden. It was not to be spoken of except in euphemisms, like Mother did, to soften it and keep it from exploding and ruining lives. *Chinelo was defiled by three boys.* Defiled cloaked the ugliness of the act and made it possible to be spoken of.

I could feel Ephraim watching me dress, his eyes soiling every part of my body they landed on. My hands were lead as I pulled the blouse over my head. This really could not be me. It had to be someone else, someone whose pain I could feel as intimately as if it were mine, the ache between my legs mimicking that of the someone else. There was the taste of something unidentifiable on my tongue, something acrid. My throat burned as if I had drunk acid. I wished I could throw up just to rid it of the burn. A dozen hooves were stomping all over my chest, cutting off my breath. I thought I would pass out. I could not breathe.

I dressed and in a haze stumbled out. Ephraim followed me. He hailed a taxi and got in beside me, to make sure I got home okay, he said. Every time I opened my mouth to say something no sound came out. Saliva spooled in my mouth. Ephraim sat in the back of the taxi with me, sitting so close that I could hear him breathe. All through the drive he spoke into my ears. He quoted Bible passages denouncing the Devil and reeled off names of prophets before him who had been tempted. Remember King David and Uriah's wife? he asked, his breath warm and rancid. 'In Corinthians 1 the Bible says, "No temptation has seized you except what is common to man." And God is faithful; He will not let you be tempted beyond what you can bear. But when you are tempted, He will also provide a way out so that you can stand up under it. Nani, the Devil shall not prevail. First of all, He sent the taxi driver last night to tempt me after the vigil. Did you hear his blasphemy? "I am my own god"? And after I overcame that by the colossal power of the Almighty, the

Devil just would not stop. He would not stop because the Devil, he hates to see God win. When he sees Christians triumph it makes him go mad like a wild animal.' He talked and talked, filling up the car with his foul breath, his foul words. His words floated in the car, and I only half heard him, the sound of rage in my ears drowning every other sound. How could I have been so stupid? How could I kill this man? Why couldn't this taxi hit a tree and just kill us all? The taxi stopped in front of Number 47. I turned to Ephraim, aimed and spat in his face.

When Aziz let me in, his eyebrows rose as if to ask where I had been all night but he did not dare to. I sneaked into the house and went straight to the bathroom. I had to scrub off the memory of what had just happened. I could feel Ephraim's hands crawling over my body. I wanted the hot water of my bath to scald me and slough off the skin so a new one could grow in its place. If my body could forget it happened, so could the universe. What if I got pregnant? Oh God! I pushed the thought away as hard and as far as I could. I pushed it to the very bottom of my stomach where it would not slide out when I wasn't paying attention. If I got pregnant, I would kill myself.

PART TWO

The Present, 2014

Ugo

Recently Ugo has begun going to the library. She's been gorging on books about time. Parallel universes. Gravity. She tells herself that she can find a way to go back in time. Haba! She knows she can't but she's unable to stop dreaming that that possibility is there to return. Back to when they were kids watching Tom and Jerry in front of the TV, to before Udodi died and their world dizzied and their family splintered and scattered like ashes in different places. She brings the books home and leaves them all over the house.

'What's with the obsession with time?' Mother asks her. Ugo cannot explain it, she barely understands it herself, this crushing loneliness that has taken hold of her, this wanting to see Nani that suddenly has her waking up at night from dreams in which her sister is screaming her name. Here in America, Mother doesn't rush in and out like she did in Enugu, consumed by her clinic and her patients, so she has the time to pay attention to Ugo even though the girl thinks she is too old to be babysat. Mother often says she's been forced into an early retirement. 'I'm not yet ready to live like a grandmother!' Ugo never responds when her mother says this. She lets the word 'grandmother' bounce around the room. She doesn't catch her mother's eye when she looks at her. The words they do not say fill the house and swirl around like dust to enter every crevice, and so they talk about other things, easier things, like things that confound them still about America. How one country can be both glamorous and vulgar at the same time; how animals are treated better than people; how everyone talks to you as if they know you without actually knowing you; church signs; grits and biscuits. Y'all.

In Enugu they always spent the week of advent dusting and putting up their Christmas tree, hanging decorations and heaping presents underneath it. Even after Udodi died, and Doda died and Nani left and Ugo and Mother did not feel much like celebrating, Aunty and the guard dragged in the Christmas tree and the box of decorations from the storage and left them in the parlour for Ugo and Mother. Here in America, Ugo tries to keep up the tradition. Last year they had no tree but Ugo blasted Christmas carols for days. This year she wants more. She begs Mother to buy a massive tree from Home Depot. At first Mother says no but then she gives in. They drive to the store and choose a four-foot plastic tree but when they bring it home neither of them has the energy or the will to unpack it, and so it stays in its box for weeks. When Ugo does set it up – she hires a few people she knows from college to help her out – she is shocked to see tears in her mother's eyes. 'We need decorations,' Mother says, and Ugo drives down to the Michaels at the Avenue and buys silver tinsel, shiny balls and snow stars. When they are hanging them up Mother asks suddenly, 'Have you heard from your sister?' The ball

Ugo is holding falls and breaks. *Every time I've heard her sob at night, I was always sure she was mourning Ugo and Doda. Haba! She won't even call Nani by name. I have never once believed that she thought of Nani at all.* Perhaps it is all the reading, all the thinking, all the sprinkling of her wishes for a ride back in time, but one night soon after this the dreams of Nani start, and Nani calls Ugo in the dead of the night.

Udodi, the Chorus

If one does not chew water, one does not know that water has bones. These are the things I know that nobody else does about Nani: she sneaked up behind a girl in her class who called her names and stuck chewing gum in her hair. How did she not notice? I asked Nani. *I have my ways. Please don't tell anyone.* No one knew to suspect Nani, least of all the girl whose name-calling days were at least a few months behind her. *She thought I'd forgotten. She doesn't know I have the memory of an elephant!* When the girl came to school the next day, her long braids cut close to the skin, Nani said her heart sang. *Although I felt some guilt, Udo!* Nani liked to take her time but she never forgot a wrong. I used to tell her, Nani, if people knew you, really knew you, they'd be more scared of you.

These are the things I tell myself: if I peer into the future beyond the darkness, I see Nani in a pool of light. This is the biggest lesson I've learned: the most difficult thing to do when you have all the time in the world is wait. And even when you know the end, the how eludes you still.

The Past

Nani

After my bath I burrowed under my blanket, the air conditioner in my room set so low I could feel my ears getting numb. I welcomed the cold, this cold that knocked me out, anaesthetised me so that I almost did not feel the pain that would make me remember. It hurt to breathe but this was bearable pain, the pain of breathing. My drapes were drawn so that my room stayed dark, and I had no idea what time of day it was. I had been lying like that since I got out of the bath, the clothes I had worn to the night vigil stuffed under my bed. I would never wear them again. I would tie them up in a paper bag and bin them so that there was not a chance I would stumble upon them and be brought to a remembrance. If there was a way I could incinerate them, I would. The dress with the polka dots, which I had chosen to wear for its decency, short-sleeved, came down to my knees, I now would never be able to face again.

When Ugo stuck her head into my room I pretended to be sick. That same day Ephraim came to see me, and Aunty came to fetch me.

'I don't want to see him.' His audaciousness flabbergasted me. That he would imagine that I ever wanted to see him again! That I would welcome him! Act as if nothing had happened! My own ability to maintain a casual calmness at the mention of his name surprised me too. I had expected the name to unravel something in me, to have me shouting and crying, but now all I really wanted was to be left alone to forget.

Aunty stood still as if she was waiting for something more, an explanation. Getting none, she turned and left. Before then Ephraim had come often and every time the message was brought that he was at the gate, I had always gone to see him. Aunty approved, silently, of the friendship between Ephraim and me, and I knew this. The first day that she had walked in on us – she herself was coming back from fellowship – sitting side by side on the bench outside, Ephraim reading a verse from the Bible, Aunty had smiled approvingly.

When Mother stopped the nightly prayers, and stopped the church-going, Aunty had begged her for a while to reconsider. Aunty still went to church, and prayed loudly if Mother was not home – as it was her obligation – that God would touch the heart of her employer and bring the family back into His fold. She told me that God had brought Ephraim into our family and was using him to bring first myself, and then the rest, back to Him. And so I was not surprised when Aunty asked Ugo to talk to me because I had refused to see Ephraim.

Ugo did not bother knocking this time. She sat on my bed and asked, 'Why are you refusing to see your preacher friend? What has he done?'

I thought that maybe I should tell my sister the truth. Surely Ugo would not judge me. I opened my mouth but other words came out. Convenient words, wrong words, safe words that were not heavy on the lips. Words that did not bruise me. But words, nevertheless, that still cost me an effort to speak because I had no energy left.

'I'm too tired to face anybody now, biko. I'm tired. I just want to doze.'

'You guys must have stayed up for a very long time ooo. What if Mother had come back unexpectedly and checked your room this morning?'

'The vigil lasted longer than I thought it would. I really do need to sleep.'

'Ah ah. It's almost two o'clock ooo. Will you sleep tonight at all? Hmm . . . you sure you guys really spent all night praying?'

She was teasing but it upset me. I spat out the 'Yes, idiot' before I could stop myself.

Ugo rolled her eyes, said 'fanatics', but instead of leaving she peered at me. It felt as if she could see into my soul and it both relieved and scared me at the same time. If Ugo found out, I wouldn't have to bear the burden of my secret alone. But then she said, 'Your eyes are swollen. You really do need to sleep! I don't blame you for not wanting to see anyone. I should leave you. Aunty is making moi-moi. You want me to call you when it's ready?'

'No.' The moment to tell Ugo passed. She was already halfway out of the room, continuing with her life, leaving me and the terrible secret I could not utter.

Ephraim came every day after that. And every day I sent the same message to him, hoping that he would disappear from my world, humiliated that it was my inability to report him that gave him the audacity to keep coming by. It seemed to me as if we were rehearsing for a play, repeating the same words each day.

'Ephraim is at the gate.'

'Tell him I'm not home.'

One day, instead of relaying my message, Ugo let him in. I was watching TV in the parlour when Ephraim walked in, his satchel slung from one bony shoulder. I felt the walls constrict. Ugo said 'You guys sort out your quarrel' and left, closing the door behind her before I could say a word.

He said, 'I came since morning. Your gateman said you were out.'

I increased the volume on the TV, although I could no longer tell what I was watching. The images were hazy. My head was pounding. Why did Ugo have to meddle with this?

'I've been outside waiting for you to return from wherever you went. God spoke to me as I prayed last night. He said I must see you today. I told God how the Devil pushed me and God said that we must talk. You. Me. And Him.'

He moved and now stood directly opposite me, blocking the TV. I looked through him, as if he were a gossamer ghost, willing the rage inside me to come out in tongues of fire and lick every part of him.

'God said we must talk. He said, "Tell Nani that I love her. Tell her that I have prepared a lavish banquet for her on my mountain." God said—'

I raised a hand, a gesture he understood and which stopped him. 'God said what? Have you forgotten what you did?' I switched off the TV so that I did not have to shout. I did not want Aunty or Ugo coming in to see what was wrong.

'I am sorry but you must forgive me Nani. Forgive me, so that God can liberate you from anger.'

'I swear I will never forgive you. As long as I live, I swear. Please leave. Go! Go! Go!'

'Nani,' he said. 'Why won't you forgive? I forgive you. I forgive you for seducing me. I for—'

'Are you completely mad? Leave my house now!' I did not care any more. I was shouting now. He sat beside me. I dragged him up. 'Leave my house!'

He stood up. 'I will leave but first let me tell you this. Once a man has carnal knowledge of a virgin, they have a bond. God came to me in a vision. He stood me in front of you and He spoke to me and He said, "Behold thy wife." We have a bond now. It cannot be broken. Listen to the voice of the Lord.'

'Well, God came to me in a vision too. He stood you in front of me and said, "Behold the snake. Keep away from him!" Now, Ephraim, go.' I pointed at the door. 'Go or I swear I'll pour hot water on you. Go. And never come back here!'

As I watched him leave, his steps jaunty, his satchel with his Bible slung across his front, the bottoms of his trousers swishing about his ankles, I began to see something a bit crazy about him. How had I not noticed it before? The quirks that previously were charming and amusing now took on a sinister note. I wished I had a knife and the courage to stab him and stab him and stab him until he lay dead, curled on the floor in a pool of blood. Dead. Deader. Deadest.

I told his departing back that if he ever stepped foot in the house again I'd have the gateman shoot him in the leg. 'Aziz will not hesitate to kill you! I swear to you, I will ask him to make sure he kills you!' I was shaking now. Fevered anger taking over my body. I locked the door and collapsed onto the sofa, breathing hard as if I had been running.

When I stopped shaking I went in search of Ugo. I found her in Doda's study – which we once jokingly called his sanctuary – reclining on a chair, leafing through a magazine.

'You had no right interfering. You don't even like Ephraim,' I said, startling her, my voice as cold as ice. Nobody spoke in the sanctuary.

'Abeg abeg abeg. Don't vent your frustration on me, I beg you! You were acting like a woman whose husband had just died. I couldn't care less about your preacher friend but you were depressing everybody, refusing to eat, refusing to leave your room. Even Aunty was worried about you! Go, get over it – and close the door on your way out!'

'You. Had. No. Right.' I stabbed the air in Ugo's direction with every word, reminded, even as I did so, of how Mother's grief after Doda died was nothing like Ugo just described. Doda's death had not changed her in any way.

Ugo hissed. 'Abeg carry your frustration somewhere else. If your friend upset you, you sort it out with him. Like I said, close the door on your way out!'

I hmphed and stomped all the way up to my room. Why could Ugo and Aunty not mind their business? All I wanted was time, time to erase Ephraim from my memory, and I was making progress. Now they had spoiled everything by dragging him back in. Today, the day I was finally starting to believe that I could put things behind me, they had to bring him in and cause me to relive that night again.

Mother came back later that evening in a happy mood. She called Ugo and me. 'I've heard a rumour that I am to be one of the recipients at next year's Independence Day Awards.' It was not really a rumour. Mother had been putting the word out, planting the seed that she deserved at least an Officer of the Order of the Niger award for all her contributions to Nigeria. If she got this, it would be a coup for her, something else to rub in the face of her husband's brothers – those men who waited and hoped that she would stumble so that they could tell her 'We told you so'. We will all have to go to Abuja for the ceremony, she said, looking pointedly at me. 'All of us will go!' She noticed that Ugo's enthusiasm was muted and she stopped. Ugo was her biggest fan. 'You'll get to meet Yar'Adua!' We said nothing. The thought of meeting the president did not rouse us from our apathy. Her excitement thinned. She sensed the tension in the air.

'Spit it out. What's wrong, girls?'

We said nothing, reverting to our childhood manner of keeping silent around each other after a quarrel. Besides, how could we speak of our argument without speaking of the vigil? Ugo did not want to put me in trouble by revealing that I had spent the night away from home, and I wanted no reminder of that night at all.

Ugo was the first to grumble, 'Nothing. There's nothing wrong.'

And I, keen not to dwell on it, said brightly, 'Nothing, Mother. I can't wait to go to Abuja. It'll be fun, right, Ugo?'

If Mother thought my tone suspicious, she said nothing.

I had not been enthusiastic about anything she had to offer lately. Now I said quickly, before I changed my mind, 'I'd also like to take exams . . . for . . . for America. I want to go.'

Ephraim

Everything worketh together for the good of those who love the Lord. The stone that was cast away has become the corner stone. Who says that my Lord doesn't have the ability to reverse the impossible? He works in mysterious ways, His wonders to perform.

The medulla oblongata of my God is bigger than any man's comprehension. The birds of the sky do not work, yet He feeds them. Do not be anxious, the Bible tells us, for God will make ways where there are none. He has provided the way for this, His humble servant. A man shall lie with a woman and the two shall become one flesh. No evil fashioned on earth can untie the bond with which God joins a man and a woman. Nani and I have become one. Praise the Lord!

Nani

Four weeks after the attack I was back to my normal self – or as close as I could possibly come to that person. I threw myself into preparing for my SAT, swallowing my fears of leaving the country and dying like Udodi had, swallowing my disgust of Mother. I'd let her pay my fees but, once I could, I would pay her back so that I would never have to owe her anything. I needed a physical distance, oceanwide distance between Ephraim – although he never returned to the house after I threatened to set Aziz loose on him – and me to be able to forget the hell that Ephraim had dragged me to. It was all my fault, breaking Mother's rule and going out with a man at night. I made several promises to myself, punished myself by going over in my mind all kinds of alternative endings. I could have got pregnant. He could have killed me, which was hardly any different from getting pregnant. There were stories, I had read those stories in the papers, of women going missing and months later, years even, a body or a part of it turning up. How could I have been so stupid? 'Good girls do not go to men's houses.' I could hear Mother say this if she ever got to know.

I was grateful for the cramps and lower back pain of

an impending period, the harbinger of good news. I wore a sanitary towel every day in anticipation. Ugo and I threw what we called 'mini parties', which was just us and whichever friend was around and could visit, dancing in her room or mine, drinking endless cans of soda, pretending it was beer. Ugo promised to throw me a huge send-off party when I left for the United States. 'We'll convince Mother to let us have beer. We'll have the entire estate come!' I said. Ugo and I spent days drawing up plans for this party she'd throw, and I waited patiently for my period to arrive.

The familiar cramps stayed for another three weeks, and I thought maybe I was ovulating and if I waited a bit longer my period would come, but I knew – and my diary confirmed – that I should have had my period three weeks before. I did not want to think what that might mean. Had I not read somewhere that stress could delay a period? It had to be the trauma I went through that kept my period at bay. I examined my diary daily, calculating and recalculating. Maybe it was possible that I had messed up the date of my last period. Maybe I was not counting right. It happened all the time. Women getting their dates mixed up.

Deep down inside, I knew. Yet I asked myself how that could be? There was only one reason which made sense. It had to be God punishing me. I was a bad girl, and He was punishing me for it. I'd got myself raped and pregnant all in three months. Just when my future was starting, after all those years of school and now university to look forward to, I had to go and ruin it. Something was wrong with me and I needed to be punished. Normal, good people didn't attract the kind of bad things that I did. Some people were born bad, rotten, and I had to be one of them.

I kept telling myself 'I don't want to be pregnant. I don't want to be pregnant' over and over again, chanting it like a mantra. Maybe if I said it enough times, it would become the truth. Maybe my period would start, bright red staining my towels and giving me cramps. I would never complain again about menstruating. I would never again call it 'the curse'. I would welcome it as a sister, cherish it, love it even. I prayed to God to forgive me and grant me a miracle. I would make amends for whatever wrong I had committed. All I needed was another chance.

I knew that before I began to show, before Mother found out, I had to take care of it. I wrote a note for Ugo telling her to cover for me for as long as I was away ('shouldn't be too long!') and, because we were taught to always let someone know where we were, I wrote down Ephraim's address, never imagining that she'd need it. I had to fix things. And the only adult I knew who could help was the one responsible. And so I found my way back to hell.

Nani

I did not know what Ephraim did. I did not even know if he worked. I had not been curious enough to find out, and so had never asked him. I knocked on his door. I did not know what I would do if he was out. Then I decided that if he was out, if nobody came to the door for me, I would take it as a sign from God that I should return home and confess everything to Mother. But Ephraim was home. When he opened the door to me his lips curved into a smile, parted as his smile grew wider. He stood aside to let me in. I saw his eyes move from my bag to my face, swollen with tears. He smiled again, this time a smirk which spread slowly across his face. I tugged at the strap of my duffel. Being in this house again suffocated me.

Ephraim began to speak even before I had said a word.

'My God is a faithful one and I knew He'd bring you here.' He had been expecting me, he said. He wiped his face several times, as if he were sweating. 'I am so glad to see you, Nani. I saw this in a vision: you in my edifice. God told me, "Prepare. Nani is coming today, the woman I have prepared for you." See? I even tidied the whole house for you. God has already started the beautiful work in us. The Devil has been shamed.'

He smiled as he said this. He tried to take my bag from me but I held on to it, clutching it close as if it were an essential part of me. He let go and motioned to me to sit down.

'No.' I shook my head. I came just deep enough into the house for him to shut the door. I suddenly felt claustrophobic. The smell of the air freshener, like something dead, clogged my nostrils. Doda told me once of some flower that smelled like rotten flesh. I had never seen it but I imagined that the air freshener was its odour. My palms itched. The back of my knees begged to be scratched. I thought of a way to begin what I had to say.

'God showed me to you on a mountaintop. He said to me, "Dear son whom I love, this is the woman I have handpicked for you."'

How dare you? I wanted to ask. 'How . . .' I began but then I thought of why I had come, and the words I was going to say died in my throat. Instead I said 'I am pregnant', before words failed me. I did not want to cry in front of this man but I could not control it. It was the first time I had ever said it aloud, the first time I had said it to anyone. Pregnant. The word was a mountain on me and it crushed me. I began to cry again, and for a moment Ephraim looked astonished, as if he could not understand why I would be crying. The mountain was strong and I could not lift it off me and it was crushing me and crushing me and I could not breathe unless I opened my mouth wide and let out a cry. I willed the tears to subside, I swallowed my cries, I gathered myself and as calmly, as clearly as I could, I said 'I want you to help me get rid of the pregnancy. My mother . . . she must never find out.' It burned my tongue to have to ask him. He said nothing. His smile spread.

'I'll forgive you. Forget what you did if you help me,' I said.

His smile discomfited me. I continued, searching for the vocabulary that was close enough to his to shake him into action.

'It was the Devil. I understand. But the Devil must not win. If you do not help me, what happened will come to light. The Devil will win.' I was clutching at straws. I did not stop to think about what I was saying. I just kept on talking. And if I had to stand there talking until the sun went down, I would. I could not, would not, quit until I heard from him that he would help me. I would talk him into submission. But he said nothing, just stood opposite me, looking at me with that smile on his face, his hands behind him like a school headmaster on patrol, his eyes shining in amusement.

'Please. Help me,' I said.

Ephraim's smile deepened but even though he was still silent his lips began moving as if in prayer. Finally he said loud enough for me to hear, 'It is God's handiwork. Praise Him. Elevate His holy name. He ordained this. In the book of Amos, the Bible perspicuously proclaims, "Do two walk together unless they have agreed? Does a lion roar in the forest when it has no prey? Does a young lion growl in its den unless it has seized something? Does a bird get caught in a snare if the snare has not been baited? Does a tiger spring up from the ground unless it has caught something? If a trumpet sounds in a city, will the people not be frightened? If disaster strikes a city, has not Yahweh caused it? Yet Yahweh does nothing without revealing his plan to his servants, the prophets. If the lion roars, who will not be afraid? If Yahweh speaks, who will not prophesy?" This has been ordained by God. You shall be my wife, Nani. There is nothing any man can do about it.'

Each sentence he uttered jumped out and kicked me in the stomach, punched me in the chest, stabbed me in the eye. I could not see. My knees were buckling. Maybe I should sit down after all but I did not. If I sat, I would not have the energy to get up and would be stuck to the chair, in his house forever. The smell of death pervaded everything so that I could not breathe properly. This was how I had been in the days after Udodi's death. I tried to breathe through my mouth but it was impossible to do that and speak at the same time, and I needed to have him hear me. I held on to his shirt. 'What? I can't. Please. I am begging you! Please!' I was yelling now. He was saying something but I shouted above his voice, panting from the effort. 'Please. Please. Please.' My head was bursting from the pressure inside it, pressure that could only be relieved by my screaming. He prised my hands free from his shirt and pushed me onto the sofa. I landed on it hard and the walls closed in around me.

'God abhors abortion. He has given us a child to seal the bond between us. The Bible says that. Sit. I will marry you.'

'Marry? Are you mad?'

'That is the only way. This baby, our baby . . .' He seemed gripped by emotion. 'Our baby will have a father and a mother.' He began to clap his hands and sing,

112

dancing like a deranged man. If he would not help me, I would go back to Mother. I would face her anger and scorn. Not even she would make me marry this man to save face.

Ephraim

Doxology!

Nani

In the weeks before I realised I was pregnant, when I began to dream again of a normal life, I imagined returning to Enugu after medical school. I'd set up my own private hospital, marry some man I'd fallen in love with and have a big, beautiful wedding.

This was how I had dreamed of my wedding: a white gown of the most delicate lace with a V-neck bodice with sparkly sequins; a veil, long and diaphanous, over my face; a long train trailing the ground as I walked up to the altar; silver, satiny pumps; a bouquet of flowers picked by my own hands; a groom in a three-piece suit; six brides-maids and the same number of flower girls with ribbons in their hair throwing confetti and rice at my back. Ugo would be the maid of honour. Mother would have to give me away. I could not think of anyone else who could replace Doda. I would have the best of everything: a twelve-tier cake ordered from Genesis and an all-night party at the Brown & Brown Centre with DJ Blox (whom everybody knew was the DJ to have) performing. It would be a wedding everyone would talk about and pictures of it would make their way to local papers and magazines. My groom and I would be on the cover of some of the magazines, dazzling, looking like film stars, the sequins on my bodice throwing off light like diamonds. Sometimes, inspired by pictures in bridal magazines and in *Ovation*, I sketched my ideal wedding, shading in the details with brightly coloured glitter pens: the big hall, the glamorous clothes; the multi-tiered cake in the shape of a tower, the flowers.

Yet the wedding had come sooner and was as far removed from all the things I had dreamed of as it could have been. There was no DJ, no fancy cake from Genesis, no dancing until midnight with my new husband in a hall festooned with balloons. Not even my mother knew I had got married.

I did not expect that going to Ephraim's for help would culminate in a marriage ten days later. He'd trapped me and left me with no energy to fight when he said we were going to the registry. It was only much later that I'd regret not even putting up a fight: he couldn't have dragged me into a car. Regrets do no good, Doda used to say, so I tried not to think of the fact that I had walked into the cab he hailed and into the registry office with him, that I hadn't summoned up the energy to resist.

The only witnesses at the sham affair were a man who looked like a rodent, in an ill-fitting suit, and his wife, who seemed undecided as to whether she should smile or cry. Ephraim said they were friends of his, he knew them from church. I had never seen them before. The man kept looking at his watch, complaining every couple of minutes that he would be late for work if the court registrar did not turn up soon, and if he was late he would get a warning and his supervisor was a wicked man and before he knew it he would lose his job and where would he be without a job, eh? Ephraim asked him to stop complaining, nobody would sack him, although he too kept asking the pimply-faced, rather yellow-looking receptionist when the registrar would turn up. She promised him each time, without looking at him, that 'Oga will soon return. Five minutes. Don't worry.' She sounded bored. Her words came out with the practised air of someone who was used to saying the same thing over and over again. The room was suffused with the smell of roast groundnut, which the receptionist was eating while furiously typing something, her keypad going tak-tak-tak like a bird pecking at the bark of a tree. The entire floor was her dustbin as she dropped groundnut shells nonchalantly on it. Mother would never have stood for such careless disregard of cleanliness. She would have asked the woman to pick up after herself. I could almost hear Mother say in that authoritative voice which no one had ever been known to ignore, 'Will you stop behaving as if you were in a pig sty? Stop this rubbish now, and clean up around you! And while I'm here, I'll take my daughter home. What's she doing here?' I almost smiled at the impossible thought of Mother striding in to save me.

Entering the registry office was like walking into a cloud of dust. It hit your nose before you even saw that the chairs were coated in a film of thick grime. We could not sit without wiping the wooden chairs first, so Ephraim asked the receptionist whether he had accidentally walked into the Sahara Desert.

'What?' She chewed slowly, insolently. I had never seen anyone so light-skinned. She was lighter even than Aunty Enuka.

'I enquired if this is perchance the Sahara Desert, or

do you people export dust? The chairs. Everywhere. Dust. Dust.'

He laughed. The man who had accompanied Ephraim laughed a little. The man's wife and I did not. The receptionist rolled her eyes at Ephraim, hissed and went back to her typing. Tak. Tak. Tak. It was as if Ephraim did not exist, as if all four of us there did not exist. Her lips, outlined in black, her purple eyeshadow, the eyebrows waxed and then pencilled in, the huge blond mane on her head, so high it looked like she would tip over, and which made her face seem comically small, the red rouge on her cheeks, all gave her the look of a cartoon character. But I liked her, liked that she rolled her eyes at Ephraim without caring if anyone saw her or not, that she hissed loudly at him. The eye-rolling and the hissing avenged me in a small way for all the humiliations I was suffering at Ephraim's hands.

He said, 'Is this how you treat a prophet of the Most High? A servant of the living God?'

His voice was gentle but I was starting to know him well and I could hear the menace folded into it. He brought out his Bible from the leather satchel he always carried. A dimpled smile spread across his face and he offered to pray for her, for forgiveness, if she was willing. 'And if you do not want my prayers, sister, I'll do like Jesus commanded His disciples in Matthew 10, verse 14: "And whosoever shall not receive you, nor hear your words, when ye depart out of that house or city, shake off the dust of your feet."' He snorted out a laugh as if he had told a joke but the receptionist looked scared, chastened. My admiration for her ebbed. Even as I willed more impudent behaviour from the yellow-faced woman,

118

she flicked her mane from side to side, stood up and began to apologise.

'Sorry, I had no idea you were a Man of God. Please forgive me.' I hissed under my breath. She brought out a rag from under her desk, all the while saying, 'Sorry. Sorry. I did not know you were a Man of God.' Her voice had taken on a wheedling note. 'Forgive me, Man of God. The chairs will be cleaned now-now. Sorry about the dust. The cleaner hasn't come in almost two weeks. I am going to ask my oga to sack him! Sorry, Man of God.'

It was as if Ephraim was a big politician, or her boss, someone with the power to take away her job and make sure she never held another one again as long as she lived. It amused me, this respect for anyone who claimed to be a 'Man of God'. If I told this woman the conditions that had forced me to be there marrying Ephraim, would she still have so much respect for the 'Man of God'?

The receptionist told Ephraim that she had 'issues at home' and could he please pray for her. Afterwards, buoyed on the prayer, the receptionist's attitude to our party, but especially to Ephraim, changed. She became fawning, solicitous, offering us her groundnuts, complaining of how hard she was worked and asking Ephraim if he could ask God to get her another job, somewhere where her education could be put to better use, where she could earn more money.

'I even want to act. Nollywood. I can act well.'

'No!' Ephraim said. Nollywood was a den of iniquity. 'You must forget that, sister! A new job, a job sanctioned by God, a good job and prosperity will find your name and address in Jehovah's mighty name!'

119

The receptionist shouted an amen that sounded as if it came from a place of pain. She smiled as if Ephraim had already delivered the job. If I had not been feeling so sorry for myself at that moment, I would have laughed at the ridiculousness of it all. I imagined sharing the story with Ugo. How we would laugh. I would also tell Ugo of the woman's hair, 'So huge that you could not even see anything behind her!'

I looked down to hide the smile which had formed in spite of myself, and caught sight of the dress I was wearing. It was a green polyester dress with black dots which Ephraim had given to me that morning with the instruction that I should wear it. He said he had bought it the day after the vigil, in anticipation of my coming back. It had no tags and smelt washed, so I was certain that he had picked it up from a BBB – bend-down boutique – one of the ubiquitous secondhand stores at the market. I tried not to imagine which dead white person had owned it before me, remembering how my sisters and I had often felt sorry for Aunty, who sometimes bought clothes from such stores, boiling them in water to wash away the smell of the 'dead white person' all pre-owned clothes were said to have come from. I could not stand the thought of it touching my naked body. I had thrown it back at Ephraim. In this new life where Ephraim ruled, with his fists if his words did not have the desired effect, I was soon naked and the dress forced on me.

Ephraim had a long caftan of an indeterminate colour. He was the only one who was in a good mood, humming under his breath, smiling occasionally and saying how he could not wait for 'this man to come so I can begin life as a married man'.

'I don't blame you, Man of God,' the receptionist said. 'Your woman is beautiful. God has blessed you.'

The scene seemed to me to be covered in a wrinkled polybag like an old magazine cover, too ersatz for it to be real. I couldn't be here, surely. I was at home sleeping and that (real) me would soon wake up and tell Ugo about this absurdly ridiculous dream. An itch started from the back of my neck and travelled slowly, teasingly, to the back of my legs. I could not stand it any longer and so I began to scratch. I ignored the four pairs of eyes watching me curiously as I scratched. This was a dream after all, I said to myself, luxuriating in the release the scratching gave me, and none of these people mattered. The only thing that was real was the itch and I was getting rid of it.

It was another hour before the registrar strolled in, a thickset man with a face Mother would have called 'jolly': full cheeks and bright, wide, alert eyes. He wore a surprisingly fashionable pin-striped shirt, a tie which seemed too elaborate for the surroundings, and held a handkerchief to his forehead to soak up sweat. He looked out of place in the room, like someone who could be Doda's friend, someone I would have to call 'Uncle'. He barely glanced at the people waiting for him, nodded absentmindedly in response to Ephraim's greeting, spoke to his receptionist in a low, confidential tone, and then turned to us, shook hands with Ephraim and signalled that we should follow him into his office. He switched on the air conditioner, sighed and sat down behind a desk.

'So what can I do to help you? Who's getting married today?'

He had on a high, cheery voice which I assumed he used

for occasions like this. I could imagine him telling his wife at home, or his friends when they asked how his day went, in a different voice about how he put nervous couples at ease with his cheerfulness. My head throbbed.

And now this registrar was asking for names, and 'Who are your witnesses?' He still had the false genial voice he felt he ought to use. And now he was asking for the new couple and the witnesses to sign. And now he was saying 'I declare you husband and wife' and he had another appointment and to have a happy married life.

'You may now kiss the bride,' he said, putting a file away and almost walking out the door, his voice already changing back to the one he used when he was not performing marriage ceremonies.

I had a feeling of having been hit in the head with a blunt object when Ephraim grabbed me and planted a furious wet kiss on my mouth. I wiped my lips. The receptionist shouted 'Congratulations, Mister and Missus Man of God' as we trooped out of the office. Ephraim shook the hands of his witnesses, waited for me to catch up with him and nudged me into the bright, blinding sunlight to look for a taxi to take us back to his house.

'Today you have become mine, both spiritually and by law. No one can tear us apart.'

It felt to me as if I was playing a part in a film. I couldn't be married. And not to Ephraim. If I decided to walk home now, he wouldn't be able to stop me. I quickened my steps. I imagined my mother's face at my return, imagined telling her why I'd left in the first place, and my steps slowed. But maybe I could go to Aunty Enuka? I began to walk faster again. Who was I kidding? Not even Aunty Enuka would be able to convince Mother to forgive me. The invisible chains around my ankles tightened and I could only take short, slow steps.

On the drive back to Obiagu Road he whispered into my ear, 'What God has joined together, let no man tear asunder.'

I felt a sharp pain in my chest. With some luck, I thought as the pain continued, I was having a heart attack which would finish me off.

Udodi, the Chorus

A story is a coconut you crack open to see the world.

The Devil never makes a good friend. Doda told us the folktale of the dog who befriended a ghost against good counsel and paid for it with his life. The day the Ezemmuo of ghosts needed a sacrifice of flesh and blood and demanded the dog, his ghost friend had not even pleaded for the dog. Nani should have remembered this story before going to Ephraim's.

His *Shout Hallelujah! Hallelujah!* pierced my heart. I could see his thoughts forming.

He began to dance, this man with no edges, just one long swirling, menacing thing.

'We will marry!' he said.

I closed my eyes but I saw still. Nani's repulsion, her fear crawling up my own arms.

Nani kneeling in front of him, hanging on to the hem of his trousers.

Please, Ephraim, Please, I do not want this . . . I don't want this . . . this baby. You cannot want it. Just help me. Please. I forgive you for what you did to me. I forgive you. I will never tell anyone about it and I forgive you from the bottom of my heart. I swear! I am not angry with you any more but you must help me, I am pregnant now and I don't want it. You must know someone who can help me. Please. We can't get married. I can't have a baby. My mother . . .

Ephraim's weedy leg jerking as if he was dancing. The smile on his face wiped out as if it had never been.

'Not a hair on the head of this baby will be harmed.'

His voice a sharp cutting into the room, into Nani's flesh, into the world. I saw into his heart and I knew even before he locked Nani in, before the breaking of things (by her): a flask against the wall disintegrating into particles of shininess, a drinking glass on the floor, cushions scattered all over. I knew.

Ephraim walking out while she wailed. Ephraim returning into his kingdom. Kicking and trampling on broken things. His eyes settled on Nani amidst the wreckage and the splinters.

'Crean this up.'

Nani, standing up to him:

No. No. No. You can't make me do anything! Do not push me! Don't you dare!

When she slapped him, my heart soared. Take that, Ephraim! Fuck you!

But I closed my eyes against the fist that descended on her like a judgement.

Striking. Again. And again. And again. Breaking her. She joined the broken things on the floor.

Begging: *Stop! Stop! Stop!*

The body is a traitor. Feels pain when you want to feign supernatural strength so that you do not break too. And as she begged, I knew she remembered Chinelo. She would not go to Mother, broken and bruised, a baby swelling her stomach.

125

She would not go to Mother and be asked, 'Where did he rape you?' She would not return to Number 47 because she knew her mother well.

Nani knew when a battle was lost.

Ugo

When Nani doesn't return that night Ugo leaves early the next morning to look for her at the address she left behind. She tears into her for not coming home when she should have. 'Haba! How long do you think I can cover for you, ke? The driver is outside, let's go!'

'Did Mother send you?'

There is something hopeful in Nani's voice. Ugo shakes her head. 'Mother doesn't know you're gone yet. She thinks you went to bed early. She doesn't even know I'm out.'

Ugo is impatient to leave. *Why's Nani wasting my time? Abi, she wants two of us to be in hot soup?* She hopes that she and Nani can get home before Mother wakes up. If not, she will tell Mother that she and Nani went for some early morning errand and hope Mother believes her. The room is hot. Ephraim has his head bowed over a book but Ugo can tell that he is listening. There is something malevolent about him she's only noticing now. It gives her goose pimples. What on earth is Nani doing with this man?

'It's too late, Ugo.' The hope in Nani's voice is gone. Her voice is a squeak.

'For what?' Ugo asks. Ephraim looks up and holds her gaze.

'You heard her,' he says. Ugo has never seen Nani look that small, as if she were somehow diminishing before her eyes, a song fading into nothing.

'May your scrotum shrivel to the size of a cockroach's. I was talking to my sister, not to you!'

Nani shakes her head at her. She whispers, 'Go.'

'No! What's wrong with you, Nani?'

Ugo wonders if her sister has been jazzed. She's read about it. Aunty calls it remote control. 'Someone puts juju on you and they can control you from anywhere!' Aunty used to warn them about accepting food from strangers when they were much younger. Ugo has never believed it but now she's not so sure. She tries to drag Nani out but Nani pulls her arm away.

'Go!' she says again to Ugo, this time in a strong, clear voice. 'Go before you get into trouble with Mother.'

'Nani?' Ugo calls, confused. This is not her sister, willingly choosing to be with this man. Ugo begins to cry, to plead. The day Ephraim came to the house and she let him in, Nani's anger scared Ugo. She knew then that he had done something to Nani. It doesn't make sense to her now that Nani is choosing to stay with him. *What kind of nonsense dream is this?* She cannot imagine a life where Nani is not at Number 47. Not in America. But in Enugu with a man like Ephraim. Living in a house like his.

'This is my choice,' Nani says. There is something in her voice Ugo can't place. Nani places a hand on the small of Ugo's back. 'Please. Please go. I love him.'

And that is what reverberates in Ugo's head all through

the drive home. 'I love him.' *How can Nani love this person? Haba!* Maybe she is too young to understand love. She cries all the way back to Number 47. She doesn't care that the driver can hear her snivelling in the back seat.

In the weeks following Nani's departure the flowers in the front yard wilt and die, drooping their heads as if in shame, or in accusation, or in defiance, as if they've refused to bloom if Nani, who of all three daughters was the one who took most joy in them, was gone. Aunty complains that the roses have developed black spots, she can't pick any for the dining room. Ugo, too, is withering inside from guilt. She cannot believe that Nani loves Ephraim. When has this love happened? Maybe, she thinks, she shouldn't have agreed to cover for Nani the night she went for that vigil because Nani returned from that outing quiet, quieter than she used to be. Ugo has a feeling that whatever it is that has Nani living with Ephraim, that night was responsible for it.

When the car pulls into the front of the house and Mother is there, arms on her waist as if readying for a fight, Ugo braces herself to tell Mother that Nani is gone.

'Gone where? And where are you coming from so early in the morning?' Mother asks.

Ugo tells her everything. Maybe Mother will march into Ephraim's house and drag Nani back. Mother lets out a *hia!* She raises her head to the sky, mutters something and spits out 'Nani is no longer my child.' Then she turns and walks back inside, taking whatever hope Ugo has that she will bring Nani back.

Ugo spends her days playing loud music to drown out

the thoughts in her head. She hates Nani for leaving and shrinking their family of five to two.

When Cordelia comes to the door to ask for Nani, Ugo tells her Nani's gone to visit an aunt of theirs in Lagos.

'When is she coming back?'

'Soon,' Ugo says and pretends that Mother is calling her.

Soon after, Mother lets her wrath loose on Aunty because the maid told the Mbagwus' son who came calling for Nani that Nani had been kidnapped and Mother was still negotiating the ransom, millions of naira. Aunty was only trying to mitigate the rumours that she was sure had started making the rounds. It was better for people to think that Nani had been abducted than that she had run to a man's house, she explained to Mother.

'You do not get to decide,' Mother screamed at her. 'How long are these kidnappers supposed to be holding her for? Where did they kidnap her from? From inside this house? You think Mrs Mbagwu, who stopped me today to offer her condolences, believed the cock and bull story you told her son?' Mother tells the gateman to tell whomever comes to look for Nani that she is out, it doesn't matter what time of day.

A few months later Enang corners Ugo at the supermarket.

'It's been a while since any of us has seen Nani. Is she okay?' Enang asks, and in the way she asks it, the way her eyebrows shoot up, Ugo knows that Aunty is right, the entire estate knows that something is up. She spreads her ten fingers at Enang.

'Waka. Carry your gossip elsewhere!'

She runs out of the supermarket without the apples and the bell peppers Mother asked her to get. She wonders what exactly people know, how much. The driver who drove her to Ephraim's house, and Aziz, who let Nani out the gate, must have blabbed. Aunty would never. She is almost family. Drivers and gatemen are not to be trusted. Everyone knows that. When Chibuogo's father had a baby with a teacher at Chibuogo's school, when the father bought the teacher a house in Trans-Ekulu, and moved her and the baby into the house, it was his driver who told the Ugokwes' washer-woman (who was his girlfriend), swearing her to secrecy, and she in turn swore Enang's gardener (who was her cousin) to secrecy before telling him, and he told the Ojukwus' cook, who told the Ifedibas' cook (who never liked Chibuogo's mother because she was always threatening to have him fired), who was only too happy to bring his madam down a peg or two, and then all hell broke loose. Chibuogo's mother – whose father was some big-shot military man – went with military police to the teacher's house on the day of the baby's christening and had both her husband and his mistress handcuffed and doing frog jumps while a mocking crowd watched. Aziz must have told someone of the preacher who visited often, and then one night Nani left with him and spent the night and then one day she left and never returned, and the estate would have done the math, putting two and two together and coming up with a disgraced family, a daughter who's run off with a man. And what a man. A preacher. Ugo could imagine the conversations around dinner tables on the estate.

'A preacher?'

'Yes ooo. Not one of those Gucci-wearing, funky ones ooo, some random guy with dust on his shoes.'

'I always knew that that Nani's head wasn't correct.'

'If she wanted a boyfriend, why didn't she find someone suitable?'

'Why move in with a man?'

'You don't suppose . . .?'

'Who knows . . .?'

Nani, like Chinelo, a cautionary tale told on the estate. 'Don't let any yeye man turn your head and drive you to foolishness! Just look at Nani.' At school Ugo is sure people are pointing at and whispering about her. 'That's the girl whose sister . . .' She hates Nani.

A few days after Nani leaves, Mother asks Aunty to box up all of Nani's clothes and books and shoes and give them away. 'Whatever that Ephraim has on her is her own business,' Mother says but she grips her glass of water too tightly. She shouts instructions at Aunty from outside the door as if she were afraid of entering the room. 'Clean it out! I want the room to be spotless!' By the time Aunty is done, there is no trace of Nani left in the room, and Mother installs three baby cots in there. She christens the room 'the nursery'. When babies arrive, all Ugo hears is 'Go to the nursery and feed the babies!' 'Come to the nursery and see the babies.' 'Clean out the nursery.' The room takes on the smell of baby powder and diapers and Johnson's baby lotion. Yet each time Mother says 'nursery' her voice trembles, as if the weight of the word is so heavy she could not speak it. As if the word is the world, and her tongue Atlas's shoulders carrying it. Despite the cries of babies and the laughter of visitors and Mother's growing wealth, visible in the new cars she buys and the generosity of her pocket money to Ugo and in talks about new clinics, Number 47 retains a sombre mood. When Udodi died, and then Doda died, that sombreness was there but Ugo knew the grief would never lift. With Nani's absence it has become one tinged with frustration and sometimes hope. *One day Nani will come back.* Ugo waits for that day. She imagines her sister walking in at midnight, standing in the middle of the living room, and she, Ugo and Mother hugging her and asking, 'Is this really you? Is this a dream?' As days segue into weeks Ugo has dreams of Mother going off to look for Nani, scouring the earth for her prodigal child and finding her, hugging her and bringing her home. All forgiven. And all forgotten. Ugo knows that that is too much to hope for.

Ephraim

All praises to the Lord who guides my trajectory.

I, Ephraim, have become the husband of the most beautiful rose in the universe. The son-in-law of a woman whose money will not be exhausted in one lifetime. Nani's mother has acquired a son, and what she has shall be mine too. Maman! God has buttered our bread. He has rescued us from this valley of tears. Hallelujah.

Nani

At the beginning, never having had any use for it, I could not cook. At home, at Number 47, Aunty did the cooking. Once, Mother had floated the idea of hiring a proper cook, one of those in white uniform and chef's hat like some of the families on the estate had, but Doda was against it. He said it was too elitist. He did not want a cook who made foreign dishes he could not stomach. Had she forgotten, he asked, the trouble the Odogwus who lived at Number 55 had with their cook? White-aproned and hatted, the cook constantly served food that his employers neither recognised nor could pronounce the names of when told. 'It was as if we were dining at a high-end restaurant with a particularly recherché – a term I picked up from the chef – selection of food,' Mr Odogwu said. 'Cromesquis. Poutine. Boeuf Bourguignon. All those names that mean nothing to us and food that did nothing for our palate. My wife said we were paying him good money so we might as well enjoy the new experience he was bringing. When the children whined, she asked them how many of their friends could boast of gourmet dining every day of the week. We persevered. But . . .' he paused, looking theatrically distressed, 'the day he served egg on creamed bitter leaf was the day my wife decided he had to go. She had had enough! Bitter leaf should only be in onugbu soup, she said!' Laughter.

Mother countered that those cooks were very often adept at making Nigerian dishes too. 'We will interview them before we hire.' Doda said Aunty already made the best egusi soup and as long as she was with us he did not want to sample anyone else's. None of us expected to live a life where we would ever have to depend on our own cooking and so, not having the slightest interest in it, I never asked Aunty to teach me. While I had a general idea of what went into making most dishes, I did not know in what quantity or sequence.

That day after the registry wedding, Ephraim asked me to make him yam porridge.

'I can't,' I said. He hit me behind my neck.

'A wife cooks for her husband!'

He dragged me to the kitchen. There were two other women there, chatting as one pounded crayfish and the other stirred a pot beside her. I stood in front of Ephraim's stove.

'I can't cook,' I said. 'I don't know how.'

The pounding stopped. The chatting stopped. Ephraim's mouth opened, closed, then he let out a bellow. The women looked at us and began to titter. I had been spoilt at home, Ephraim said, but he would undo the damage. It was his Christian duty as my husband.

'How can this one be a proper wife if she cannot cook?' he asked, addressing the kitchen, abandoning his high-falutin language. 'Here, begin by cutting the yam.' The women went back to pounding and stirring and chatting in low tones but I knew they were paying attention to Ephraim and me.

Every day, for the next few weeks, Ephraim did not stop instructing me in loud, derisive tones, regardless of who else was in the kitchen as he did his 'duty'.

'Stupid woman. One handful of egusi, not the entire bag. Are you cooking for a political rally?' 'You always fry the tomato in oil first, Nani! How many times do I have to tell you? I'm not even Nigerian and yet I know to make your food!' 'Your parents had money but very little sense if they couldn't even teach you that egg is not deep fried!' When words alone would not do they would be accompanied with a slap on my back. Ephraim did not slap with his palm. When he slapped my face he used the back of his hand, and when he slapped my back or my neck he used the edge of his hand, deliberate attempts to inflict maximum pain. Once, he forced me to eat burned rice 'because good wives do not let their minds stray when they cook, so much so that food burns!'. I spat the rice out at him and so he clamped my mouth shut until I swallowed. And then he dragged me to the kitchen to start all over again.

Sometimes other women gathered to view the unusual spectacle of this new wife being taught to cook by her husband. They giggled, they called me 'ajebutter', mocking my wealthy background for not preparing me well for a life of marriage. They never offered a hand in friendship. They did not plead with Ephraim not to humiliate me. I would not have taken their friendship in any case. I did not know what I could discuss with these women, many of whom had never seen the inside of a classroom. I felt superior to them, I was better than they were in every way, I told myself, pretending that their snobbery did not hurt me. I had never had to beg for friendship and yet here I was with women who would not talk to me. I looked for flaws in them and magnified them, flaws I could not discern in myself (poor dress sense; crass, vulgar tongue; poor grammar). I would think later how much easier it is to be nice to other people if one's life is exactly as one dreamed it would be.

Ephraim did not speak directly to any of the neighbours, even as he pandered to their curiosity by announcing loudly to nobody in particular, while I cooked, that 'my wife comes from a rich family. Her mother never taught her the rudiments of cooking!' They, in turn, never spoke to Ephraim, even though they laughed and kept returning to watch the anomaly that was a grown woman who could not cook. It was obvious that they did not approve of him. And that their disapproval extended to his strange wife.

One day while I was cooking with Ephraim supervising as usual, and the group of women gathered to watch, sometimes commenting loudly and laughing amongst themselves, Ephraim suddenly turned off the kerosene stove. He pulled me away from it by the neck and dragged me, stumbling across the yard, towards his flat.

'What have I done? What have I done?' I shouted.

I could see some of the neighbours snickering, although I also saw Philo, whose name I did not know then, her clothes flowery and blazing with colour, colours Mother would have approved of, look away, as if she were too ashamed to witness the spectacle of a grown woman being pulled like a child.

'What have I done, Ephraim?' I asked again, twisting

free as he locked the door behind me. I might not like the neighbours but being shamed in front of them was more than I could bear.

'Search yourself. I should not have to tell you.' He slapped me hard on the back of my neck. I scratched his cheeks.

'Tell me what I've done!' I demanded. I wished he would kill me. I dared him to kill me. He slapped me. I reached out to scratch him again but he preempted me, holding me by my wrists.

'You make me a sight for ridicule in front of all those stupid women. Do you see any other man in the kitchen? No. Only Ephraim. You hear them laughing at another man? No. Only Ephraim. You make a raffing stock of me.'

It was not the first time there had been a crowd watching, and he had always seemed not to mind, acting out for them even, giving me instructions in a tone that suggested by its loudness that they were not meant for me alone, so I could not understand why it had suddenly bothered him today. But I was also starting to learn that Ephraim had a temper as fractious as it was unpredictable. Both the temper and the unpredictability he clothed with a cloak of righteousness once he was outside the house.

His outburst ended as suddenly as it had started and he pushed me onto a sofa. He came and sat beside me.

'I rove you, Nani, but you make me so angry sometimes. You are so beautiful, my beautiful wife, but you must be taught to be a good wife too as the Bible wants.'

His breath was hot and uncomfortable. I could still feel the pain of his slap on the back of my neck. I did not feel beautiful. When I looked in the mirror I saw a woman of indeterminate age with dry, scaly skin and a scarf covering her head.

Every beating I got from Ephraim ended with his declaration of love and, if he was in the mood, with sex. I learned to take myself far, far away and let someone else be the one on the narrow bed, a man I could not stand grunting like a pig on top of that person who was not me, taking her nipples in his mouth and biting hard enough to make that woman wince in pain and finally, when he was done, resting the weight of his body on her and saying ' I rove you very much, Nani.' It wasn't me he was with, it was the rag doll. I was back at Number 47, eating beans and fried plantain or ukwa with fish at a dining table too big to fit into this house.

Nani

I, who had not been prepared for marriage or for pregnancy, began to watch in horror as my stomach grew, distending like an alien growth, something that was not a part of me. I woke up from dreams where I stomped through a garden full of weeds, pulling out the weeds by hand, and woke up sobbing. I execrated this thing which drenched me in sweat each night. It was nothing like Mother told us it was when she was pregnant with each of us. Mother had had food cravings which sent Doda to the kitchen late at night, making her chicken pepper soup and jollof rice. Mother said that for each of her pregnancies she added so much weight from eating that she never thought she would ever regain her waist. 'I was always like the Michelin Man!' With Udodi she had a craving for goat head pepper soup but, being in Washington DC and not Enugu, Doda could not find goat head anywhere. 'This was in the eighties, you know, not like now when there isn't any major US city without an African store or a Nigerian restaurant!' So poor Doda had had to make use of lamb instead. 'I managed it,' Mother said, laughing at the memory, 'although all that packaged supermarket meat hardly tastes like meat!'

If I had any food cravings, I disregarded them. Ephraim would never have gone out of his way to get me what I wanted to eat. And I would never have brought myself to ask him. I could not let him think that I accepted that we were an ordinary couple, doing ordinary things. We ate what he bought, which was mostly yam and rice. I made huge pots of rice and stew; pots of yam porridge and vegetable yam; jollof rice and fish – food I had not known how to cook before – and warmed up portions at a time in a small pot. No matter how tired I was, no matter how unwilling I was to cook or eat, I did both under the hawk-eyed supervision of Ephraim. I suffered from indigestion which kept me awake at night. When I fell into uneasy sleep, it was usually to dream of ways of excising that growth that was a demon eating me up inside. Once awake I fed it evil thoughts, hoping to send it back into nothingness. I remembered Aunty saying that a cousin of hers had killed her baby by thinking bad thoughts. I gobbled up my hatred of the baby taking over my womb, sending it down in thoughts and harshly whispered words while I rubbed my stomach. 'Evil child. You're not wanted. Die!' It did no good. The baby was determined to grow once it had taken root. Even my indigestion was getting better, although the morning sickness remained. I learned not to fight Ephraim but to eat whatever he asked me to, not tasting the food, not even willing to. I was a rag doll, limp and helpless. I missed Ugo. I even missed Mother. I missed my bed. I wanted my life back.

When I slept I dreamed that I gave birth to a monster with two faces. I woke up sweating and shivering from fear. Trapped in the house with Ephraim, who followed me around throwing out names, asking if I had a preference for any of them. Abednego. GodsOwn. PowerinHisname. Redeem. He said I should ask Ugo to be the godmother. 'You should invite your family to the Ark for the christening.' I dared him with my silence.

His biggest obsessions were Mother and America. All the questions led to them. Would Mother still send me abroad? Would the baby be American as I was American? And he, was he American now too? I marvelled at how easy it was for him to pretend that ours was a normal relationship, that I had married him of my own choosing. He seemed to have erased the memory of his crime. He never mentioned it and neither did I. It still shamed me that I had been so easily taken advantage of.

He asked 'Will your mother give us money for the baby? Her pioneer grandchild!' I rolled my eyes at him. Ephraim flung the paper he was reading away, strode over to where I was sitting and said, 'When I talk to you, you do not roll your eyes. You use your mouth. You speak.' I hissed. I smelt his fury and hissed again. With some luck, I would lose the baby if he beat me. He growled and punched the wall behind me.

It pleased me that Mother refused to have anything to do with us for the simple reason that it denied Ephraim a chance to get close to her money. The bigger my stomach grew, the more reckless I became in how I spoke to him, no longer caring for whatever punishment he would invent, hoping that he would snap and do something that would bring an end to the monster in my womb. When he said maybe he should go and see Mother *properly*, now he was her son, I laughed and told him, 'How stupid are you? Mother won't even employ you as

143

gardener!' I watched him slam the back of a chair to keep from hitting me. When he asked how soon we could go to America, I mocked him. 'Do you even have N100,000 to pay for the visa?' An American visa cost way less than that, no more than N18,000 of course, but what did he know? Ephraim did not like to admit to his ignorance. He did not ask anyone to verify my claims, he was too proud to do so. He bought my lies, and not having the money I claimed was needed, no longer asked me about it. It did not stop him from telling people in church that I was an American citizen, though, as if that extended him special honours.

Udodi, the Chorus

There was once a land where the gods demanded a sacrifice of eyes. To keep the gods happy, the king had the eyes gouged out of citizens who did not use theirs well. 'Ehe! If you have eyes but refuse to see, those eyes are useless,' the king said.

Would Ugo and Mother have survived that land?
I would have seen.
I would have felt it.
Nani with no flowers in her hair.
Nani ascending her room like a wandering, forlorn
    spirit.
Nani under her blanket.

Akaliogoli:
The restless one
Causing mischief
Get thee away from Number 47

I would have seen the pestilence that visited Nani
    arrive.
It would not have been hidden from me.
And if it had, Nani herself would have told me.

Don't tell anyone, but I've been raped

And I would have promised but I'd have known to let
    my tongue loose:

Mother.
Aunty Enuka.
Somebody.

I would have broken the bond between her heaven and
    his hell
pursued justice for her.

And when she had become pregnant
I would have thrown myself between Mother and Nani
Rolled back the dark clouds
Or stopped them where they were.

Nani

Holy. The baby that I had fed toxic thoughts to kill in my womb announced her approaching arrival to me with a slight discomfort. I went to bed with heartburn and woke up before dawn to a soaked bed. I thought that I had peed in bed and a wave of shame washed over me. I could not allow myself to think of what Ephraim's reaction would be if he found out. I had not wet the bed since I was six years old and could not understand why I would suddenly begin again now. No one had mentioned to me that pregnancy might induce bedwetting.

I had to find a way to slip out and wash the sheets before Ephraim realised what had happened. It was a good thing, I thought, that he had taken to sleeping in the parlour so that I could have the bed to myself and my ever-expanding stomach. I started to pull at the sheets when an intense pain took hold of me and caused me to shout out Ephraim's name. Ephraim ran into the room, rubbing sleep away from his eyes with one hand.

'What's wrong?'

I screamed again. It was as if giant secateurs had grabbed my insides and were squeezing hard. I was dying. I was going to be with Doda and Udodi, and I was afraid. I had thought I would welcome death but now it seemed close I discovered that I was too scared to face it.

Ephraim filled the room, asking, 'What's the matter? Why are you shouting? What's the matter?'

The pain slowly ebbed, and I regretted ever having shouted out his name. I hated him. He repulsed me and yet when I thought I was dying he was the only one I could call. The thought made me cry.

I knelt down and began to strip the sheet off the mattress. He asked why I was stripping the sheet. It was only three a.m. I ignored him but as soon as I had it off he snatched it from me. I tried to snatch it back, thinking it would kill me if he found out that I had wet the bed, but another wave of pain clutched my insides and I buckled back onto the bed.

Ephraim ran out of the house and when he came back in he picked me up and carried me, protesting and yelling, into a waiting taxi. He shouted the address at the driver several times, as if the driver was hard of hearing. I knew Ephraim. He wanted the driver to know that he was going to an upscale hospital. The Ark had raised money for the bill. Ephraim had spoken of nothing for weeks but the money he had been given to make sure his baby was born in comfort.

The pain became more frequent in the taxi. I felt the urge to use the bathroom and shouted for the taxi to stop. I wanted to go to the toilet, I said. 'I can't hold it.' From far away I heard the driver reply, 'Madam, abeg, no have this baby for my car ooo.'

Baby? It had not occurred to me that it might actually be the baby coming. This thing I had no wish to meet but which I hoped would buy me freedom from Ephraim.

I heaved my buttocks up and, balling my hands into fists, placed one under each thigh so that I did not sit with my buttocks touching the seat. It had become uncomfortable, feeling as if I was sitting on something. Pain came in waves and drenched me in a sweat. I tried to take my mind away from it, to think of other things. I had been sleeping in a wrapper, as usual, but now I had a dress on. How had that happened? I wracked my brain to remember but could not. Ephraim must have helped me but when? How? My mind wandered to Number 47. What was Ugo doing at this exact time? Probably sleeping, her life uncomplicated. Why had I not listened to Ugo when she tried to dissuade me from going to that night vigil?

Pain. A fire wrapping itself around my body.

I might have been in my own bed now, far away from Ephraim and this taxi driver who growled at me every time I screamed. I thought of the dog I had owned when I was a child. I had kept asking for a dog, finally wearing Doda down until he bought me one that looked like a sausage and had no hair. What was its name? What was its name? How could I have forgotten its name? How? Impossible. Whatwasitsnamewhatwasitsname?

Pain. Thunder rolling through my body, violently and without warning.

The driver stopped in front of a hospital and Ephraim carried me out, shouting 'My wife is about to have a baby! Nurse! Nurse! Where are you?'

I kicked my legs and pounded his chest but he held on to me as if he had just saved me from drowning, his morning breath fouling the air as he kept asking for a nurse, a doctor, anyone. He was asked to take me to the labour room, to let me walk, walking was good, a nurse would be with us soon.

'She's in great agony. Take a look at her!'

'Ah, all these new fathers, sef! Your wife will be fine. Women give birth all the time. Even ones younger than your wife. Ah. Love!' I heard the female nurse who had directed us to the labour room saying, her laughter indulgent and tender, mocking this young husband so obviously devoted to his wife and devastated by the pain she was going through, running through the hospital corridor with a grown woman in his arms.

I was relieved when Ephraim released me and transferred me to a bed. The mattress was less thin than the one I used at Ephraim's house but nowhere near the plush luxury of what I had at home. I could not believe that this was happening to me. I had long accepted the pregnancy, was living with the consequences of it, had willed time to pass so that I could have the baby. I wanted to be rid of the growth. When I daydreamed, I waltzed back home without a pregnancy and a baby, inserting myself – no questions asked – back into the life that I had been robbed of. But I had never really thought of actually birthing the baby. I remembered all the horror stories I had been told of giving birth. Somewhere in my mind I had imagined that one day I would wake up and the pregnancy would be miraculously gone, my stomach back to its normal size and Ephraim and his baby in a past I would erase no matter how long it took. If I ever dug it up, it would be to remind me never ever to trust so rashly again.

'I've learned my lesson,' I screamed, bent over on the bed – for the pain would not let me lie still – and it was in this position that the nurse found me when she entered.

She addressed herself to Ephraim. How long has your wife been like this? Has her water broken? How regular would you say the contractions are? She asked me to lie down and spread my legs. She inserted an expert gloved hand into my vagina. I thought again of that night in Ephraim's room when he tookandtookandtook and he was a mountain crushing me and I could not move him.

'Keep still. Don't move, please,' the nurse said.

I had not realised that I had tried to shake her off. I did not want Ephraim in the room. I did not want this excruciating pain tormenting me. I did not want to have a baby. I did not want to be in a hospital room with strangers putting their hands up my privates. I did not want to live. I did not want to die.

'You've dilated almost fully. I can feel the head,' the nurse said.

'Is that good or bad?' Ephraim asked. His voice shook.

'Birth is imminent.'

She rushed out and rushed back in with more people in uniform and I was wheeled away to another room. Ephraim walked alongside me, speaking, saying something I could not hear because the pain that had been searing my insides had worsened. He might have been praying, because the nurses sighed an 'Amen' every time he drew breath. Ephraim was good at that. Plucking prayers out of his hat at every occasion. Prayers and Bible quotes. The nurses must have thought *What a good husband, what a good prayerful man, what a righteous man.* If they knew him like I did, they would have kicked him out of the hospital. At least that was what I liked to imagine would have happened.

The pain colonised my body so that I became one with

it, so that I was nothing but this wave after wave of pain causing me to clutch at the bedsheets and yell 'Get him out of here! Get him out of here! He's evil!'

The nurse who had checked me earlier on said to Ephraim, 'Don't mind her. She doesn't mean it. When women are in labour, they say all kinds of crazy things. Once the baby is out they forget the pain and stop blaming you and the sweet loving continues. Women in labour say the craziest things! Pay her no mind. Once the pain wears off, she will spread her legs again!'

She laughed, a coarse sound that sounded like the neighing of a horse. It embarrassed me.

The nurse asked me to breathe through my mouth, it would help the pain. She said, 'The obstetrician will soon be here. You're doing fine, breathe, breathe!' She wrapped something around my arm, put a pillow under my back, asked me to sit up with my thighs and legs spread and drawn up to my stomach.

'I want to push! I feel like pushing!' I shouted.

'No. Not yet. Let the doctor come.'

Some other nurses came in, and then a doctor. I had hoped for a female doctor but with my luck, of course, I was not surprised that I did not get my wish. The universe seemed to be conspiring at every turn to keep me from getting a break. The gynaecologist, a man not quite as tall as Ephraim, about Doda's age at the time he died, without saying anything to me, inserted a cold, gloved hand into my vagina. I yelled and clamped my knees together.

'Please don't,' he said, his voice surprisingly gentle.

He parted my thighs and kept his hand inside me. I was convinced I was in a nightmare. This could not be happening to me. Not to me, who should have been training to be a doctor by now, somewhere in America, and dreaming of starting up my own private practice one day. Tears, fast and furious, ran down my cheeks as the doctor asked me to relax, pushed my knees apart and asked the nurses to stand on either side of me to make sure that I kept my legs sufficiently spread. He had one hand on my stomach, one inside me. He kept pushing on my stomach, asking questions in his kind voice: 'How are you feeling? You think we can get this show on the road?' Show on the road? What was this man talking about? This was not a game! I fumed silently, hating every single person in that room, every one of them witnesses to my humiliation. I imagined I was a witch, a god, someone with some superpower, and I plotted revenge in my mind. They'd all grow tails. Lose everything they held dear. And Ephraim? He'd die a slow, painful death. I cursed my mother for making it impossible for me to come to her. If she hadn't had that business dabbling in selling babies, I might have risked going to her once I found out about the pregnancy. She couldn't have killed me. I now called on death to take me. To spirit me away to Udodi, my beautiful, beautiful sister. The doctor removed the hand that was inside me and said with a smile, 'You can push now.' It was a relief to be able to push and I groaned, held my breath and pushed until he asked me to stop.

'Catch your breath. You're doing well. Good girl.'

He pressed a palm on my stomach with one hand and asked me to push again. He said I was doing well, take a break, push again. I was sweating and panting, pushing and taking a break and pushing, and when I thought I could not bear the pain any longer I felt a numbness and a slithering out and a baby being pulled out of me in a mess of blood. It felt like I had evacuated a huge watermelon.

'Well done,' the doctor said. 'Good job.'

He sounded like a parent complimenting a child. He sounded like Doda when I brought back craft I had made at school – like the time in elementary school when I brought back a Father's Day pencil holder made out of an empty tomato tin covered in plain coloured paper and decorated with drawings of 'my family'. Doda had the holder on his table for as long as he lived. Who removed it? It suddenly bothered me that I had not thought of it before now. I wanted that holder back. Who had it? I wanted Doda.

The doctor who spoke like Doda was looking at me and holding out a bloodied mess which was now bawling over Ephraim's singing.

'You want to hold her before we clean her up and weigh her? Do you have a name for her?'

He had started sounding impatient even though his voice was still gentle and kind, and he was smiling. He placed the baby on my chest. I fought the urge to shake her off. She smelled of something off, maybe sour milk. It turned my stomach. The baby had something white and mucus-like covering her head. I did not want her. The stench of her filled my nose. I wanted to escape. Far away from the baby, and from Ephraim, who was grinning. And from the nurses and the doctor who were smiling and seemed pleased with the world. A nurse was saying, 'Let her feed. Her first meal in the world! Breastfeed her and afterwards we'll have her cleaned up and Daddy can hold her too.'

Daddy! Ephraim was not Daddy. Ephraim was my abductor, the stealer of my dreams, my rapist. This baby was an unwanted consequence of a horrendous event.

The doctor was gone. I held the baby out to the nurse closest to her. I did not want to hold her. The nurse regarded me strangely, her eyes looking over her glasses to the other nurses, but she took the baby from me, saying it needed to be cleaned anyway. I closed my eyes. I willed my thoughts to take me as far away from that hospital room as possible. I wanted no part of this . . . this farce. That was what it was after all. But I wondered if a farce was always comical. I could not remember. Perhaps a better word, then, was 'tragedy'. I did not deserve this much ill luck. The baby was still bawling. I could not keep my eyes shut. I felt cold and my body started to shiver. I saw the nurse to whom I had handed the baby say something to the other nurses and I saw one take a quick look at me. They passed the baby around. They weighed her. They cleaned her. They gave her to Ephraim. The nurse who had the baby, who was now wearing a romper, said, 'Not every new mother wants to feed their infant straight away. I'll bring a bottle. Congratulations.' As she spoke, the other nurses managed to lift my buttocks and put an oversized pad between my legs, held in place with netted underwear. All the while Ephraim was in the room. I could feel his eyes probing, watching. He did not have the grace or the kindness to look away. My humiliation was complete and unequivocal, made possible with the complicity of the nurses.

Ephraim held the baby wrapped tightly in a blanket like a huge chunk of meat and walked alongside me as I was wheeled away, raw and hurting with a mountain crushing me, into another room. He said, after the nurses left, 'It's our baby, Nani. She is beautiful. Exquisite like her mother. God has done a wonderful thing for us. We shall call her Hory.' He was crying. He held the bundle out to me. I turned my head away from the two of them. Holy! What a stupid name. He could not even come up with a real name but what did I care? I hated Ephraim. I hated the baby. This ugly, old-looking baby. I shut my eyes so that I did not have to see anything that would remind me of where I was. There was no air in the room. Ephraim was sucking it up. The baby, grunting like some animal, was sucking it up too.

Udodi, the Chorus

Anyi bu umu Komosu
Anyi nwelu ako na uche
We are Komosu's children
We have wisdom and common sense
We know this:

If you wish to trace the path to the river, follow the
    footpath strewn with pieces of broken clay pots.

So:

Nani at eleven
Her Spanish teacher corrected her pronunciation while
    she read a text
He was rude, Udo! He made the entire class laugh at me!
    I'm never taking Spanish again

Never mind that:
She liked Spanish

You do not cut your nose to spite your face
Nani did.

You'll regret it
What do I care?
And, Udodi, I'll get back at that teacher!

Finger to tongue, flicked up to Heaven, she swore.

Nani

We brought Holy home two days later, on a Saturday afternoon. I was relieved that Ephraim wanted to carry her. She was swaddled in a knitted blue baby blanket he said was a present from a church sister. Everything we had for Holy came from people I did not know. The day we left the hospital the nurses laughed to see him so eager to do the carrying. They laughed as they observed him cover the baby's head with urgent little kisses, as if he were performing a ritual. They laughed as he pushed back my scarf with one hand and held tightly on to the baby with the other. Their laughter was long and envious. One of them, a woman whose uniform, although standard, looked stylishly fashionable on her, said to Ephraim, 'I should bring my husband to take lessons from you!' It was the same nurse who had told me jokingly, 'When you get tired of this man, please send him to me. We all deserve a man like him!' I looked at her, horrified. Ephraim, who hardly left my side while I was in hospital, said from where he sat beside the cot, 'No chance, sister. My wife and I are forever' in a tone as jocular and as light as the nurse's was. But through the lightness I pared down his voice and the seriousness

159

of it increased my horror. Forever! His voice a million thorns on my skin.

Once we got back to Obiagu Road, Holy began to cry and Ephraim said, 'She's hungry. Sit down and breast-feed her. My mother will bring food.'

I wanted nothing to do with this hungry thing but I sat and took Holy in my arms and guided her mouth to my breasts, which had begun to hurt and leak. I wished my milk would sour and kill her. Ephraim cooed to her, saying '*Hory! Hory! Hory!*' in a squeaky high voice which grated on me. I could not stand the baby so close to my skin.

While I was in hospital Ephraim's mother had arrived from Cameroon and settled into the house, getting it ready for me. She came in now from the kitchen, carrying a bowl of food. She placed it on the table and smiled widely at me. I hated the woman on sight. Ephraim was a faithful reproduction of his mother. They had the same straight stature, the same dimpled smile. She stood beside me, smiling as if that was all her face was. This huge grin, so uncannily like Ephraim's. Ephraim said something to her, she stretched out her hand and I handed the baby over. She held Holy across her shoulder and rubbed her back gently. Holy let out a burp and Ephraim's mother laughed and said something in French. She passed Holy over to Ephraim, who carried the baby into the bedroom. Ephraim's mother pulled me up. She was full-fleshed but when she hugged me, a hug I did not return, standing stiffly with my hands at my side, it was as if I was being bumped against something hard. She released me.

'Me, Mrs Ebosse. You, Mrs Ebosse. Enchantez,' the

woman said, stabbing at her own chest with a stubby finger, her smile growing but uncertain.

I said nothing. The older woman spoke very little English and I spoke hardly any French. The effort it cost her to dredge up the few words she had just spoken was evident on her face, in her uncertain smile, in the careful way in which she had enunciated her words, in her eyes waiting for me to show that I understood. Yet I did not say a word to her in return. I could have said 'Oui' or 'Je m'appelle Nani, et vous?', even 'Voilà Monsieur Mayaki', or any of the other nonsensical phrases I retained from years of French classes at school. They might not have been the appropriate response but at least they would have shown that I was keen to make friends with Ephraim's mother. I did not utter a word, though. I could not like anyone connected to Ephraim, no matter how much they smiled, no matter how much of an effort they made, no matter how innocent they looked. They were tainted by association and his mother most of all. I could certainly not like the woman who had given birth to the monster. I glowered at her, watched as the dimpled smile became tighter and tighter and then completely disappeared, as if it had been a drawing on a blackboard which was slowly being erased.

Under my breath I muttered, 'I am not Mrs Ebosse. I have never been. I never will.'

I filled the air with so much hostility that it stood like a barrier in the gap between myself and his mother.

Later, Ephraim told me that his mother said that his wife was beautiful but that she had a pinched face, that she looked as if she was sucking on an ant. He laughed as he said this, amused at his mother's creativity. 'She said,' he said between laughs, 'I should tell you to smile more. Spit out that ant!'

She might not have known the circumstances of how I ended up with Ephraim, there was no reason to suspect that she did, but I blamed her still. If she had never conceived him, sheltered him for nine months in her womb, if he had never been born, he would not have infested my life. Ephraim's mother expected me to behave like a grateful daughter-in-law. A complement to her perfect mother-in-law act. She did all the chores. She cooked, she cleaned and bathed the baby. I never thanked her once, even though I knew enough French to say 'merci'. She changed Holy's diapers, soaked them in hot water and washed them, singing as she scrubbed away at baby poo. She was on hand to take Holy from me once Holy was fed. I, who wanted nothing to do with Holy, was happy to hand her over to the woman who burped her and sang to her in a language I did not understand. She carried Holy on her back all day, the baby's head resting snugly on her shoulder, so that I could rest. I was not grateful. All I could think of was, What sort of a woman gives birth to a rapist? I turned my back on the woman and on her grandchild with a resolute air of indifference.

The week before Holy arrived Ephraim had moved us into another flat. This new one had three rooms, each as small as the rooms in the one we had moved from, but there was more space than we had previously had. His mother stayed in one of the rooms, Ephraim stayed in another and I shared the last with the baby. I was tempted some nights when Holy cried to pinch her nostrils and quieten her forever. I saw that once in a film. A new mother who killed her own child. I remembered thinking what an unnatural, terrible thing it was, a parent wanting to kill their own child, but now all I could think was that if I had the strength, I would do it. This child had been foisted on me. I had never wanted it, had not asked for it, could not love it.

I did ask him once to keep Holy and let me go. I said he could keep the child, I just wanted to return home to Number 47. I convinced myself that Mother would be willing to give me another chance without a child raising awkward questions from people. She could tell people that I had been abroad, taking a gap year, that sort of thing. Ephraim adored the child after all. His mother did too.

'Your mother can stay and help you out,' I said. Holy clearly trusted her grandmother, for she was less fussy in the woman's arms than she was in mine. Even when she cooked, Ephraim's mother kept Holy firmly tied to her back.

Ephraim acted as if I had not even spoken. Then, in addition to watching my every move, he must have got his mother to keep an eye on me, for I noticed her watching me with a new wariness in her eyes. She tailed me whenever Ephraim was away, talking, talking in that language I did not understand. If I walked towards the door, she sprinted towards it, a challenge and a question in her eyes. She made me so uncomfortable that I began to wish that she would go. My solitude grew. Ephraim and his mother talked in their language and laughed. Holy was passed from one hand to the other. I was ignored. I was a cactus that needed no care, saying nothing, asking nothing. Ephraim's mother, rebuffed, did not proffer friendship again.

After she left, Ephraim began locking the baby and me inside whenever he went out. When he was home he shadowed me. One day Holy was crying and Ephraim asked me to get her to shut up, he wanted to sleep. I went over to Holy's cot and her hands and legs – chubby despite my ill will – flailing reminded me for an instant of Udodi. How had I never noticed that she looked like Udodi? The high forehead and the eyebrows that ran into each other – unmistakably like Udodi's and Doda's. I peered closely and observed her with new eyes, suddenly seeing how Holy was very much like my side of the family. If I looked hard enough, I could see that Holy actually had very little of Ephraim in her. I felt a new love for her creeping up and sweeping over me like good news. I lifted Holy and, as if she felt the love, she stopped crying and seemed to look at me with a certain wonder in her eyes. I felt a rush of tenderness come over me that day, the wonder of a love that I had not known I was capable of. I was sure the baby could feel the transformation in me, even at three months, and I began to whisper in her ears how much I loved her, how sorry I was and how I would never abandon her. I promised her that I would look after her so that the fate that befell me would never befall her. For the first time I felt what it was like to be willing to die for another person. At night I wondered how I could protect her if I left Holy with Ephraim to pursue my own dreams. Then I realised that my own dreams had changed. I still dreamed of escaping but I could not leave without Holy. If I took Holy, Mother would never have me back. I was trapped.

★　★　★

PraiseHim was born exactly a year after Holy. Ephraim had left me alone the two months after Holy's birth while his mother was with us. He never came to the room where I slept. For those two months, apart from Holy's cries, the bedroom was my haven. I closed the door – I had no key with which to lock it – and I could pretend to be back at Number 47, even though the walls were dark purple and the paint was peeling and the room smelled of poverty. And there was no room for flowers. Still, it was my sacred space. I had hoped that he would never touch me again but one night, as I was descending into sleep, Ephraim walked in naked. He lay beside me and began to paw me. I pretended to be asleep but it did not deter him. I begged and cried but he was a mountain I could not push away and so I lay under him and he took and he took and he took.

The year after PraiseHim came Godsown. Ephraim named the children. Names that reflected his own farcical self-righteousness. Names I would never have chosen but which Ephraim said were given to him in a vision by God. He made it sound as if God had written them out on a sheet of paper each time and instructed him in a deep voice, 'This is what thy child must be called.' Had God nothing better to do, I wanted to ask him, than to figure out names for newborns? 'Three for the trinity,' Ephraim said whenever anyone asked him how many children he had. 'A holy number,' as if he decided on three children precisely for that reason. Three children born in quick succession. A girl and two boys, each pregnancy plunging me into a darkness so deep I thought I would never ever see light but startling me with the ability I had to love them. It was as if my love for Holy

– unexpected and delayed – prepared me to love the ones who came after her, for I had fallen in love with both Godsown and PraiseHim as soon as I laid eyes on them. Even when Godsown's features smoothed out and it was plain to see how much he looked like Ephraim, and I believed I could not love him, that love had come anyway.

After Godsown I became cleverer at not getting pregnant. Ephraim did not believe in birth control. 'You'll stop getting pregnant when God says that it is time.' I could not go to our family doctor, even if I had the money. 'God's ways are not our ways. If he wants to give us twenty children, we must accept them with gratitude.' I imagined twenty children living in that small house, stuffed away under beds and in pots and pans and drawers, and the image panicked me.

I knew that I had to be the one to ensure I did not have any more babies. Without access to pills, and with Ephraim against condoms – 'Raincoats are for men who sleep with ladies of the night, not for Christians with wives at home' – I had to find a way to save myself. I started faking periods to keep Ephraim away from me. Luckily he either had no idea how these things worked or was too lazy to calculate it but he did not seem to cotton on to the fact that I appeared to be having more periods than the average woman. Nights when I told him I was 'on', he grumbled and rolled back to his side of the bed. The times when I could not use that to keep him away, I crossed my fingers that I was indeed 'safe'.

Something had changed in me with the births. My thoughts were no longer of myself but of them, children I vowed to protect from the monster that was their father. I knew, however, although I hated to acknowledge it, that

166

Ephraim worshipped them. It hurt me to see his love for them, for it legitimised his claim to them, and to see how easily they returned it too. If I could, I would have ordered them not to think of Ephraim as anything other than an interloper. In church other wives poked their husbands to watch how Ephraim carried Godsown, how gently he wiped snot from Holy's nose, how preciously he picked up PraiseHim, who, just learning to walk, toppled and fell between the aisles. I hated it when people just looked on the surface and told me how lucky I was to have such a devoted man, a man who loved his children with a maternal passion. 'How many men do you know who change diapers and rock their babies to sleep?' they asked me. I was the only one who could lay claim to such love of the children. I was the only one they should love back with the same fervour. It was unfair that Ephraim should have that too. Unfair because, apart from everything else, I was sure I loved them more than he was capable of doing. It was my heart that broke the first time Holy fell ill, malaria giving her a fever so high I spent all night with my heart in her own hands. Once the medication kicked in and the fever broke, I began to breathe again. Every scar on their legs and arms from mosquito bites, cuts and scrapes, I knew intimately. When they cried and preferred to be carried by me, arms outstretched reaching for me rather than for Ephraim, my heart soared and I felt vindicated. They belonged to me, these children, and I wanted Ephraim to have nothing to do with them. I loved them. I loved them. I loved them.

I loved all the ways in which they were different. Godsown was a very clever boy. He had inherited Mother's razor-sharp tongue. I could imagine him being popular at school. One of those children other kids were drawn to, a natural leader but not a bully. PraiseHim was quiet, like me, and it was difficult often to tell what he knew, although it was obvious that, like his brother, he observed and knew a lot. At Bible school he always answered all his questions correctly. Holy was the inquisitive one, always asking What's this? What's that? What's your name? What do you do? She knew so many Bible verses off the top of her head. She could recite the Ten Commandments, and because Ephraim thought it important that she be trained well in her 'duties as a woman', at not quite seven years old, she was a competent cook and a good house-keeper. I quietly determined that Holy would know that her 'duties as a woman' had nothing to do with cooking and cleaning. I would remove her from Obiagu Road and give her the tools to decide what her duties would be. The day Ephraim told her that at her age her mother had not known how to even boil an egg, Holy had thought it was a joke and laughed. Ephraim, laughing along with her, told me, 'See? Even your own daughter thinks it ridiculous. Tell her. Tell her how useless you were when I married you.' Holy had never worn a hair bauble. Ephraim did not believe that little girls should grow their hair or *beautify themselves.*

'The Devil dances when they do so,' he said the day Godsown asked why his sister's hair was not like that of a little girl he saw at Bible study. 'And the girl at Bible study, nko? Is the Devil happy with her? Yes! She'll be dragged to Hell, screaming and begging,' Ephraim said.

I was elated to see in Godsown's scrunched-up face that he did not entirely believe his father.

'Is it true, Maman?' he asked. Ephraim looked up at

me as if he were the one asking the question and not Godsown. I gave a little nod, my happiness draining.

I wondered where Ephraim got his doctrines from. The pastor of the Ark did not talk about Hell as much or with as much relish as Ephraim did. Ephraim had never hidden his ambition of becoming a pastor. The thought of a bigger share of the tithes paid in the church coming to him had him drooling when he prayed and asked God to 'bless' him.

The first Sunday of every month was the Day of Joy at the Ark. That was the Sunday when every working member of the church brought their tithe offerings – a tenth of what they have earned the month before. The pastor blessed their offerings and there were always extra-long prayers for their pockets to be replenished. The Sunday after the Day of Joy was the Sowing Seed Day. That was the Sunday when people gave in the hope of getting it back multifold from God. The Datsun the pastor's wife drove was sown by someone petitioning God for money to buy a Range Rover. As long as he held on to his old car, the pastor warned him, he was blocking the way for the blessing of a Range Rover. 'When the angel of God brings that Range Rover, where is he going to place it? Your old Datsun would confuse him!' There had been scattered laughter in church when the pastor said this, and he had laughed along too so that I was not sure whether he was joking after all, but the very next Sunday the pastor's wife drove into church in that Datsun.

'If I were the pastor,' Ephraim said, 'that car would have been mine!'

But the pastor did not need a new car. He already had

one. Some kind of jeep which he taxed every member for, for an entire year, to buy for him because 'the Lord said so'. When he heard that there had been mutterings of discontent amongst some of the members of the church he had taken to the pulpit to remind everyone that 'Pastors, Men of God, are not to be touched. Touch not my anointed, says the Lord!' And then he had listed ten pastors of other churches, counting off on his fingers – Okotie, T. B. Joshua, Oyakhilome, Fireman, on and on he went – who had luxury cars. 'Not just one! Fireman has five Hummers! Each of them yellow because yellow is his favourite colour! Okotie has a Rolls-Royce! Oyakhilome has his own private jet. T. B. Joshua wines and dines with presidents all over the world . . . Is our God a poor God?' he asked. A resounding 'No' shook the walls of the Ark. 'Clap for our God.' A strong applause broke out. 'Our God is not a poor God, and his representative on earth must not be poor. Do I get an amen?'

'Amen!'

He had got his jeep.

Ephraim wanted all of that. And more. I did not care what he got, as long as I had my children. At night, when he had us all kneel down for prayers, when he asked loudly for God to bless him with prosperity, I prayed silently to Him to make a way for me to escape this nightmare with my children, so that when I said amen loudly at the end of Ephraim's prayer I was sealing not his prayer but my own.

Udodi, the Chorus

The man plants yam and knows yam will sprout. The man who plants the future, does he know what it will grow?

Nani

On Holy's third birthday I said to Ephraim, 'I'd like Holy to start kindergarten.'

At Holy's age I was already learning to read. Even now I still remember my own kindergarten days. If I close my eyes and concentrate really hard, I can sort through the layers of memories and taste the sweetened milk Mrs Ezeokoli served her pupils at Joy of Faith nursery school. I wanted to go to school especially for the milk. And for the sandwiches smeared with a mixture of butter and brown sugar that it was paired with. I can still recite some of the rhymes I learned at school, even the silly one about Old Roger who got up from the grave to give an old woman a knock which made her go hippety-hop. I can even still do the hop of the old woman, one hand on my waist like I had been taught over twenty years ago. I wanted Holy to have such memories too. She would not be able to go a fancy school like Joy of Faith, she would probably not be served sweetened milk and sandwiches with the crusts cut off at the public kindergarten on Onyuike Street, but at least she would be out of the house. She would make friends, be a child. I imagined her walking out of the house every morning clutching my hand, a backpack on her back, and returning at the end of the day with excited tales of new friends and with songs and poems that she had learned at school. I imagined her bringing home arts and craft she had made at school, roses made of construction paper with straw stems, pencil holders from empty toilet paper rolls, nonsensical gifts with huge sentimental value. Holy would love school, I was sure she would.

I waited anxiously for Ephraim to speak and watched him eat, my own spoon held above the plate, the yam pottage scooped in it cooling down. Ephraim chewed on a piece of fish almost contemplatively. There was no way he would say no to this. Whatever else he was, Ephraim loved his children. I relaxed, threw myself fully into the daydream of Holy's life somewhat replicating mine at her age.

Ephraim spat out a bone, dug out a handkerchief from his shirt pocket and in a slow, deliberate movement began to wipe his mouth. It was only after he replaced the handkerchief that he turned to me and asked, 'This school, who will be taking her to it?'

'You. Or myself when you can't.'

'Really?' He drank some water and cleared his throat. 'So you spend your days plotting for ways to meet with other men, eh?'

Before I could decide whether or not to respond, he said, 'Let this be the last time I hear of this nonsense in this house. Holy will go to school when I say so.' He picked out another piece of fish and plopped it into his mouth.

The next day I handed Holy a pencil and paper and began teaching her myself. We started with numbers.

Holy was a fast learner. I felt an exaggerated pride in watching her cautiously, slowly, lips pursed in concentration write a perfect 1; two rounded O's on top of each other for 8; a 3 that was somewhat wobbly. I rubbed her head and she looked at me as if angry that I had broken her concentration. How could this girl, my bright, bright girl, grow if she never left this house? Ephraim had to see sense. I would have to talk to him again. I would have to quote his Bible to him. That passage about not lighting a lamp and hiding it under a bushel. Holy's light needed a school where it could shine. If Holy broke free of this catacomb, then in a way I would have broken free too. If I failed her, then I would have failed where it mattered the most.

Two days later, Ephraim came back from a church committee meeting and thundered into the room where I was teaching Holy the alphabet, our voices loud enough to penetrate the entire house. Holy was an enthusiastic learner.

A is for Apple.

B is for Book.

C is for Cat.

He scooped Holy up from the bed where she sat beside me, a pencil in her hand, scooped up Godsown in his other hand and deposited both in the parlour beside the cot in which one-year-old PraiseHim lay sleeping.

'Wait for Papa here,' he said, kissing both children quickly. He strode back into the room and closed the door.

'You think you can disobey my rules?'

'What's wrong with teaching my child to read? I haven't taken her to school. All—'

174

My words were truncated by a sharp slap across my face. 'S is for Slap!' Ephraim said, his 'slap' coming out as 'srap'. Sometimes I had fought back, halfheartedly, mostly just defending myself because I wanted to shield the children from witnessing the horror of their mother being pummelled, but this time the slap snapped something in me. Before I could even think about it, my hand reached out and slapped him back. I put my back into that slap. The effort of it paid off, for I saw Ephraim touch his cheek as if he was not quite sure what had happened. Then he pushed me back onto the bed and began to punch me. 'Don't you ever raise your hands to me.' My entire body went into rebellion. My back refused to feel the pain of the punches he rained down on it. My ears refused to heed his warning. I raised a leg and kicked him, hard. Rage blinded me but my hands and my legs developed their own eyes and sought their target. I had never fought back as committedly as this but now it was as if I was an elastic band and all those years in Ephraim's house I had been stretching and now had reached my breaking point. A snapped band feels no pain. And it was only afterwards, much later, that I felt the pain of the beating. That evening, in the room in which Ephraim had locked me and through the walls of which I could hear him playing with the children, PraiseHim's laughter ringing in the house like an alien thing, I made up my mind. I would kill him. I would kill him and then I would take my children and I would leave. I refused to think beyond that, the killing and the absconding, because I knew that if I allowed myself to think further than that I would see the mountains in my way and never make a move.

The next day I slipped a knife from the communal kitchen into my pocket. A small knife, not much bigger than a table knife but so sharp that it cut through beef tendons as easily as it sliced onion. That evening I hid it under my pillow. All day Ephraim had stayed out of my way, as if he suspected what I planned to do. When he spoke to me he was uncharacteristically solicitous, almost to the point of deference, as if, by fighting back as heartily as I had, I had earned a certain level of respect. 'You know I love you, Nani. But a man is the head of the family.' 'Eat, Nani. You have hardly touched your meal. Here, let me feed you!' I ignored him and he did not push it as he would have usually. When PraiseHim cried he lifted him out of his cot and cooed him back to sleep. After putting Holy and Godsown to bed, I went to bed without saying a word to him. I could feel my heart pounding against my ribs. Pound. Pound. Pound. It was a wonder that no one else could hear it. It was like a sound coming through an amplifier. I shut my eyes and pretended to be asleep when Ephraim came in, praying that the sound of my heart beating so loudly was not enough to alert him, listening for his breathing to settle deeply into that of someone who was dead to the world. Once I was sure that he had fallen asleep, I slid out the knife and began to stab blindly, stunned by how deep the knife went, how much flesh was on this man who had the stature of a stalk rather than a tree. I heard him scream, heard something fall over, imagined a river of blood drowning him. I felt his hand encircling my wrist, shaking it until the knife clattered out of my hand.

The commotion woke the children and I could hear them crying in the dark. Ephraim dragged me into the parlour and pushed me into a chair. He switched on the light, flooding the small room with a light so bright that I was blinded for a moment. When I recovered my sight again I saw Holy sniffling, standing beside Ephraim, holding him around one leg, her eyes wide with fear. Ephraim had a small cut on one shoulder. All I had done was cut him a little bit. Not even enough to send him to hospital. I was disappointed. But heavier than my disappointment was the weight of my daughter's scared eyes. I tried to smile at Holy but the child's face did not crack into a smile. She looked up at her father instead and held out her hands to him to be carried. He hoisted her up, resting her head on the shoulder without the cut, as if he wanted to keep her from looking at me, as if she needed protecting from her mother.

'If you try this again,' Ephraim whispered slowly, 'I will kill you.'

He drew a finger across his neck. I had no reason not to believe him. I had to get the job done properly next time.

Nani

Five years after I had last seen Ugo she appeared, a luminous and beautiful apparition at my door. Ephraim was out. He no longer locked me in when he went out. There was no need to. He knew I would not leave. The children kept me stuck in the soil of this place which had never felt like home. Even the children knew not to let their curiosity drag them beyond the front door without their father. They did not talk to the other children in the compound when they ran into them outside. Ours was a family that kept to itself and the neighbours came to accept it. No one knocked on our door asking to borrow salt or a pot; no one asked me if I could watch their baby while they ran some errand; no one asked if I could plait their hair, help them carry their shopping inside. None of the men came to ask Ephraim if he wanted to watch football with them; play table tennis with them; help kill a goat. We were left in our state of self-imposed isolation. The children, who had never known another kind of life, accepted it. And I, who had lived another kind of life, swallowed my sadness and floundered in this cocoon of lies and impenetrable darkness which Ephraim had spun over us all, showering my children with love, my heart breaking for them, while I waited for the right moment to strike. This could not last forever. When my sister turned up it seemed to me that the darkness lifted a little.

I hadn't seen Ugo in five years – not since that first time she came – but when I opened the door to her time stood still. A cascade of memories came pouring in, rushing out of my mouth in an excited scream. Haaaaaaaaaaaaah! It brought the three children scrambling to the parlour to see what had possessed their mother. Ugo tumbled into the house because my arms wouldn't let go of hugging her. My sister held me tight too.

'This is your Aunt Ugo,' I said to the children, when Ugo and I let go of each other. I wagged a finger at Ugo as if I was scolding her as I spoke. 'My sister.' I was breathless, speaking as if I was talking through an asthma attack. I grabbed her again to make sure she wasn't a mirage. I screamed a second, a third time. Haaaaaaaaaaaah! Haaaaaaaaaaah! Ugo grinned. It would be later, only after she had left, that I would wonder about the miracle of her finding me in the new flat. 'This. My sister.' I could hardly believe it. My children looked at me and I could see them trying to make sense of their mother's words. Holy laughed in disbelief and said with all the certainty of a child her age, 'No. Maman doesn't have a sister.' PraiseHim and Godsown stared at me before shuffling back into the bedroom, each clutching a bottle counter with which they had been playing.

Holy came close to Ugo, and for a second it seemed as if she wanted to hug her new aunt. Instead she asked Ugo what her name was but did not wait for a response before running back into the room to continue playing with her siblings. Did Ugo flinch when it looked like

Holy might reach out and touch her? I saw my children through my sister's eyes and was upset at my embarrassment. They looked nothing like Ugo and I did at that age. They were beautiful children, I knew, but while they were standing there, staring at Ugo and she staring back at them, I scrutinised them the way a stranger might. All of them had short hair, cropped to the skin because Ephraim insisted that was the only way to keep hair clean. Holy's dress was at least two sizes too big. It was not really a dress. It was a T-shirt for a much older child and came down to below her knees. Across its front was a print of the Eiffel Tower, with 'Paris' written underneath it, but it had been ironed over and the grey of the T-shirt was blotched with the red colour of 'Paris'. PraiseHim had a dress on, inherited from Holy, a year older. Ephraim did not believe in throwing away serviceable clothes, and it did not matter that PraiseHim was a boy: when he was home he wore Holy's discarded dresses. Godsown had been having trouble with heat rash, and so for a while Ephraim ordered that the two-year-old be left to run around naked at home, his whole body coated in white powder so that he looked like an alien ghost.

Ugo did not gather them into her arms like an aunt would, like something loved, like Aunty Enuka did each time she had visited us when we were children. She did not say, 'How beautiful your children are, Nani. Wow! Mother would be so proud of them.' She said, 'I can't believe you are a mother. And that . . . that you live like this. How did it get to this? How did this happen?'

She sounded like she might burst into tears. I did not want her to cry because then I would start crying too. How did I get to this? How could I begin to tell my humiliating story? Where was a suitable beginning? The night of the vigil seemed like a different century. That memory, like the memory of my wedding, I had successfully learned to suppress so as not to go completely crazy. I had supplanted it with other memories, less painful in their remembrance, like the first time Holy wrote her name on a sheet of paper and showed me, the letters splayed all over the page to fill a foolscap sheet.

Ugo looked around the crowded sitting room, an improvement on Ephraim's former flat but still nowhere near the standard my sister and I had been raised on. It was a bigger parlour than the previous one. The red velveteen sofa had been joined now by two armchairs with cushions of striped pink and red. Beside one of the armchairs was a standing fan which circulated air around the room. I, who had always been indifferent about the house, now felt a deep shame, as if it was a failing on my part that had earned me such a dismal room.

Ugo said she could not stay but she could not go without seeing me. They – she and Mother – were leaving the country. A police raid. Something about Mother's baby business. Mother's friend in the judiciary had advised her to leave 'until this whole thing quieted down'.

I did not care about Mother. Or about her business. I would be happy to see that baby factory burned. But I cared that I was being left, that Mother had not – as difficult as it would have been for her, as unrealistic as it was to expect it – come herself to see me, to ask if I wanted to leave with them.

'When will you be back?'

'We don't know yet. Mother's cleared all her accounts.

I will start school over there.' Ugo sounded pleased and paused before she continued. 'Me sef, I can't wait. All these strikes here, I'm still in second year when I ought to be in third. Mother will stay for as long as she needs to. She doesn't expect it to be a long stay, though. I wish you could come . . .'

I was not listening. Or rather I was but at the same time was being eaten up by my own resentful, suspicious thoughts. I was upset that Ugo had not made more of a fuss over my children; they were her niece and nephews after all. They might look like the sort of children we pitied when we were kids but they were mine. I hated Ugo. She had not told me how beautiful they were. Instead she had me think of Aziz and his son. Until Ugo came I had not thought of Aziz's son, whom he brought once at Christmas to eat at Number 47, even though they were Muslim and did not celebrate Christmas. Mother had seen our guard's son once when Aziz's wife brought him to the house, and decided that it would be a good idea to have him over for Christmas dinner. Udodi, Ugo and I, in matching dresses and shoes we had picked out ourselves, with little heels that went click-clack-click when we walked and hair plaited and decorated with dozens of plastic barrettes in a multitude of colours, sat at the table with this boy who was about my age then, eight years old, and could not think of a single thing to say to him. The little boy spoke in whispered monosyllables when he was spoken to, and his English was mostly pidgin, which made us snicker when we gathered in Udodi's room to dissect the day. We giggled after he left about his shoes which were so loose on him that they kept slipping off his feet, and the fact that he could not eat with a fork and a knife, 'and his shirt had buttons missing!' Udodi said, as if that was the worst crime anyone could commit.

Did Ugo really think that being forced to lose a school year because of the ASUU strike was a disaster? What was losing a year compared to my own tally of losses? I had not had the chance to go to university and here was Ugo complaining of a government which did not pay lecturers so that they constantly went on strike, a government which removed oil subsidy so that the price of everything rose overnight ('Even the price of sugar cane has risen! What was N50 the day before suddenly shot to N150'); complaining that Mother had not wanted to send her to America to go to school on her own, she wanted her close to home, and now she was just so relieved that she was leaving. 'I'll have to start from the beginning but I don't care. Ah! Nani! I'm tired of this country. And now I really need to go!' Ugo was just concerned – after five years of being separated from me – with getting home before the driver became impatient and before Mother wondered where she had been. I did not think that at twenty, and an undergraduate, and being Ugo, that she was as much controlled by Mother as she claimed. I suspected that the reason she was eager to leave was because she could not bear to be in the house . . . could not bear to see me like this. She had said that she was supposed to just go and pick up their tickets and return but had convinced the driver to let her see 'a friend'. This driver was new, acquired since I had been gone. He had probably never even heard of me and it hurt that my mother and Ugo had gone on with life as if I no longer existed. Ugo should have been happier to meet my children. She should have lifted them up and tickled them under the arm like Aunty Enuka used to do to us. I hated Ugo and yet I could not stop looking at her like a fawning stranger might. She looked healthy, her skin smooth and a shiny brown. Her single brow was now separated, skilfully waxed. The acne she had before seemed to have cleared. She was carefully made-up, her eyes rimmed with black liner. Whatever foundation she had used on her face suited her perfectly. She looked like a sculpture, buffed and polished. I envied her her glowing skin. Her hair was even straightened. Held in a ponytail, parted in the middle like Mother used to have in old photographs of herself. Ugo had been wanting to have her hair permed for years but Mother would only let her daughters have their hair straightened once they finished secondary school. Ugo was so jealous when Mother took me to the salon, on my last day of secondary school, to have my hair straightened and styled. When we returned Ugo's jealousy filled her stomach so much that she would not talk to me for days, and when she did it was to tell me 'You look like a drenched rat!' Five years, and now she threw out 'I really need to go' so casually. I wanted to shout at her to go, to ask why she had bothered to come after all. My children's laughter trickled in from the bedroom and Ugo looked uncomfortable. I hated her again and yet I wanted her to stay. I wanted her to ask to see the children again, to love them, to tell me that Mother had begged her to bring me and my children with her. I searched for something to say. Something meaningful and life-changing that would make her stay.

'So you've finally permed your hair? You couldn't wait!'

I wanted to reach out and touch her hair, her face, her

neck, every glistening bit of her. She laughed but it was not a familiar laughter, there was something sad and contained about it, the way one laughs at a funeral when someone tells an inappropriate joke.

'It's already been a while since I permed it sef,' she said.

Of course. It seemed strange to me that Ugo was already older than I had been when Ephraim happened. In the way of a disaster, Ephraim happened to me. I laughed along with Ugo but the laughter tasted like bitter leaf on my tongue. If Ugo and Mother left, then truly I had nobody any more. Even though I could not return to Number 47, knowing that Mother and Ugo and I were in the same city had comforted me. It meant that I was not completely alone.

'Why?' I asked Ugo, not knowing quite what I was asking her to explain.

She said, 'I told you already. We can't have Mother in jail.' She was shaking her legs, in her mind already out of the country, I was sure. She dipped her hand into her handbag and brought out a polythene bag through which I could see rolls of naira notes held together with thick black rubber bands. She gave me the bag. 'All my savings, Nani. In case you ever need cash.' She dug in her handbag again and brought out a mobile phone, a set of keys, and a card with Aunty Enuka's phone number. 'Keep these. I will try and call you. No. I will call you. I hope that one day . . . I'm sorry . . . I'm . . .'

She didn't finish her words. She got up and walked to the door. 'I have to go.' Ugo might have been trying not to cry. My own eyes were misting too. 'Look after yourself, Nani. And . . . this isn't you. The children . . .'

She ran out, and I ran after her but Ugo did not look

back as she entered the car, driven by the new driver I did not know, and slammed the car door.

I ran back inside, collapsed on the sofa and sat still, as if I had been hit with a pestle. My head hurt. My body ached. My skin itched. I could feel the tears rushing to come out. I replayed the visit in my head. I analysed everything Ugo had said and done. I thought how easy it would have been for Ugo to have said the right things, to have made it easy for me to bundle the children and myself into that air-conditioned car of Mother's and away from Ephraim. She had not even asked me to. Ugo had told me that Mother had warned her that if she ever went to visit me she would be thrown out of the house and disinherited. She was afraid that Mother would carry out her threat and she could not take the risk. 'You know Mother doesn't make idle threats ooo. I couldn't come. I'm sorry.' I, patron saint of anyone in need of under-standing, I, Nanichimdum, told her not to be silly, there was nothing to be sorry for, that I might have thrown away my future but there was no reason for her to throw away hers as well. 'I understand, Ugo. I do.' But I did not. Not really. Had our roles been reversed, I would have stood by Ugo. That was how it had always been. When we were growing up, and Ugo upset Udodi and was banned from Udodi's bedroom in punishment, I would always – unasked – beg Udodi on Ugo's behalf. Ugo had never stood up for me. Not even back then. 'Don't apolo-gise, Ugo. There's no need,' I said. Mother was worried that I would 'negatively influence' her remaining daughter, the smart, beautiful Ugo, her trump card in the world, to show them that being widowed and cast out by her husband's family had not affected her ability to be a good parent. Ugo would exculpate her. 'You don't have to explain to me, Ugo, I understand.' I tried to make my voice sound light. 'Mother said you did this to hurt her. I don't believe her, Nani. I know . . .'

'It's fine, Ugo. Don't be silly, go on. Go back before you get into trouble with Mother.'

I gave her a little push, laughed a little too loudly. Inside me an anger at her whirled. Ugo had abandoned me and was doing it again now by leaving.

'I'll keep in touch,' Ugo said, as though reading my mind. 'I'll call you every day.'

She was already leaving, already sounding like a stranger, like somebody I would have nothing to talk about with. I feared that she would forget me as soon as she left, as she had done in the years I had already been away, the promises mere words to fill the air.

I was relieved that Ugo had caught me on a day that Ephraim was not home.

I had to make sure that Ephraim knew nothing of this visit. I fought my way through the stupor that was enveloping me and dragged myself up to the bedroom to hide the evidence of Ugo's visit. I told the children not to mention the visitor to their father when he returned. 'Why?' Holy asked. I told her God would not like it. I hated using Ephraim's line to get her to keep my secret but I could not risk him finding out. He would want to know what Ugo had come to do, why I had let her in. I didn't know yet what I would do with the money, or with the phone, but I did not want Ephraim having any access to them. It was nice to have something which was mine, even if they were things I could not use. Who did I know to call? And as for Ugo, I did not believe that my self-centred sister would remember to call. And if she did, and Ephraim discovered the phone, he would destroy it. It was safer for me to turn it off and hide it where there was no danger of it ever being discovered but somewhere close enough for me to be comforted by it. Ephraim never went through the woven tote in which I stored my underwear and old clothes. So I put the phone, the money and the keys in an old purse and hid it at the bottom of the Ghana Must Go bag, zipped it up and pushed it under the bed. Just knowing it was in the house, something my sister had given me, was some consolation. It was not enough but it would have to do. In the early days that followed, every time I lay in bed I imagined it glowing red and filling the room with its light so that Ephraim, curious, would upend the bag on the bed and discover my secret. Whenever I retrieved an undergarment from there, I resisted the urge to dig out the purse and look at its contents. Yet, despite the fear of discovery, I could not resist checking it. The first week, every time Ephraim left home, and the children were playing by themselves, I'd bring out the phone, switch it on and call random numbers. Sometimes I called numbers I could remember but whenever anyone picked up I'd pretend I had dialled a wrong number. After the first week the excitement of it died down. It was almost a month before I brought it out again and there was an icon of a message. Ugo had kept her promise. *Nani! How are you? Miss you! Call me!* The exclamation marks made me imagine Ugo shouting so I could hear her, her voice loud enough to reach me from across the ocean. I did not respond to her. Ugo's message depressed me. It would have been easier had she not kept her promise, if I could forget that her visit ever happened.

Nani

Ephraim disapproved of visitors. None of the neighbours
came to the house – not even the woman with the one
good eye, Philo, who had spoken to me once – no friends,
only the chief pastor now that Ephraim had been made
one of the assistant pastors. He came for Sunday lunch
once in a while and had discussions with Ephraim, occasionally praising him for finding such a 'nice, submissive,
Christian wife' – for I was a submissive wife. I did not
talk back to Ephraim, served him in silence and did not
interfere in the conversation when he had a guest. All
Ephraim had to do, the pastor said once, praising me, was
say the word and his wife would do it. 'Where does one
find such a woman these days? Our brother Ephraim has
struck gold with his mate. He is so richly blessed.' In
several of his Sunday sermons 'the family of one our
brothers, a holy family with a woman as quiet and submissive as wives should be' was used to typify the model
Christian family everyone else should aspire to. Everyone
knew it was Ephraim's even though it was never said, and
I despised the respect I could feel grow for him from the
other members of the congregation. If only they knew,
I told myself at such times, picturing myself rushing to

the microphone, snatching it from the pastor and booming Ephraim's sin into the church packed full of people. I would, I told myself on the days when I felt brave, but even on those days I knew that I never would. I would be ridiculed, not Ephraim. And those who did not ridicule me would pray for me, for the demon in me to be exorcised. I remembered the many people who had been prayed over, sometimes being whipped to send the demons said to be possessing them out. I did not doubt that there would be people who believed me but those I knew would remind me that whatever happened was in the past, why dig it all up now? Some might even tell me that Ephraim had after all stepped up to his obligations. He had married me, had he not? He had performed his duties as a husband and given me more children, had he not? So what was my problem? And of course I would be reminded that 'the Lord admonishes us never to touch His "anointed".' And Ephraim, whatever else he might be, was a 'Man of God'. He had been anointed by God and by the pastor and was only a few rungs down the ladder from becoming a full pastor.

We hardly went anywhere apart from church. And every few months Ephraim bundled everyone into a taxi to the General Overseer's house for an appreciation party. The General Overseer, who was the boss of all the pastors of the Apostolic Church of Jesus and His Twelve Disciples Keeping Us Safe in the Ark scattered over the five states of the southwest, lived in a big house with two sitting rooms and seven bedrooms, they said, and while I listened to the others praise its opulence I could not help thinking that Number 47 was far more opulent. At those times my loss hit me with a renewed force.

Ephraim

My woman's heart is as hard as stone, yet, for the love of God, I remain dedicated to my job as a good husband. The master of the house must guide the household in the ways of the Lord, lest he be doomed.

Nani's materfamilias, accursed witch, has no yearning to behold her very handsome grandchildren. Her wealth has turned her head. The Lord rewards patience and I know that one day I will be elevated to chief pastor. Has He not given me everything I have desired? I have a beautiful wife, the finest children earth has ever seen. Will He not make me chief pastor and give me the wealth that comes with it? Praise Him! Praise the Almighty. Amen.

Ugo

In her wallet Ugo carries a picture of Nani taken the year before Nani left. Her sister doesn't know this, Ugo's never told her. In the photograph Nani is not smiling, she's looking at someone or something else, but her face is turned towards the camera. She is in her favourite outfit at the time, polka-dotted shorts and a red T-shirt with a raised fist in the middle of it. The picture was taken at one of the neighbourhood parties but Nani looks contemplative, like someone at church instead of a party. Ugo lifted the photo from one of the family albums and soon after Nani left she would talk to it, as if she could conjure her back into Number 47. She takes the picture to school with her, everywhere. The first time Ugo went to see Nani, and Nani said she couldn't come back, Ugo went home and cried with that photograph in her hands. When Mother found out she had broken her rule and gone to visit Nani, she sacked the driver. 'If I ever hear that you've gone to visit that no-good sister of yours again, I swear, Ugo, I'll have you pack up and join her!' Mother didn't threaten her often, not even back then, but Ugo was afraid that she meant this. What would she do if Mother kicked her out to go and live with Nani and Ephraim in

Obiagu? Now Ugo knows that Mother wouldn't have done it but at that age she believed that she would. And Ugo still wanted to go to America. Haba! She still had her own dreams to pursue and she wasn't going to give them up because her sister had fallen in love with a man (she had to believe it was love).

That first time, she went to see Nani for all of their sakes. She wanted her family back together. The second time she went – before she and Mother left for America – she went for the same reason. She hoped that Ephraim would not be around, that she'd catch her sister alone and somehow deliver her to Mother and they would all cry and their tears would cleanse the past and the future could begin with all three of them in America. She did not count on three little children who looked like urchins staring at her with Nani's eyes. Seeing Nani with children made her seem even less like the Nani of Number 47 and more like someone Ugo had once known in a distant past. The children were raggedly dressed and Ugo did not feel any familial connection to them. She went to Obiagu hoping that once Nani heard they were leaving she would beg to come back with her and beg Mother to take her with them but, seeing those children, Ugo knew it was impossible. Mother would never have taken them on. She, Ugo, could not even look at them. This wasn't the life that Doda and Mother had planned for them. Ugo still can't understand that sort of surrender, giving up everything Mother could give them for Ephraim and his shack. So what if she didn't approve of how Mother made her money? Haba! She could have sulked. But going off with that man? That was too rebellious, not something she would have thought Nani capable of.

A cramped flat, a husband and three children before getting any university degrees. If Nani really wanted to return to Number 47, she could have come back, fallen at Mother's feet and begged before having not one but three children! It didn't matter what Ephraim did to her, she chose this life.

It is only when they are on the plane, so safely away from Enugu, that Ugo confesses to Mother about seeing Nani and about the three children. And it is only now that it dawns on her – and she sees the realisation come to Mother too – that Nani was probably already pregnant when she left Number 47. She watches Mother's face shut down. *Ah! I think she's just washed her hands of Nani completely.* Ugo realises now what Nani meant when she said it was too late, on Ugo's first visit. But it wasn't, not then. She could have told Mother. Mother is old-fashioned about a lot of things, and worried constantly about her daughters slipping and showing her up as a widow who could not control her children, but Mother loves them. Ugo knows this. Mother would never have let Nani throw her life away on a man like Ephraim if Nani had come to her for help. Her sister ought to have known that.

Nani

'I'm taking the children to Udi for evangelism,' Ephraim announced casually as we ate breakfast on a Wednesday morning, two years after Ugo's visit. 'You stay home and look after the house.'

Udi was an hour away. I had never been away from the children and evangelical tours outside Enugu were always for three days at least. Ephraim always went alone. Why did he want to take the children now?

Holy dropped her spoon into the bowl of akamu she was drinking and started dancing. 'Will we go in a bus, Papa?'

'Yes, ma petite chérie.'

Holy clapped her hands in delight and did another dance. 'Did you hear?' she asked her siblings. 'We are going in a bus with Papa.'

'Sit down and finish your food, Holy,' I said, trying to keep my voice even.

I brought my little finger to my mouth and began to bite the nail. Wild thoughts darted across my mind. I did not want to imagine what he might do to the children, left alone with them for three days. You heard these stories all the time, parents disappearing with children or killing them. Ephraim doted on the children, but still.

'I'll come too,' I said.

'No. Why pay for the two of us when one will suffice?'

I knew that he had done the calculation. He was better off not paying for two adults and maximising the charm of three children alone with a father. He would get more money if he toured Udi with them, a single parent, than if he had me with him. My sullenness put people off. If I had learned anything about Ephraim in these seven years together, it was how his mind worked. Everything, every action of his, was calculated in terms of naira and kobo. Yet it would also be the first time in seven years he was leaving me in charge. He was sure that I would not leave him. He would come back and find me exactly where he had left me. It made me sick to think that we had reached a point in our arrangement where Ephraim was confident that he could leave me in an empty house for three days and I would not make a break for it. It was almost as if he were mocking me, daring me. And when he told me I was not coming with them, had he not said it with a certain smugness? The same smugness with which, in the early days, he used to throw my mother's abandonment of me in my face but even in those days he did not trust that I could be left on my own.

One day, when I was pregnant with Holy, and trying to escape an airless May afternoon inside Ephraim's house, I stood up and made slowly, cautiously, for the front door.

'Where are you going?'

'Outside. I am hot.'

'If you want to go outside, you say. You do not leave the house without my permission.'

He had been lying on the sofa. He got up then and followed me outside where we sat on a bench, not talking to each other. Anybody seeing us would have noticed nothing amiss. We could easily have been mistaken for a young couple in a normal relationship who had just come out for some air. Even in those days, when he must have realised that the pregnancy made it impossible for me to return to Number 47 where my real life was, he was still wary enough of me to worry. How had I become the sort of woman that he need not worry about any more?

The arrogance of his certainty riled me but the fear nagged at me still. He had to know that he had the trump card: the children. What if he never brought them back?

The morning they were to leave, as the children chattered excitedly about the trip, how big the bus was, how many packets of biscuits I had packed for each of them for the trip, I tried to change his mind.

'The children, will they be able to cope? Away from home for three days?'

He did not answer me.

At the bus I feigned a brightness I did not feel, waving them off, making sure to call the children by name as I waved so that it was clear that Ephraim was not included. The two boys held on to Ephraim's hands as they boarded, Holy beside them. A normal family to anyone looking. Tears gathered behind my eyes but I did not want my children to see me cry. I would hold on until the bus drove off. It was a surprise then to me that as soon as the bus left I exhaled rather than cried. I had not known that I had been holding my breath. I missed the children already but that missing was bearable because Ephraim had taken with him the malevolent spirit which lingered in the house every day. I was dizzy from breathing too quickly, greedily gulping as if Ephraim might return any minute and stifle the air again. It was only after I calmed down that I realised that skirting around the edges of my exhilaration was anger. The same recklessness that had taken hold of me when I stood up to Mother in my former life raced its way through me now, filling my veins. Ephraim was gone, there was no reason for me to stay. I paced the parlour, wondering what to take. I picked up the framed photograph of the children on the centre table and sighed, dropping into a chair. Not even a drowning mother saves herself without trying to save her children. Unless that mother was my own. I had to be better than her. I had the money from Ugo. I had the phone. I had three days in which to plot.

I stood up to go the room to retrieve the bag then heard an insistent knocking on the door. For a moment it crossed my mind that Ephraim might have sent someone to keep an eye on me. I took a deep breath. Could he have asked his mother to come? I could not be alone with the woman. I would kill her, I swore. She had come for a few weeks with the births of Godsown and PraiseHim, each visit a cross I had to bear. My rebuttal of her friendship at Holy's birth was neither forgotten nor forgiven, and the older woman sought revenge in small ways. She scolded me in a language I did not understand, gesticulated wildly to point out failings I seemed oblivious to, and once, when Holy pinched the month-old PraiseHim and I spanked her, Ephraim's mother had pretended to spank me to console the crying Holy. How stupid of me to imagine that Ephraim would actually leave me on my own. I could choose not to open the door, couldn't I? I knew I couldn't. If indeed Ephraim had sent someone and I did not let them in, they would tell him once he returned, and I'd get beaten. I had never got used to the punches and slaps. My skin did not harden to accept them without flinching or without a sense of humiliation, especially with the children looking on. I did not want them to grow up with the image of their father beating their mother. I wanted to save them, to protect them as much as I could, so I tried not to provoke Ephraim. I became the most subservient wife (how that word curdled on my tongue) on the planet.

I opened the door and was relieved and surprised to see not Ephraim's mother but Philo, the short woman with a kind face and one good eye who always wore brightly coloured clothes. In her green and yellow dress, she looked like an exotic flower.

'May I come in?' she asked, smiling up at me. I swung the door open and shut it behind her.

'I saw your husband leave with the children. He was carrying a suitcase so I assume they have travelled?'

'Yes. Please sit down.' The last thing I wanted was a guest but I was raised to be polite.

'My name is Philo. Please do not think me too forward but I have always wondered what a girl like you was doing here. I said to myself, "Philo, this girl doesn't belong to this yard. She doesn't belong with that man." The day one fine girl came, dressed expensively, saying she was looking for her sister, I was the one who pointed out your flat to her. You hadn't been long here. That day I knew. You could not have a sister like that and belong here. That day I said to myself, "Philo, find out her story." I did not have the courage to come until now because I saw your husband leaving with a suitcase. Nobody in this

199

compound likes him. There is something about him which everyone agrees is bad.'

She slipped her feet out of her flip-flops and moved deeper onto the sofa. The brightness of her dress seemed out of place in the dark room, like the sun at night. She made a steeple with her fingers under her chin, her one good eye fixed on me. She was waiting for me to speak. She would not, I knew, get off the sofa until I had spoken to her. But how could I excavate memories I had buried long ago and lay them bare before this woman I had hardly spoken to before today? The silence stretched and threatened to snap. Philo sighed and spoke.

'There are some burdens one must never carry alone. We are taught from when we are young girls being prepared for marriage never to share our problems. We are told that if the old woman talks too much of how she trampled the chick to death, the mother hen would be given to her too. But you know what Philo says? I say that that is the problem we have as women: we do not talk enough about what we suffer.'

Her Igbo was the lyrical dialect of the Wawa, which made it seem like she was singing. It was a pleasure to listen to. It soothed me. It delighted me. It wormed its way into my heart and asked to be trusted.

'If we do not talk, how can we get help, eh? It is only a fellow human being who can be your chi. God is not going to descend from the clouds and fight our human battles for us.'

I liked this woman, and the longer she spoke the more I began to trust her. I had thought it a miracle that Ugo had found out which flat was ours. Philo's concern gathered in her good eye that would not look away from my face. Her deliberate, paced voice encouraging me to talk broke down my barriers. I never thought I would tell a stranger how Ephraim happened.

'Philo,' I started, shocked by my clear voice, not muted in response to Ephraim, not high and foolish in talking to the children but an adult's clear, concise voice.

'One day, Philo,' I said. 'One day I will tell you. But now I need to get out of this house.'

I did not mean to be rude, to push her out, but she stood up and gave me a quick hug. She smelled of fresh ugu and egusi, as if she'd come straight from the kitchen. She held my hand.

'If you need anything . . .' She stopped. She did not let go of my hand. 'I didn't come for gossip, you know. My husband and me, we can help.'

'I know. I'm grateful.'

With Philo out of the house I could think better. I felt a momentary panic. How could I leave the children? But I had to. It would not be forever. In fact, Ephraim did not even need to know that I had left. A compromise. I could go, stay at Number 47 for two nights and return before Ephraim did on Monday. What if Ephraim suddenly returned? What if something happened on the way? One of the children got ill? Ephraim forgot something? What were the chances that an entire bus full of people would turn around just because Ephraim forgot something at home? Calm down, Nani, I told myself. Calm down. First things first.

I went into the bedroom and dragged out the Ghana Must Go bag from under the bed. I brought out the phone. I had not charged it in almost three months. Would it still work? The last time I had it Holy had come into

201

my room before I could put it away. 'What's that, Maman?' she had asked but it was not a question. She was asking to whom it belonged, what it was doing in the house, how come she had never seen it before. Was it something her papa would agree with. Of course she knew it was a phone. I told her a sister at church had given it to me to keep for her but it was a secret. 'Not even Papa must know.'

I plugged it in to charge, sure that it would not. I'd learned not to expect things to go right for me. But I heard a click and saw a light come on. I fell on my knees before the phone, as though it were a god demanding my worship. I pushed the centre button to turn it on. Nothing happened. I tried again, this time more firmly than before, and a battery icon appeared. It was one per cent charged. Happiness washed over me and made me weak. I brought out the money Ugo gave me and, half running, half walking, ran to a small kiosk near the house and bought a phone card. I could not bear to think that, if everything went well, I would be able to speak to my sister before the day ended.

It must have charged the phone for about half an hour before there was a power outage. Scared that it might not have been long enough, determined to leave whether it had charged or not, I unplugged the cord and checked. Seventy per cent full. I switched it on. A multitude of messages popped up, all of them from Ugo, each one asking the same thing: *How are you? This is my number. Call.*

I wrote Ugo's number out, twice so that I could be sure I had it right. My hands shook so much, as if I were drunk, that the pen slipped several times. I wiped my sweaty palms on my dress and then carefully, very carefully so that I would not make any mistake, put the numbers in, calling each one out as I punched it in. I held the phone to my ear with both hands, one to keep the other steady as they were both shaking uncontrollably.

I listened as the phone rang at the other end, a long interminable ring, and then a voice – heavy with sleep – skipped over the distance and shouted my name. It shrieked a second time, the sleepiness quickly receding to the edges.

'What time is it there?' I asked.

'Haba! Who cares what time it is. Oh my God! Is this really you? I've waited for this call forever!'

Udodi, the Chorus

When a bird perches on a hanging basket, it swings
    when the basket swings:

The day Mother laid the foundation for her clinic, I
    saw these things:

Thing 1 that I saw

The Debe Enugu Ocha Campaign by a new governor
    making scapegoats of low-hanging fruit
Low- to mid-ranking fraudsters and criminals
419ers who operated out of muggy internet cafes,
    letter-writers to European and American men and
    women professing love and asking for money
or pretending to be princes or widows of some
    government official;

Thing 2 that I saw

A doctor who had a baby factory near Holy Ghost
    Cathedral on Ogui Road
nothing on the scale of Mother's

luring and keeping pregnant women hostage, shamed
   on TV
Hands manacled behind his back

A journalist shouting in a thick apoplectic voice into
   the microphone.

'Dr Okeke and his team of criminals were kidnapping
   young girls! Targeting university students!'

One of the young women rescued from his clinic,
   recently delivered
Her voice thick with anger
At being cheated, saying

She had been promised N50,000 but had been paid
   only N10,000 – less than $100, the journalist
   interviewing her interjected –
and given a few days to leave the clinic.

Thing 3 I saw

People like Edu Gburugburu
Rumoured to have his own private jet,
A mansion in every world capital
Fraudster par excellence
Dining with the highest and the mightiest only

And Mother, whose wealth too
Has bought her proximity to power

were tipped off
Given time – not enough time that others would catch
    wind of it –
to get their affairs in order and
like magic, disappear for a short while.

Thing 4 I saw

Mother expecting to be back within a year (she will
    not be back for many more)
Sending Aunty and her guard and drivers off 'on
    holidays,'
Princely bonuses –
Keys and deeds to the house, hugs and a drawn-out
    bye-bye to her best friend, Aunty Enuka.

Nani

The day I left my husband's house the world continued as it always had. The Harmattan wind was mild. As I walked away from that life the mist that had earlier covered the skies cleared, dust swirled and plastic bags discarded on the street danced around my feet. There was nothing to suggest that something momentous had happened, that something had shifted in the order of things, a seismic shift which caused my heart to beat so quickly it made me faint. How had everything else remained so ordinary? As I neared the part of Enugu where traffic was slower, and houses had shrubbed fences and carefully manicured lawns, I slackened my pace. Instead of mechanics' garages and hasty zinc constructions lining the streets, here there were flowers and trees with pink and purple and yellow blossoms, a luxury hotel and high-end beauty salons. Even the air seemed different. Everything was unhurried, generous. Obiagu was a concrete jungle: houses built so close together that it seemed as if they were standing on each other's toes. After all the years there I had almost forgotten that Enugu was beautiful.

As temperatures inched up sweat dribbled down between my breasts, behind my neck, puddled under my armpits. I felt like someone who had been bedridden for so long and was now recovering from an illness. How apt that I felt that way. Ephraim was an illness. A seven-year sickness that had just lifted. My throat itched from thirst. Luckily I still had three out of five bags of pure-water that I had bought earlier from a street hawker peddling them in a wheelbarrow. Mother and Ugo would have been appalled to see the expertise with which I tore open the bags. They would have been shocked to see me drink it. I could imagine Ugo saying, 'Surely that water can't be safe to drink?' What did they know of a life without an indoor tap? I removed the sweater I had been wearing and stuffed it into my bag. I drank one bag of water and splashed a second one on my face and neck. My eyes fell on my feet. The flip-flops I wore had seen better days. The state of my feet – dry and cracked – amused me because I could imagine what my mother would say: 'Thieves' feet.' As if you could tell the character of a man from his feet. As if everyone with soft, moisturised feet was the epitome of goodness. Ephraim had soft, baby feet. He was meticulous in keeping them soft, first soaking them in a mixture of warm water, vinegar and mouthwash for several minutes, and then having me scrub them with a pumice stone, rubbing the bottoms in slow circular motions while he directed and scolded me. 'Haven't you had any sustenance today? Employ force! Rub it well!' I never thought of treating myself to the same care, even when Ephraim was out. I could not bear for him to think that I was making myself look nice for him, softening my skin for his pleasure.

The duffel bag hanging from my shoulders was light. I did not have much that could fill a bag. Having been forced to live a spartan, austere life by Ephraim, I had got used to it. What weighed me down was inside me. No bag would be big enough to carry it. I had got used to that too. But now I hoped that I would begin to discard that internal weight, shed it bit by bit until I once again became that Nani whom teachers had said was so light on her feet she could fly. 'You should run for Nigeria. With the proper training, you'll make a superb athlete,' my sports teacher had told me. If he saw me now, I thought, dragging my feet – where the burden inside me settled – as I walked, he would not recognise me. My husband was responsible for slicing me open, scooping out the essence of me and filling me up with all that dead weight.

I called Ephraim husband because he was the man to whom I was married but 'husband' has an intimacy to it which I never had with Ephraim. I did not choose Ephraim. His house had never felt like home. Not even after the children came. Number 47 Osumenyi Street was home. And there I was returning, sweaty, damp under the armpits, heavier and more broken than I was before I left. Feet cracked and knuckles calloused. I should have taken a taxi. But I had wanted to walk, to take in Enugu, to have space on either side of me as I walked back to Number 47, and now on sighting the house the heaviness lifted. This must have been how the Israelites felt on seeing the promised land. The analogy came easily. After seven years with Ephraim, I could not even make a comparison in my head without referencing the Bible. I hissed and wiped my mouth as if to wipe the taste of his name away. My lips, too, were cracked from the Harmattan and felt like sandpaper to the touch. I should have dabbed some Vaseline on them this morning. But I had not thought of anything else beyond walking out, afraid that any extra minute spent at Ephraim's would coat me in a viscosity that would make it impossible to leave. Ugo had said I would find peace here, in our childhood home, as if peace were a surprise birthday present Ugo had hidden waiting for me to discover, the way we used to do when we were children.

In the years that I was gone the essence of Umuomam Estate had not changed. It still screamed its affluence even from afar, houses wide and huge, satellite-dish masts floating like ghosts above the roofs. The road to the estate wound past a school, the private secondary school I went to, protected by its high fence with barbed-wire edges, through which, as I walked past now, I could see students in familiar pink and blue pinafores running around, blissfully unaware that the future did not always unfurl in the way one wanted. The flashes of pink and blue took me back to a time when life had been a smooth and shining thing, its glimmer a promise of a future so different from what it had eventually yielded me. Thinking of it now brought a familiar tightness to my throat.

I could hear the school bell ring for the end of break as I reached the gate leading into the estate, as if signalling the end of my life with Ephraim. Or the beginning of a new one without him. With sudden, unexpected excitement, I pictured an existence without Ephraim darkening it; saw myself working in a hospital, a stethoscope around my neck; imagined myself stretched out in front of the TV, a glass of wine by my side after a long day's work, like my mother used to do. The bell crashed into my daydream. Ding! Ding! Ding! Each ding an inner voice telling me *Leave. Leave. Leave.* My feet obeying. Ding! Ding! Ding! My pace increased. The guards at the gate barely glanced at me. They must have imagined that I was someone's maid. Once I went through, I swore to myself, there would be no turning back. This was it. I stopped, looked around, took a deep breath and, as if I was diving into water, I held my breath and walked in. The heaviness – as heavy as ice – which had suffused my body fell away completely, dissolving and gathering in pools of water around my feet as I exhaled. I was setting foot finally in the promised land. I resisted the urge to kneel in the middle of the road and kiss the blessed ground. I stood for a second to honour the moment. I did not want to attract any attention. Even though I doubted that anyone would recognise me when even my own sister had been shocked at my appearance the last time we met – and I knew that I had not improved since then – I would not take the chance. The houses on the estate were humongous, with ornate gates beside which uniformed guards sat or stood announcing frightening levels of wealth. Many of the houses still looked the same, as if time had stood still for them, but the house at Number 47 had shifted. It was nothing like the fantasy that I had carried within me: a stately, beautiful mansion with wide, sliding windows. It had transformed instead to a big, rambling object I barely recognised. One window had a crack which was plastered over with duct tape. My mother, punctilious to the point of obsession, would never have allowed duct tape on her windows. It looked like somebody else's house now, a house on the right street but one I had never been to before. On the outside it was no longer the dark chocolate brown of my memories – a colour chosen by

211

my ever-pragmatic mother for its ability to absorb the dust of Enugu and hide it – but the dull, stained yellow of a decayed tooth.

In all the time that I was gone I had never once passed by the house. I never even came anywhere near the estate. What was I avoiding? At the beginning I could not have come even if I had wanted to but much later, when I could have, I still did not. Was it embarrassment or fear that had kept me away? In any case, what would I have come back for? What friends I had here, I had lost touch with. Nkiru, Ugo told me, lived in Canada now. Montreal. The Ejimofor twins moved to London. Ugo said they were doing well, she could tell from the pictures they posted daily on Facebook. Bob and his sisters left for Berlin even before Ephraim happened. Ours was an estate in constant motion. I was certain that nobody I knew seven years ago was still around. I certainly did not recognise any of the security guards and so far nobody had recognised me, or they would have been at the door. I was grateful for that.

The house looked bigger than it had when I lived there, as if it were dough rising and expanding, spilling off the kitchen counter. Was it magnified because I had become used to small, narrow spaces? Rooms in which I could not stretch out without hitting something or walk without stumbling – like one walking in the dark – into one of the many objects crowding the space: a suitcase, a table fan, a Bible. And shoes. Children's shoes. Men's shoes. I had kept mine under the bed, hidden from view, and would have kept everyone else's under beds too but those were crowded as well. Pots. Pans. Bags. The house spawned more things than it could contain, cluttering every nook and cranny. When I saw the children stumbling and falling into the chaos, and was helpless to pull them out of it, I closed my eyes and imagined I was back home. To be here now without them, under these circumstances, felt like a betrayal. They would return to Obiagu Road, expecting to find me waiting, having no idea that I was gone. They would call for me and search for me, shouting 'Maman? Maman?' But I would not be there to love them with my hugs. They would cry for me and Ephraim would be the one they would turn to, to console them. He would be the one to hold them and tell them, 'Shhh. Stop crying. Papa is here! We do not need Maman.' They would be comforted. He would make them shriek with laughter and forget that they were missing their maman. They were children after all. I could not do this. How could I have thought that I could? Leave without my children. The heaviness that I had shaken off earlier began to sneak back in. But I had to do this. I willed my thoughts away to a future where Holy, PraiseHim and Godsown were with me at Number 47. I tried to imagine them running around in the front yard. My chest felt heavy, like I was about to cry. I swallowed to force down the lump forming in my throat. I must not think of the children now or I'd be tempted to go right back to the place I had just escaped from. But I had to get them somehow. I could not live without them.

The rose bush outside the gate was now a wasteland of overgrown thicket. The bench was mottled with bird droppings. The guava tree was gone. It was now a stump with tiny mushrooms growing wildly all around it, an amputated limb sticking out of the earth. Who would have cut it? It could not have been Mother. It would have broken her heart to see it cut down. Mother loved that tree like a child. In turn, the tree had been faithful to her, producing baskets of sweet seedless guava which she liked to peel and freeze. We made fun of her because of it, of course. We did not know anyone else who peeled guava or who ate the fruit frozen. She did not mind the teasing. Not about the guava or about any of her other habits which we found strange. Mother made her own rules and did not care what other people thought, except when it came to her daughters, where her readiness to show what a great mother she was made her even tougher. There were times I wished I had a bit more of Mother's toughness to me. Ephraim would not have been drawn to me; he would have left me alone.

I slipped the key into the padlock that kept the gate to the house locked, turned until I heard it click, and pushed the gate open. The gate too had changed. It had become arthritic and creaked louder than I remembered as I closed it behind me, pushing against it with both hands. A memory came of being carried through these gates when they still swung open noiselessly. I was about eight years old and had gone walking around the estate with Doda. I must have stubbed my toe or something along the way and Doda had to carry me back.

The guard's room was open and I looked in. The room was empty. Of course. Even though it had been several years, I felt guilty about Aziz and the punishment he suffered for letting me out that morning when I left for Ephraim's. I had never wanted him to lose his job. Old newspapers and rodent droppings carpeted the floor. Obviously Aunty Enuka, whom Ugo said came in regularly to check on the house and frighten potential squatters away, had not been in the guard's room for a while.

The jacaranda tree under whose electric blue shade we sat in the dry season was thankfully still there in the front yard, still dazzling in its blueness, but the orchard in the back yard – my mother's pride and joy – was now a sprawling graveyard of broken things: a kitchen stool; a magazine rack; a baby swing. I spied something that looked like the decapitated head of a doll. It rolled over when I nudged it with my foot and two plastic blue eyes stared at me from out of a dirty, smudged face. It looked as if someone had tried to burn it. The sight of it triggered a memory, the smell of burning hair deep in my nose. I was here to pick up the shattered pieces of my life and make it whole again. But how could I if I kept walking into memories I had no wish to unearth?

Goose pimples crawled up my arms and I half walked, half ran, dragging my bag behind my back like an indolent pet to the front of the house, through the front door and into the parlour where so much of my childhood had unfolded. But this had acquired a new smell: the sickly sweet odour of something wrapped and locked away in a suitcase full of mothballs – specifically camphor – for many years. I could not imagine where the smell came from. Mother never even used camphor. The smell disgusted her. Whenever Aunty Ichida, my father's aunt who came round often before the family fell out with her, visited, Mother would complain that she smelt too much of camphor and that it took a long time to get the smell out after she left. 'Does she bathe herself in camphor?' Mother asked once, emptying canisters of air freshener into the rooms, asking the maid to vacuum and scrub and clean as soon as Aunty Ichida left. Once, she gave Aunty Ichida a bottle of perfume, an expensive-looking bottle with a fancy French name, but Aunty Ichida had just laughed and told her, 'My dear, perfume is for young women. Who does an old woman like me hope to ensnare with scent?' Even though it is bad manners to give back presents, Aunty Ichida had done just that. 'If you want to give an old woman something, give her money, not scent.' Mother, seething, had taken the perfume back but pretended not to catch the hint about the money.

Ugo and I used to joke that whomever had designed the house lacked imagination. Ugo, budding architect then, called it 'a child's drawing of a house': a gate, a front yard leading up to a door that led you right into the living room. One door off the living room led to a guest toilet; a second led to the kitchen (which had a door leading to the back yard), a third to the study and a fourth to an annoyingly narrow hallway – a frustrating fact in our childhood when we wanted a hallway to run around in like we had seen in films on Channel 8 – with stairs to the second floor, the bedroom floor. Five bedrooms in a row, each with its own toilet and bathroom. The rooms – despite smelling different – had retained their colours but the effect was muted now. No longer bright and shiny and electric, so that Doda complained that he got a migraine from being inside and why couldn't Mother have used such bright colours for the outside of the house instead of inside where he couldn't escape it? It was like the sun shining in your eyes, he said. The walls looked almost timid now, shrinking violets of colours, not daring to show their faces. I had expected to be comforted by the familiarity of home but nothing was as I remembered it. The shift that had occurred in my own life was replicated in the house. It wore the look of having been abandoned for years, accumulating dust and grime, yet it had only been two years since Mother and Ugo left. I could not stay here. Was the electricity even working still? I switched on a light but it did not come on.

I had messaged Ugo before I unlocked the door, to tell her that I was at the house. I had not been inside more than five minutes when my cell phone began to ring. Ugo. Seven years had changed the balance of our relationship. I am older but anyone listening in would not have suspected that. Ugo sounded like an older sibling. Earlier that day, after Philo left, I had called Ugo to tell her I was leaving Ephraim. Her shout of excitement trilled through the phone. She sent me money through Western Union, 'for your ticket' she said. It was so much money the Western Union agent had refused initially to give it to me in cash. It had to be paid into a bank account, he said. I didn't have an account. I had no driving licence, no proof that I was who I said I was. He had had to call Ugo on the phone and ask her to scan her own proof of identity.

'Have you bought your ticket? When are you coming?' Ugo asked now.

'I've only just arrived. I've left him. Isn't that enough? I've left, Ugo.'

'It is not enough. What is it? You still love him? In some twisted way, do you still love him?'

'How could you?'

I had always thought love would lead me to marriage. I wish it were so. Love that so thoroughly and so completely turned my life upside down and inside out.

Love that made me lose my head and produced Holy, Godsown and PraiseHim, thoughts of whom consumed me now, wondering if I would ever see them again. That is how every story like mine begins: butterflies in the stomach. Heart palpitating. Love like a raging fire consumes you and you think you will live happily ever after but then this and this and that happens and the fire cools and you drift apart. Except that with Ephraim and me it was nothing like that. Not even close. When we met there had been no love. No fire. No palpitating heart. No butterflies. On his part it could not be love. Maybe he had been to the area and noticed me sitting outside as I usually did in the afternoons. Maybe it was not co-incidence that brought him to our house that day but a well-orchestrated plan. With him I have learned to rule nothing out.

'How could you?' I hung up on Ugo. I wanted to scream, to kick something, to wring Ephraim's neck. Why would Ugo ask that after everything I had told her? My mouth was filled with a bitter taste. I needed air. I walked around and began to open all the windows, throwing them wide open to relieve the bitterness in my mouth.

Nani

Ugo called back. 'I'm sorry,' she said. 'I'm glad you're out. Next stop is America.'

'I am just catching my breath,' I answered.

'You'll catch your breath in America. Plenty of time for that. It isn't right for you stay there, to be so close to . . . to . . . You said he threatened to burn you? Actually lit a candle and brought it to your hair? Nani, leave this minute. How. Did. You. Get. To. This? Leave!'

Ugo's voice was tight and packed. There was no space for mine to snake in. When we were younger Doda nicknamed his youngest daughter Ugo the Stubborn, the 'stubborn' soaked in tenderness. I was the Peacemaker; always afraid of confrontations, I had been the more compliant child.

'I cannot leave for America. Not just yet.'

What did Ugo know of a mother's love so strong that she stayed in hell for them? Ugo responded as if I had spoken this out loud.

'You're stronger than you think. You can. You will. Look what you've done already. Mother and I have been talking . . .'

The mention of Mother spoiled my mood. Why

couldn't Ugo talk to me without bringing her into it? I pretended that her reception had gone bad and shouted 'Hello! Hello!' into the phone, shouting above Ugo's own insistent 'I can hear you. Can you hear me? Mother and I think you should join us here.' I shouted 'Hello! Hello!' some more, drowning out her words, and then groaned for good measure, complained about the poor reception before hanging up on her. Almost immediately the phone started to ring. A ringdringdringdring that pierced through the silence of the house. I threw it in my handbag to bury the sound. I was drained. Forty minutes it had taken me to walk from Ephraim's to the estate. Forty minutes in the sweltering heat. Every part of me ached but this was an ache I welcomed. There was no point to freedom if it was painless.

I could not clear my head with Ugo telling me what to do, ordering me about. And bringing up our mother. After everything, Mother was the last person I wanted to be in a room with. I started working on my fingernails, biting them, one finger at a time. I had to get my children. I couldn't stay here. Not without electricity. I wandered from room to room, still out of breath from the walking, imagining an America where I could 'catch my breath', an America with the penumbrous calm of Doda's 'sanctuary'. Doda's study was always quiet, clean and seemed in its quietness, in the smell of books which permeated it, to require obeisance. I always felt like genuflecting whenever I went in there. We called it Doda's study but it was really the family retreat room. When we were younger we had done homework there, sitting at its enormous table on plastic chairs which hurt our buttocks. The chairs had in later years been replaced by grainy leather ones, and the table had gone, but the shelves had remained stacked with the same books: classics our father encouraged us to read and huge encyclopedias with embossed lettering on their spines and an especially expensive bible. No one spoke above a whisper in there. It was empty now, the shelves layered in dust. I felt a sense of loss so unexpected it seemed as if the ground was opening up underneath me.

Upstairs, the doorknobs were as cold as death. I bit my fingernails until they bled. I stopped in front of my former room but my hand suffered a paralysis and would not reach out to push the door open. I stood there for a while, tears gathering behind my eyes.

Ugo

In the days after Nani left, Mother, confused and dazed that a child of hers – and Nani, the quietest of all her children – should run off to live with a man, had thumped around the house, banging doors and shrieking orders at Aunty and the driver to make sure that 'Ugo does not go anywhere but to school and back'. At night she drank bottles of wine and Ugo caught her once, stumbling from her room to the living room downstairs, wobbling like an old lady, holding on to the banister to keep from falling. To save her any embarrassment, Ugo sneaked back into her room. She has never told her of that night.

Or of the nights much later, here in this house, when she's heard Mother crying softly in her room, unaware that she was not crying quite as softly as she had assumed. Or of the days when Ugo takes out the trash bag from the dustbin in the kitchen and it weighs more than normal, bottles clanging merrily against each other. And yet every morning Mother dresses up and strides out of the house like a woman for whom the world was exactly as it should be, her concealer doing a good job of camouflaging the dark rings under her eyes to everyone but Ugo.

'We'd be looking to sell in a year or two,' Mother had

told the realtor, a tall, blond woman who sold them the house. The first time Ugo and Mother came down into the sub-division to view the property, driving down from Paper Mill with its multimillion-dollar houses and lion statues standing guard at their front gates, sprawling green lawns and high trees, Mother was convinced she wanted to live here even without seeing the house. 'So much greenery, Ugo,' she said, pointing at the trees which lined the entrance to the neighbourhood. What a joy it was to her, who swore she could not live anywhere without greenery, to find an abundance of trees in the back yard of the house they had come to view. The realtor smiled, and Mother smiled back, but Ugo could see in the way Mother's lips stretched that her smile had something weighing it down.

The trees in the yard remind Ugo of Enugu and of Number 47. In the spring the leaves turn a dark green and sway in the breeze the way they do in films about serenity and joy. Fucondo, a jolly Mexican man who has mowed the lawn since they moved here, fifty bucks a week, keeps their yard as clipped and tidy as the neighbours'. 'But why the flowers no grow?' he asks Ugo each time, befuddled that the roses and the purple coneflowers and the daisies that he plants do not yield any fruit. Their yard should be a burst of colours. She chose this house with Mother, certain that they would be happy here, but the happiness Ugo expected to feel is slippery, constantly out of touch, like Mother's smile, like the flowers Fucondo plants that do not root.

The rooms of this house are large, lots of room for Mother to fill, but Mother has not tried to fill it up, uncharacteristically prudent and muted in her choice of furniture. Two loveseats in the sitting room, one side table between the two. Two of the four bedrooms are completely empty of furniture and the covered deck has a set of four wicker club chairs around a table with uneven legs which the previous tenants had left behind. At first Ugo thought it was because Mother was confident that they – or at least that she, Mother – would move back home after a year. A year was, after all, long enough for the trouble that brought them to the US to go away, to be taken care of. But even now, when it's clear that that is no longer the case, when Mother begins to talk of setting up a childcare business in East Cobb, she still makes no attempt to fill up the house.

Between Udodi's stories of humongous malls and the weekly dose of the *Fresh Prince of Bel-Air* the girls watched in Enugu, Ugo had imagined America as an expansive shopping mall full of light and laughter. The first day she took the MARTA from Buckhead to Lindbergh Center, to visit a former classmate from Enugu who was at Emory, she was sure she had ended up in the wrong country. She had to hold her breath. The station smelt like a public urinal, and at Lindbergh, where her friend was waiting to pick her up, a man walked up to her and asked if he could have the leftovers of the McDonald's lunch she had in a paper bag.

'You have beggars too in America?' she asked Joy, her friend.

'Beggars. Homeless. Cold callers. Racism. Thieves. Everything,' she said, dragging Ugo to her car, telling her to hold on tight to her purse.

'Racism, ke? Haba! But Obama is president!'

She had only been in America maybe a week by then

and had seen little of it beyond the massive Buckhead home of one of Mother's friends that they were renting while the family was away. Glass doors and a kitchen that looked like it slipped from the pages of a glossy magazine. It was easy to think of America as all sheen and glamour but the reality of it is different. The sheen of it has worn off and Ugo wishes she could return to Enugu. Not to Number 47, with its memories of familiar rooms without the people who ought to be in it – Doda, Udodi, Nani – but to a new page, a sanctuary, a new beginning. A different city. Lagos. Abuja. Port Harcourt. Or a different African country. Maybe Ghana? Mother has the means to set them up anywhere she wished. Somewhere where there is no fear of running into Cordelia or Chibuogo or Enang or any of the neighbours of Umuomam Estate. Somewhere where she can have the life she has here – imagine that back at Number 47 there is a parallel life where Udodi and Doda are still alive and Nani hasn't gone to live with a man – but without its anxieties. Nani's phone call disrupts that dream.

Nani

'Tell me about Atlanta,' I asked Ugo when we spoke again. I didn't want to talk about me, to rake over the past. I wanted to pretend that Ephraim did not exist.

'In the summer, it gets so hot that they call it Hotlanta!' Atlanta, so hot and so full of Nigerians, Ugo said, that it was easy for her to forget that she was abroad. 'It's just like living in Nigeria, only with no power cuts.'

Every week, she got an invite to a Nigerian celebration: graduation party; birthday party; anniversary; memorial; funeral; celebration-of-life parties for parents and grandparents who died in Nigeria, which Ugo went to with $50 sealed in an envelope as her 'contribution'. The pharmacist at Ugo's local CVS was a Yoruba woman, Yinka.

The nurse who saw her the day she rushed herself to the ER thinking she was dying of appendicitis (it turned out to be a really bad stomach bug) was an Igbo man named CJ who, once he found out she was Igbo too, asked her if she was married. He was looking for a wife, he said, and although America was full of beautiful women, Mami Wata women who looked like Halle Berry and Beyoncé, women any man would be proud to put up photos of on Facebook and show off at parties, finding a marriageable one was torture. A marriageable one, he said, had to be not only black but Igbo. It would break his mother's heart if he brought home a foreign wife, and he – despite their beauty – could not deal with akata. 'These black American women are nothing like our women ooo,' he had told Ugo. 'They don't have the patience our women have. They are too intense. And they can't stand pepper. Why marry a woman who can't stand a bit of spice?' Ugo looked like she would make someone like him a really suitable wife, he said. Ugo lied and told him that she was already married. It freaked her out, she told me. Someone proposing to her just like that. How could he after two hours decide that he wanted to marry her? 'Crazy,' she said over the phone, and I could imagine her shaking her head at the incredulity of it all. 'Who marries someone they hardly know?' she asked over and over again, as if pressing me for an answer. I ignored the question and asked her if she missed home.

She didn't answer immediately and I knew she did not miss home even when she said, 'A little. But I miss you. I wish . . . I wish we were all together.'

Ugo might miss me but I was sure she did not miss home because there was a farmers' market where the antidote to homesickness was weighed out in pounds and ounces, packaged and sold: 'Plantain. Guava as big as an adult fist and as sweet as Mother's guava. Yam. Nido. Even kerosene mango, can you believe it?' she had asked me. 'There is nothing to miss. The shop smells like a fish stand but I don't mind it. It's like being planted right in the middle of Ogbete market. I can close my eyes, inhale

227

and believe I'm back in Enugu.' When she had a yearning for suya she went to the store on Roswell Road owned by a Nigerian, where the best suya ever was to be found. 'It's not the same as the estate suya but it's not bad.' Trust Ugo to find ways to make up for what wasn't available. I wondered if she'd found a replacement for me.

I wished I had never asked her about Atlanta. What was I expecting? That she would tell me that she and Mother cried every day? That they thought of me every day? She hadn't even asked about my children. I stood in front of another door and twisted the doorknob to open it. It was my mother's room. The brown rug on the floor swallowed my feet. It caught me by surprise. I had forgotten how deep Mother liked her rugs, how my sisters and I used to pretend we were stuck in a quicksand in this bedroom, toppling over each other, enjoying the rug swallowing our feet. Mother's bed was still there, complete with the mattress, but the sheets had been stripped off. 'Vono Foam' was written in huge red letters across the mattress but the letters looked scrubbed out, as if someone had gone to work on them with soap and sponge intent on obliterating the red print. I had coveted this room as a child, its high ceilings giving it an elegance I thought would never be matched by any other room in the entire world. The mosquito netting covering the windows was clogged with dust. I beat a hand against the net. The freed dust flew into my nose, into my eyes, into my mouth and dragged in another memory from seven years ago.

Seven years and a lifetime.

I did not want to be sucked into the vortex of that recollection so I fought my way out of it, coughing, spluttering, arms flailing to wave the dust away from me. I held the memory and cast it as far away from me as I could, held my breath and ran out of the room.

I only exhaled when I entered the next room, the room right beside Mother's. It was as dusty as the rest. There was a reading table against a window with an empty candle wax-encrusted Mateus Rosé bottle on it. We had had lots of empty Mateus Rosé bottles used as candle holders for when there was a power cut and the generator was out of fuel. I had spent many childhood hours picking dried candle wax off them like scabs from a healing wound. I had forgotten that until now. 'What we forget,' I whispered into the room. I wondered now who drank all that liquor. Mother would drink sometimes but she was not a heavy drinker. Or maybe I had not noticed it, like I had missed other things about her until they were pointed out to me (Ephraim was an expert at that).

In the middle of the room was a bed and beside it a baby cot. It was made up as if in expectation of a baby, the sheets with blue and white clown faces, faded. Underneath the cot was a tin of infant formula. It was rusty and empty. Whoever cleared the house must have forgotten this room.

My phone began ringing again. A trilling, jarring sound that still took me by surprise.

'Ugo?' I said. 'How—'

'It's me. Mother. How are you?'

My grasp on the phone loosened so that I almost dropped it. I clutched the phone tighter to my ear. Mother sounded like a polite stranger.

'I am fine, thank you.' The response learned by rote.

If she had said 'How do you do?' I would have auto-matically responded with the 'How do you do, too?' I had learned in Elementary 3 was the right response. I had asked Doda when I came back from school that day, 'Why can't I say "Fine, thank you" when someone says "How do you do?"' And Doda had said, 'Because it is a polite question. They do not ask because they really care. In polite conversation rules matter.'

'What are your plans?' she asked.

'Plans?'

'Tickets. Travel. When do you leave? Your sister tells me you're coming to Atlanta. You'll like it here.'

'I haven't got the children yet.' Nobody was going to push me around any more. I did not leave Ephraim to be told what to do.

I could hear in Mother's silence the barely concealed judgement, the temptation to launch into a speech on Actions and Consequences. I prepared myself to match her, word for word. But then she spoke as if I had said nothing at all, nothing of importance at least.

'You might even be able to go to university and study the medicine you should have years ago.'

As if my children were the minor incidentals of an unfortunate event. Irritating fallouts that must not be mentioned. She had not even asked for their names. Rage burned within me but I could not find the words to articulate it.

'I have to . . . I have to go.' My voice was shaky. I could not break down now. If I cried now, they would be tears of fire. There would be no stopping it until it completely incinerated me.

'Okay. You know. When you're ready, let us . . . Let

your sister know. I hope you understand how important it is. This is. That you come. Call your Aunty Enuka. She'll help.'

I hung up without saying goodbye.

Nani

Holy, PraiseHim and Godsown. How could Mother think that I would abandon them in exchange for whatever her wealth could get me: distance from Ephraim. A chance to pursue my dream. It might have bought Ugo, kept her away from her only sister, but I would not give up my children for anyone. I bit my fingernails until the pain replaced my anger.

The phone began to ring again, insistently, angrily, loudly even though it was in my handbag. I dipped my hand into the bag and fished it out.

'Ugo.'

'You need to speak to Mother again. Ask for her help.'

'Please. Please, Ugo. I can't. Not on her terms.'

'What are you going to do if you don't? What are your options? You have to come here! Just ask Mother, please.'

'I do not want anything to do with her wealth.'

'How are you going to escape?'

'I'll find a way.'

'How? Did you find a way all those years your husband was abusing you? You will find it now? Nani . . .'

I did not respond. Nobody hurts you like the people

who know you the best. But nobody knows you the least like people who think they know you best. I did not tell Ugo of the day I tried to kill Ephraim. All those years he was abusing me, I did try to find a way. What did Ugo know about fighting and fighting until there was no strength left in you? What did she know about giving up because everywhere you looked you saw walls? The first sign of trouble and she and Mother dusted off their passports and ran away to America.

'I'm sorry, Nani.'

'I have to go.'

'I'm sorry. I was just—'

I hung up before Ugo could finish her sentence, so that the words hung mid-air and dissipated. I switched off the phone. I was exhausted. I was angry with Ugo. But I also felt something else for my sister, something close to envy. I could feel an itch crawling all over me like a multitude of ants. I began to scratch, scratching until the itch was replaced by an image of Ugo on the phone halfway across the world telling me what to do.

Ugo, who was away in America going to school and not missing home because of the farmers' market on Spring Road with its plantain and its guava and whatever else. And because Mother was with her in a big house with a swimming pool, 'in a neighbourhood where all the women wear tennis skirts all day long, Nani, and everyone has a dog except us!' Ugo, who could stand in a store in America and inhale and be transported back to Enugu. I wanted that life too. I stood still in the parlour and breathed in. I had a desperate yearning to smell home but instead camphor bounced off the walls and wriggled into my nose. It was a punch to my stomach, this pungent smell, and it hurt so much I cried out and slid to the floor wailing with all the unrestrained wildness of an abandoned child.

Nani

The crying calmed me. It punctured holes through which some of the anger I carried leaked out. And into those holes, in the cool, quiet safety of Number 47, thoughts of my children poured in. Those children I would have to save from Ephraim before he infected them. They were innocent and I would not leave them with a man whom I knew to be evil.

I could not bear to think of what living with Ephraim would do to them. Neither Ugo nor Mother comprehended the magnitude of the sacrifice they were asking me to make. I had survived this far because of my children. They had made a warrior of me. I could have told them how I ended up with Ephraim, starting with what happened on the night of the vigil. Time might have tempered Mother's attitude towards rape but if she could not even bring herself to ask about my children was my hope not foolish? My head spun. I found being alone slightly intoxicating. I did not drink wine – Ephraim forbade it – but I knew that this was what it must feel like to be drunk. I doubled over and began to laugh. I threw myself on the carpet, dusty from years of not being used. I spread myself out, coughing from the dust, stretching out to cover the room. I stretched as far as I could. I still did not fill the room. I wanted to spread myself so thin, like chinchin dough, so thin that every part of me covered every inch of the room. I stayed there until the lightness eased. Then I got up and I rang Aunty Enuka.

It took Aunty Enuka less than half an hour to come to the house once I called her. I held the front door open even before she had parked – screeching her tyres – and walked up to the house. As soon as she saw me she burst into tears. 'You've aged,' she said and immediately covered her mouth with one hand as if she was trying to stop herself from saying anything else. If Ephraim had not trained me well, I would have been hurt. On the contrary I felt nothing but relief, which quickly gave way to happiness at seeing such a familiar, well-loved face. Aunty Enuka came close enough to hug me and I stiffened. My body less willing to accept that which my heart most yearned for: a warm, friendly embrace. Perhaps Aunty Enuka sensed the stiffening, for her arms, already opening wide for a hug, narrowed, hovered over my face and then she held it between her hands.

'Nne m, ndo. Sorry,' she said, sobbing. Her fingers worked my face as if she were kneading dough. 'It'd kill your mother to see you like this. What happened to your face? Hai! Nne, what happened to you?' Although she was the one crying, Aunty Enuka moved her palms across my cheeks as if she were wiping tears off my own face. Still, we stood in the open door. 'What happened to you, my darling girl?'

'Aunty,' I said, feeling strangely that Aunty Enuka was the one who needed comforting more than I did, 'where do I start?'

236

I led her into the house. We stood in the empty parlour looking at one another, Aunty Enuka drinking me in. She held my face again between her hands, the way she used to do when I was a child. Her hands were warm and kind, and the clean, familiar smell of them – Lux soap – finally released the tears trapped behind my eyes. I thought I had done all my crying. Aunty Enuka gently pulled me down and we sat on the rug, our legs stretched before us.

'What happened to you?' Her voice was a fierce whisper.

'Aunty, my story is long.'

'Start from anywhere. Even the longest tuber of yam gets chopped up.'

She was sniffling into a handkerchief and she gave me one from her handbag. I held it to my nose and it smelled better than anything I had smelled in seven years. I wanted to fold myself into that smell and never come out.

'This one,' I said, pointing to the huge scar on my left cheek, 'is from a pressing iron.'

Aunty Enuka clasped my hand tighter, as if she was afraid I would slip from her clutches and leave. She stared straight ahead of her, sniffling, waiting for me to continue.

'A brother at church looked admiringly at me, and my . . . Ephraim burned me when we got home. "So that no other man ever looks at you lustfully again," he said.' I could feel the pain of the hot iron searing into my cheek. I could hear Ephraim's voice telling me it was for my own good. 'The Bible says so, Nani . . . if your eye causes you to stumble, gouge it out and throw it away. It is better for you to enter life with one eye than to have two eyes and be thrown into the fire of Hell. I am saving both you and the brother from the sin of lust.'

I could feel Aunty Enuka shaking beside me, sneezing into her handkerchief and crying.

'There are bite marks and scratch marks from the times I tried to fight back when Ephraim was teaching me a lesson in obedience.'

Ephraim's punishments differed but he had a constant ruthlessness. He kept his nails long and carefully filed to inflict maximum pain.

'I wish I had killed him! I wish I had!' I shouted now.

I got that one chance and I blew it, for after that, in addition to locking me in the house when he left, Ephraim now began locking all the knives away himself at night.

I could not tell how long we sat there, Aunty Enuka and me, but by the time I stopped talking, because I was too exhausted to go on and my voice was hoarse, it was dark. Light filtered in from the streetlights opposite the house, casting shadows on the walls. Mischievous ghosts poked their tongues out at me. Aunty Enuka, whose grip never left mine, stood up, dragging me with her. She said, 'Let's go. Tomorrow we'll go to the police station and report this man.'

Police? The euphoria of leaving, of throwing Mother's help in her face, fizzled out. Fear snaked in in its wake. Maybe I had been impulsive. If Ephraim were to hear that I had reported him to the police, he would find a way to punish me in a manner that I was not sure I could even conceive of. I feared for my children. He could keep them away from me. The thought of never seeing Holy and Godsown and PraiseHim . . . My mouth went incredibly dry and my heart beat as if I had just run a marathon. I cracked my knuckles so that I did not bite my fingernails.

'What would I tell the police?'

'The same thing you've just told me. He must be punished!'

There was a woman once on Obiagu Road who ran to the police station one early morning after being beaten by her husband. She could barely see out of one eye. She had come back chastised, announcing to the entire neighbourhood that the police had told her to go home and obey her husband. When she begged them to come with her, to ask her husband not to hit her again, she was threatened with harassing police and wasting police time. 'Who did she think she was, going to report her husband? What did she expect to happen?' Ephraim asked when he repeated the story to me. I remembered this and my courage died. I could not go through with this. But I was already in Aunty Enuka's car, my bag between my legs.

'Don't worry, Nani. He'll get what's coming to him. I'll make sure of that.'

She did not take her eyes off the road. The gold band of Aunty Enuka's watch glittered as she drove. I caught sight of it and remembered that hers was a world where the rich were used to getting what they wanted. Hadn't Mother escaped justice because of her wealth? Living with Ephraim, I had forgotten how this world operated. I leaned back into the seat, closed my eyes and let the smell of opulence which filled the car give weight to Aunty Enuka's promise.

Ephraim and the children would return on Monday. Two more days. I tried not to worry. Above all, I tried to believe. For the children. And for me.

Nani

Aunty Enuka's house was exactly as I remembered it. Smaller than Number 47 but so much better planned that my sisters and I used to daydream we lived there when we were growing up. It was a bungalow with a broad front porch. Flowers sprouted out of the dozen flower pots on the porch. The house had white metal railings running up both sides of the stairs that led to the front door. I remembered playing on that porch. Once, when I was visiting, I had got my head stuck between two of the rails. My cries had brought the grown-ups from inside the house. At first Aunty Enuka covered my head and neck with gobs of Vaseline in the hope that it would slip through. I remembered crying and being comforted by Doda's gentle voice, and Mother scolding Ugo and Udodi for giggling. Finally it was Doda who took over from Aunty Enuka, and instead of trying to release my head he had managed to slip the rest of my little body through the rails. I had to wash my face and neck several times to get rid of the Vaseline.

Aunty Enuka's parlour had wide doors at one end through which you could see her pool in the back yard. The pool shimmered like a jewel in my memory but I could not see it now in the dark as Aunty Enuka led me to a room which she assured me was mine for as long as I needed it. 'There is nothing for you at Number 47,' she said. The bedroom opened up to an indoor hot house with plants I did not recognise. Aunty Enuka had a degree in Agricultural Sciences but she worked for a rather prestigious estate agent. She had never been married and Mother used to say it was because she was too picky. 'Don't be as choosy as your Aunty ooo,' she'd warn us, teasing Aunty Enuka, 'or you'd never find a husband.' Aunty Enuka would say that she was very happy being single: 'I can't imagine tying my life down by marrying anyone.'

Aunty Enuka lived alone, and as children we had felt sorry for her because Mother said she was lonely and was to be pitied. Now I knew how misplaced that pity had been. At that age we had imagined that to be lonely was not to have people around one. In Ephraim's house I had discovered the real meaning of loneliness. One day, a few weeks after Godsown's birth, he told me that I ought to be grateful that God sent him to me to save me from the spirit of lesbianism which possessed 'your Mother and your Aunty Enuka'. I regretted ever telling him about Aunty Enuka. Everything I told him in those days when he'd come and sit at the gate, he'd filed away to use against me later. Ephraim was fond of telling me all the reasons I should be grateful to him for all the things he had saved me from. And then, to make the humiliation complete, he would ask me to thank him. If I did not, he beat me. He knew with the years, and especially after the children, that I acquiesced easily to save the children from being witnesses to his violence. When I could not, when I did not obey, and the beatings came, I tried to take them with as much compliance as I could muster to keep the damage to a minimum. I did not get out much apart from going to church but a part of me was still vain enough to want to look good there. How could I face anyone with teeth missing? I might be ugly and nobody else would ever want me, as Ephraim began to tell me frequently, but I did not want to lose my teeth. Doda used to say I had his mother's teeth: straight and even, with a front gap. I had always taken my teeth for granted but now I protected them as best I could. My face was gone. The teeth, I was determined to save. When I had terribly bad days, seeing those teeth in a mirror gave me the courage to carry on. They were not just teeth, they were a symbol of survival.

I looked around the room and the pictures on the wall seemed to be mocking me. There was a framed photograph of a little girl, smiling, underneath which was written the single word 'Happiness'. The picture next to it was of a man who might have been Aunty Enuka's father when he was young but he looked very much like Ephraim. Was my imagination playing tricks on me? It had been known to happen. After Udodi died everywhere Mother looked she kept seeing people who looked like Udodi. Once, she followed a girl into a store, walking the aisles, touching things she did not want to buy, so she could keep an eye on the girl, until she got close enough and saw that she was not Udodi. There was no resemblance at all between the two, so what had made her think she was her Udo? she asked.

I lay down in my clothes and covered my body up to my head with the blanket on the bed, even though it was hot and the air conditioner was switched off. I did not want to have to look at the pictures. I could have switched off the light but I was afraid to sleep in the dark. Not on my first night away from Obiagu Road. I had been in the dark for so long that I wanted to be bathed in light. That night I dreamed of my children. Holy was wearing the uniform of my posh elementary school. Her hair was plaited the way Mother used to plait our hair, 'somegaps', with a brightly coloured hair bauble at the root of each individual spiral plait. Holy was in a field full of flowers. She was kneeling down on one knee like she was posing for a picture but there was no photographer nearby, just Holy. I woke up shaking, as if I had a fever. My forehead was clammy with sweat. Even in the glare of the light it took me ages to recognise where I was. I stank like I had not had a bath in ages. I had forgotten to use deodorant that morning. I closed my eyes and tried to recall the dream to see Holy, and with some luck my boys too.

Nani

Aunty Enuka's house was quiet, as if it were a creature holding its breath. The silence unsettled me and I almost got out of bed before I remembered. At Ephraim's I had been woken at the same time every morning for prayers, first done with him and then with both Ephraim and the children. 'You cannot commence your morning until you have committed your acts for the day to God to bless.' He would say this without any trace of irony, so I knew that the day he raped me he had prayed too.

It occurred to me now that I did not have to leave the bed if I did not want to. Still, old habits die hard. I slipped out of the bed, knelt by the side of it, closed my eyes and tried to say a prayer, but Ephraim's face and voice interrupted me every time and I had to stop. In the end I gave up and climbed back into bed. It was strange, after many years, to wake to a room which was empty except for me. A room which did not have the pervasive smell of Ephraim. The room smelt of nothing. I could fill it with my own smell, and this thought delighted me.

At each side of the bed was a side table with a reading lamp. Opposite the bed was a dresser on top of which was nothing but a vase of flowers. If that had been at

Ephraim's, that dresser top would have served well to hold bibles and tattered motivational books. I did not want to be reminded of Ephraim but I caught myself constantly comparing my life with him to where I was now. Before Ephraim. After Ephraim. The story of my life. Parts 1 and 2 of a Nollywood film. Were the children asking about me, eager to return to 'Maman', which did not sound like me but was what Ephraim taught them to call me? I would have preferred to be called Mom. Or Mommy. 'Even if they do not speak French, I want them to have something of their country. One day, we will leave here and go back to Cameroon so that they get to know their land.' Ephraim spoke French to them sometimes but, understanding no French beyond 'oui' and 'non' (I wish I had paid better attention in class), I worried that his French was as bombastic as his English, and that his mother's might not be any good either. When she visited she spoke French to the children, which filled me with dread of their speaking the sort of French that would mark them out as uneducated. I did not want my children speaking poor French. I promised myself that once I got them, I would send them to the Alliance Française after-school programme so that they could learn proper French. And they could all start kindergarten. Holy would learn to mix with children of her age. A voice, which sounded very much like Ephraim's, asked me in a mocking tone how I was going to achieve all that. 'With the pocket money your sister gave you? Besides, Ephraim will never give those children up, and you cannot live without them, so you'd better pack up and return the same way you left.' I could consider this a short break from my real life, the voice tried to persuade me. Besides, now I was back in touch with Aunty Enuka, I could visit whenever Ephraim was out of town. If he returned before I went back, he would never leave me on my own again. If I got back before he did, he would never need to know. I might even be able to convince him to leave me with the children when next he went on a mission to another city. I could leave with them once he left. That was a much better idea. How could I have thought that I could leave him now? Without the children? And all that talk about getting the police involved. What did Aunty Enuka know about Ephraim being able to talk his way out of anything? Perhaps, right at this moment, that neighbour, Philo, was laughing at me, waiting for Ephraim to return so that she could tell him how I ran off. If all those neighbours, Philo included, hated Ephraim, then they probably hated me too. And Aunty Enuka, all she did was cry yesterday. I hadn't heard her offer any practical help, apart from the police. Ugo and Mother wanted just me. The children did not exist. Ugo spoke to me of an America that I too could discover and enjoy and speak of with confident knowledge. 'Ah! Americans are masters of both euphemism and exaggeration! They scatter praise anyhow! You enter a store and the shop assistant tells you how "preedy" you are, how "Oh my God! Your hair is fabulous", even if you have just tumbled out of bed with scattered hair. But these same people are skilled in the evasion of certain words, covering them with others so that feelings are not hurt! Fat. Ugly. Bad breath. No matter how true, they don't exist in those specific, direct terms. Ha! This is a country sustained on praise and positivity. Yesterday I went to this Naija party, eh . . .' I listened patiently, waiting for Ugo to ask about Holy, Godsown, PraiseHim, her only sister's children. She never did. Ugo had not mastered the American way of lavishing praise, even if she did not think I deserved it.

I jumped out of bed and began to dress hurriedly. There was still time to undo the damage. God please, I prayed, let me get there before Ephraim does. If I wanted a permanent break from him, I had to plan it properly.

Nani

I was at the front door when it opened and Aunty Enuka walked in carrying two shopping bags in each hand. At first she looked at me with confusion in her eyes, which moved from the duffel I was carrying to my face. But then the confusion cleared and her eyes, steely and clear, settled on me.

'Where are you going, Nanichimdum?' Even though her voice was not raised, I could tell that I had upset her. Aunty Enuka, like Mother, only used my name in full when she was angry with me.

'I'm going back to his house.'

'Eh?' She stuck a finger in her ear and pretended to clean it out. 'Say it again. I didn't hear you well. I must have water in my ear.' I knew the performance. My mother did it too. 'Say that again, I have cotton wool in my ear,' she would say whenever anyone said something so stupid she could not believe that they had said it.

Aunty Enuka pointed to the wooden table in the middle of the parlour and I sat at it, my bag at my feet. Aunty Enuka dropped the shopping on the table. Metal cans clashed against each other. She had been out buying breakfast, I could see that now. Bread. Milk. Butter. She was not like Mother, who bought everything in bulk as if she was throwing a party. Ugo said that, in America, Mother went once a month to Sam's Club or Costco to buy cartons of food. She said this as if I ought to know what Sam's Club or Costco was. Very typical of Ugo. Dropping names of places as if I was already living with her in America and all these names were commonplace for me. East Cobb. Sam's Club. Costco. Publix. Kroger. Kennesaw State University. Farmers' market on Spring Road. As if invoking the names would encourage me to leave my children behind, hop on a plane and join them. As if my life were to be lived only with them – Ugo and Mother – and my children were not real children but pencil illustrations I could erase and never have to think of again. When Holy talks, she has a habit of slicing the air with her hands. Even though she picked up this habit from Ephraim, and in whom I found it almost comical, in Holy it was endearing. Adorable, even. Whenever she recited Bible verses at church events, slicing each sentence with one hand, people oohed and aahed and told Ephraim and me that we were blessed with a special child. I swallowed to keep from crying.

'I was returning,' I said without looking at Aunty Enuka.

It was stupid being afraid of everyone. I was twenty-four years old. A mother. I did not have to be bossed around by anyone. I had to look out for myself, and more importantly for my children. Returning to Ephraim was the only way I knew to do that. Ephraim would never hurt his children, not physically. He loved them and it was that love that scared me. I feared the damage he would do to them, raising them with a love that would see him bring them up the way he saw fit. Once, I had inadvertently put too much pepper into the beans and yam I was cooking. The pepper burned my tongue when I tasted the food but I served it like that to Ephraim. I had boiled yam and palm oil for the children. Perhaps I hoped it would choke him. Ephraim took one spoonful and began to splutter and scream 'Water! Water!' He held his throat as if he could soothe it from the outside. After he gulped the water I gave him down, he grabbed me by the ears, the way he playfully pulled the children's when they got into some mischief – but there was nothing playful in the way he twisted my ears – and shouted and shouted at me. I could not make out the words because all I could hear was Holy giggling to see me treated like a child. I hated her for that, in that moment. She was only four (or maybe not even) but for a moment I hated her for choosing his side, hated her for being his, hated her and her brothers for being safe from his fists, for he'd never touch them with the brutality he reserved for me. It was a hard thing to admit to myself, this hate. And once I did, I hated myself for hating my own children. The truth was I loved them. I did not want to imagine them – Holy, PraiseHim and Godsown – years from now, walking the streets of Enugu, preying on people's goodness and judging them, seeing the world through the eyes of a sanctimonious hypocrite. I had to be a better mother. I had to be willing to sacrifice my happiness for their wellbeing.

'You were returning to?' Aunty Enuka dragged out the last word so that it came out as *Tooooow. . .?*

I could not say 'home' or to 'my husband'. Who was I returning to? I was returning to my children. I had to be there when they got home. Somehow I could not tell Aunty Enuka this. I looked down at my hands folded in my lap.

They were an old woman's hands. They seemed ossified. I could see the veins running down the back of them. My nails were bitten down to the quick. The skin around the index finger on my left hand was bleeding. I put it in my mouth to suck the blood before I remembered where I was and realised that Aunty Enuka's eyes were on me.

I could not remember when I began biting my nails but now, even in my sleep, I bit not only the nails but my cuticles and the flat face of my fingernails. I also bit around my nails, biting the skin all the way down my fingers. I sometimes bit my knuckles. Ephraim said it was a sign I had been a pampered child, over-indulged by my parents so that I lacked control (which was ironic coming from him), but he had never tried to stop me from doing it. He was wrong. It was not one of the signs of my upbringing – like poor householding – for which he beat me. I did not bite my nails when I lived at home. I did not tell Ephraim that this was a habit that started in his house. In a way, I was happy to think that there was something he thought was beyond him to try and change because I had brought it from home. The biting would have disgusted my mother, and sometimes even I had been disgusted at the sight of the damage that I had caused, but there were days at Ephraim's when sitting in the room, biting my nails and chewing on my knuckles was the only thing to offer me succour.

Aunty Enuka's eyes were no longer as hard as they had been earlier. She sighed as I hid my hands under my buttocks. She did not give me the lecture that I had been both anticipating and dreading.

'Odiegwu. Let us have breakfast. After eating, we will see what to do about those fingers of yours.'

She motioned to me to go to the table in the kitchen. 'I'll make us some tea and an omelette. Sit.'

Her voice was crisp. Starched. Sharp. I did not want to sit. I wanted to be far away from there, to be back at Ephraim's while I still had time, but I knew that Aunty Enuka would not let me go. I heard in Aunty Enuka's voice that any kind of resistance would be met with a resolute counter-attack. After all this time with Ephraim, I learned to recognise when I had lost a battle. If Aunty Enuka had to sit me down and keep me chained to keep me from leaving, she would. I knew that, and it angered me.

I said in a small, controlled voice, 'No, Aunty. Let me help you.'

I was not used to being waited upon. Not any more. I followed her into the kitchen. I could feel her eyes watching me even while she was working alongside me, whisking eggs for the omelette while I chopped bell peppers. When I was ten years old I found a stray puppy outside the gate. Even though its fur was dirty, and it had no leash, I knew the puppy wasn't an ekuke, that it had come from a good home because it had a collar. I carried it inside the house and neither Mother nor Doda scolded me because they had noticed too that underneath the dirt was a well-kept puppy used to inoculations and good food. Doda made a poster of the puppy and stuck it on the gate. Two days later a child who was about my age came to the door with her mother to say the puppy was hers. 'Ikenga's been gone for a week and I've been so worried. Come here, Ikenga!' The puppy ran into her arms and licked her face. 'Thank you,' her mother said in a British accent. 'My daughter's been inconsolable since

252

Ikenga left! Thanks.' I felt like Ikenga now. Aunty Enuka had found me and was not willing to let me escape.

We sat at the table and we ate in silence. Bread and jam and butter and tea and eggs. It might have been hot outside but the AC was humming softly, cooling us as we ate. It was like being back at Number 47. Not now, when it was all empty and changed, but before, with my family, before Ephraim. Aunty Enuka had put the chopped peppers and onions in the omelette, the way I liked. I did not know if Aunty Enuka remembered but it warmed my heart to think that it was not a coincidence, that it was a deliberate treat, that Aunty Enuka might have done it for me.

I ate, trying to think of nothing but the goodness of the food, of the cool air blowing into the room, when Aunty Enuka said, 'Nani, after food, we need to talk.'

'Yes, Aunty.'

I wished I could roll myself up, make myself so small as to be invisible. I was tired of talking, tired of excavating memories of my time with Ephraim. What was all that good for? But I owed Aunty Enuka the whole story. And I knew that she would not let it rest until she had heard everything from me, especially after the incident this morning. A part of me wished I had woken up earlier and left before Aunty Enuka found me.

I spread a generous helping of butter on another slice of bread, added a helping of the omelette and continued eating. Before I started eating I had not known I was hungry. Now I could feel the spaces in my stomach where the food had not yet got to. Aunty, at Number 47, used to say that the stomach was divided into compartments, and each compartment had a shelf onto which food went, and no matter how full you were the compartments with empty shelves would always be ready for more food. I imagined the shelves in my stomach filling up slowly.

Aunty Enuka had drunk more tea than she had eaten bread. I worried now that Aunty Enuka was not eating because she worried there would not be enough for me otherwise. The silence between us deepened. Aunty Enuka took another gulp of tea, noticed that I was no longer eating and asked if I had had enough. 'Yes. Thank you.' It was only now that I was done that I thought how my children would enjoy such a feast too. Especially Godsown, who liked eggs so much. I felt guilty that I had let thoughts of them leave me while I ate, that I could take pleasure in a meal they were not sharing with me.

I got up to clear the table. Aunty Enuka waved her hands impatiently and said something I could not catch but I knew she was asking me not to clear the table. I sat down again, and with my hands hidden away under the table I began to pick at the skin around my nails.

'I did not want to push you yesterday. You said a lot of things. Terrible things that no ear should hear. But I want to know now, why did you marry him? Why do you want to go back to him?'

'I don't want to go back to him.'

'So you say, but if I hadn't come back when I did I would have found an empty house. Your bag is still by the table. Were you just going to go for a walk with it?' Her tone was that of a parent explaining something that should be obvious to their slow child.

'I was going to go back. But not for him. For my children.'

Maybe this time I would find a way to kill him. Maybe one day he would decide he had had enough of playing families and walk out on us. Maybe one day a car would knock him down. But until then, until any of these things happened, as long as Ephraim was in my children's life I had to be in it too. Until I figured out my revenge.

'You will go back and get your children. But you cannot go back to him. Mba! Tufia!' Aunty Enuka shook her head vigorously and snapped her fingers over her head.

'If he comes and finds me gone, Aunty . . .'

'He'll do what? What are you so afraid of? That he'll stop loving you? A man who treats anyone the way he treated you does not love her! I may not be married but I have been in enough relationships to recognise love.'

'I know it's not love.'

I had broken some skin, and it hurt, but I continued peeling it. Had ours been a normal relationship, I would never have stayed once he began to hit me.

'You still love him?' Aunty Enuka sounded exasperated.

'I never loved him!'

It was the first time that my voice had risen since I had been at Aunty Enuka's. It sounded like a shriek.

'So tell me, Nani, because I am confused. Why did you marry him?'

And so I told her everything. From the night of the vigil to the pregnancy. It was the first time I had told anyone the entire story, and all at once, not in drips, and as I did I felt lighter, as if I had been walking around since it happened with a keg of palm wine on my head and could only now put it down.

Nani

Aunty Enuka pulled me up and hugged me tight. At first my hands hung stubbornly, frigidly by my side, as if they had been frozen by the cool air from the air conditioner. The only people I had hugged in seven years were my children. I would bend down and scoop them up, hug them as often as I could because that was the only thing I had to give them, something that had not been tainted by their father. Aunty Enuka now held me tight, and my hands began to thaw until they lost their frigidity and I threw them around her waist and hugged her back. It felt both familiar and strange to be hugging another grown-up.

'You'll be okay. We'll get him! I promise you. You cannot return to him.'

We will get him. I liked the certainty of Aunty Enuka's voice. I liked that she said 'we', that she was in it with me, but it also made me feel slightly guilty. How much more could I take from her before she became fed up? If Aunty Enuka gave up on me now, I did not know what I would do.

'It's all my fault. I am sorry!' I was not sure what I was apologising for but I was sure it was the right thing to do. I had after all crashed her well-organised life with my problems.

She squinted her eyes the way Mother did when she was about to say something important. I wondered if this was a habit they had learned from each other. She reminded me so much of Mother that I felt I could foretell what she was going to say but when she began to talk it was not what I had prepared myself to hear.

'Nani, nothing you did was your fault. You must never think that. I want you to get that right out of your head. That is just rubbish. I don't ever want you to say that again, you hear me?'

'Yes, Aunty.'

'Even if you had walked into his house naked, even if you were lying in his bed naked, and told him you did not want sex, he should have respected it. It is your body. He lured you. He raped you. He tricked you into marrying him. I never want to hear you say that again, that it's your fault. If you had come to me when it happened seven years ago, I would have told you the same thing. I would have made sure he got arrested and served time for what he did to you. Look at you, beautiful Nani. Look at you, and that vicious, cruel man tried to ruin your life.'

'He did ruin it.'

Mother would have said that Ephraim defiled me, would have blamed me for going to Ephraim's house, for sleeping in his bed. I imagined her sharpening her words and hurling 'Your fault! Your fault! Your fault!' at me. Three times for emphasis. No excuse would have done. Nothing, not even contrition, would have been enough. Mea culpa, mea culpa, mea culpa. Mea maxima culpa. The only response she would hear but it still would not have done. How did one put broken china together?

'No. As long as you're alive and well, you've got the chance to turn things around. He hasn't ruined it. He has delayed it.'

I thought about this. It was true, was it not? What Ephraim had done was to delay my life. I might have graduated by now, had a career, but it was not impossible to still have all of that. The way Aunty Enuka talked, it was easy for me to see that Ephraim did not have to have the last laugh.

I was now starting to feel foolish for even wanting to go back there today. Of course it wasn't my fault, I told myself, willing myself to believe it. 'But you walked into his house. You brought this upon yourself' another voice inside me said. That was the voice I was used to hearing. It had dogged my steps all these years. Mea culpa. But then, 'Even if you walked into his house, even if for argument's sake you buy this silly idea that it's all your fault, you've paid enough for it' the new voice, the one that sounded like Aunty Enuka, said. 'Just go back before you make things worse for yourself, and your children,' the old voice replied, but the new voice shut it up. 'You'd be a fool if you ever went back there.' I liked the new voice. But the old voice was insistent. It was familiar.

'Tell me about your children,' Aunty Enuka said, sitting beside me, her hands trapping mine.

I swallowed the tears that rose in me at the mention of the children. What were they doing now? They should be here with me, in a house where there was room enough for them to fly. I wiped my nose, spread my palms out, the way Doda used to do when any of us asked him a question he considered too weighty. Aunty Enuka must have recognised this gesture, for she said, 'Take your time.' She squeezed my hands gently.

How does one talk of a love that fills one's stomach like food? Of children, responsible for that measure of love but who are nothing like one wants them to be? If I heard my children outside, if I heard them speak, judging always like Ephraim, I would not have liked them. I would have wanted nothing to do with them. Holy, especially, maybe because she is the oldest. She spends her days spying out sins and presenting them like gifts to Ephraim. There were days I loathed the children but I always loved them. One day we were watching TV, I think it was a school play and the 'father' in the play came back from work and sat down to a bottle of beer. Holy, who must have been no more than four then, shouted to Ephraim, 'Papa, that man is drinking beer. He's going to Hell!' Ephraim had laughed and congratulated her on recognising sin and sinners. Holy was on a sure path to the right hand of God. Holy beamed. I tried to undo the damage whenever I could, furtively whispering in their ears when Ephraim was not looking: Godsown would not burn in Hell for lying about eating a piece of PraiseHim's meat; women who wore trousers were not 'handmaidens of the Devil'; men who wore earrings were not evil; husbands did not beat wives to teach them right from wrong, they should not beat their wives at all! But my words did not take root. They were dust. A whiff of air from Ephraim and the crew at the Apostolic Church of Jesus and His Twelve Disciples Keeping Us Safe in the Ark, where the children attended Bible school every Sunday, and they were back to their sanctimonious little selves. Even

Godsown, who was the most sceptical of the three, and therefore the most receptive to my lessons. Godsown, who at four asked his Bible school teacher why, if men having long hair was a sin, did Jesus have long hair in the illustrations of Him in the *Children's Bible*, was not immune to Ephraim's pronouncements that naughty boys and girls ended up in Hell, where they sizzled like Christmas goat. Godsown could not help himself, he questioned what he should not; he took what did not belong to him (he hid a toy car which belonged to another child at Bible school in his bag and when it was discovered – Holy had seen it and reported him – had said the child gave it to him); he slept when he should be praying, suffered long bouts of crying after each episode because Ephraim told him he was heading to Hell to be roasted by the Devil unless he changed. I could not console him. 'Nobody can save you from the Devil's fire,' Ephraim said.

Once I get them, I swore to myself, I will begin to undo all the damage Ephraim has done. I will get us a house in a neighbourhood with many children. I want them to have playmates, normal children to influence them, to teach them how to be children, to be mischievous. I had swift images of playdates and pillow fights and happy shrieks and petty disagreements, and a pet dog darting in and out. Holy, PraiseHim and Godsown climbing trees and feigning sickness to get out of school. 'I want them to be naughty,' I said. It seemed to me at that moment, when I said it, that children needed a level of naughtiness, that when people said they had a happy childhood what they meant was that they had access to a healthy amount of guilt-free mischief, which so far my children had been denied.

Nani

'I am going for a walk.'

I stood up and Aunty Enuka stood with me. She was coming too, she said.

I was not stupid. I knew she did not trust me to not go back to Ephraim's and it upset me. Everyone offering help – Ugo, Mother, Aunty Enuka – and not trusting me to do the right thing by myself.

No, I said firmly, surprising even myself by my firmness. I need to do this on my own, I said. What I did not say was that I needed to start cutting all those strings. If – *if* – I got the children, I had to be adult enough to look after them on my own. And if after all this, if we went with the police and could not get them, I had to be prepared to deal with that too. Thinking it made me feel like I was falling off a cliff but I could not let Aunty Enuka see it. Before the fear could engulf me, I walked out.

The Harmattan weather seemed harsher today than it had the day before, seeping cold air into my bones so that my joints ached. I did not want to return to the house so soon, not even to get a sweater. I walked all the way to the end of Aunty Enuka's street and turned left to where I remembered there was a park with a playground and narrow walking trails. In the past, when we visited Aunty Enuka, my sisters and I had played in that park, going down slides and climbing up tree houses. Once, Udodi was hit by a swing and had cried for so long that to console her Doda had taken all of us to Hotel Presidential for dinner. I didn't expect to find the playground in good shape, the swings and tree houses and slides still there. It made me want to cry to see that it was still as I remembered it. It was almost empty; maybe the cold kept people inside, maybe it was too early to come to the park. There was a man with a child on a tricycle. He watched as the child, most likely his, biked in circles near him. There were two children who could not have been much older than PraiseHim on a seesaw, and two women in conversation on a bench near them. In a corner of the park, if I recollected well, was a gazebo. My parents loved to sit in there while we played in the fountain opposite it, getting deliriously soaked. I began walking decisively towards where I remembered it being. I walked into the gazebo and sat on the bench. This was like coming home, not my arrival at Number 47, which was nothing like home any more. I closed my eyes and allowed memories of a long-gone past to assail me. The rest of the world could wait outside. I was grateful that this had been preserved. Tears rolled down from my eyes. At the periphery of my mind, a story Doda told us of a genie and a girl strayed. I closed my eyes, all the better to recollect it.

I could not say how long I sat there for. I might have fallen asleep, for when I opened my eyes the man whose son was riding a bike was sitting at the far end of the bench, the tricycle leaning against it, next to him, while the boy played with a bigger child near the fountain, shrieking each time they got sprayed by water.

'I feel you,' the man said to me, smiling. 'Children are a handful. I come here to escape sometimes too!'

I wanted to tell him that he knew nothing about me, to ask how he could possibly know that I was a mother, that I was a tired woman in need of 'escape'. Seven years ago I would not have thought that a twenty-four-year-old me would look like a mother. Looking like a mother had nothing to do with being one. It was a look I associated with middle age, thick waists and the onset of wrinkles. It was hurrying out of the house without making sure that your hair, your make-up and clothes were *on point*. It was, I told myself, the way I looked now. I still had the stupid scarf I wore often at Ephraim's on my head.

I got up and began to sprint back to Aunty Enuka's.

Nani

Aunty Enuka seemed relieved to see me return but she said nothing. I was grateful for her silence. She said she had been wondering what to make for lunch, did I have any preference? Did I want to go out and eat? We could go to Genesis.

'No, thank you.'

I did not want to go out. Not looking the way I did. And surely not to Genesis, where I might run into people I knew from school. People for whom life had not changed as drastically as mine had. It would devastate me to be seen like this, in another woman's clothes – for those were not clothes I would have chosen myself – looking like a much older version of the person I used to be. I told Aunty Enuka I was tired, the walk had worn me out.

'Fine! We'll eat here then,' she said brightly, in the tone of a kindergarten teacher. 'I have rice, I have fish pepper soup, I have beans . . .'

She reeled off a list of food. I picked the first because I really did not care what I ate. My mind was on other things, things I had to do. Doda used to say, 'If you wash off the dust that lands on you, no one would ever be able to tell you were once covered in it.' I needed to get rid of the dust coating me like fine hair before I could face the world again.

Aunty Enuka heated some rice and stew, and we sat to eat. Aunty Enuka was good at a lot of things but she was not a good cook. I caught myself wondering now if that was why she had never married, using Ephraim's voice in my head to mock her. *No man will marry a woman whose stew is this bland! It tastes like snuff!* I disgusted myself. Had I also changed so much inside? How had I allowed that vile man to infect me so thoroughly? As penance, when Aunty Enuka asked if I'd like some salt, I said, 'No, thank you. The food is good as it is.' Salt would have elevated the stew but I told myself that I did not deserve a well-cooked meal, not after the kind of thoughts that I had had. Also a part of me hoped that mortification might chase Ephraim's voice away. It did not. It magnified it. Ephraim was a masquerade, an unseen, impish spirit tripping my spoon from my hand so that it fell and clanked against my plate several times, causing Aunty Enuka to look at me, her face a huge question mark. I bent over my plate, gripping the spoon so tightly I feared I would bend it. I stabbed at the rice with the tip of my spoon. I had to be strong for my children. I could not let Ephraim win. He had taken enough from me already and it was time to pay him back. I scooped up more rice than the spoon could hold and shoved it into my mouth. Not a single grain fell off. I chewed determinedly. Quickly. Trying to seal the gaps through which doubts could filter in.

After the meal I asked Aunty Enuka if she could take me to a salon. I needed to get a proper haircut. In my second month at Ephraim's my perm grew out. I had always been proud of my hair. I swallowed my pride and asked Ephraim if I could go to a salon and have it retouched. There had to be a salon nearby, many of the women in the neighbourhood wore perms. Ephraim sprang up as if a bee had stung his buttocks. He reached out a hand and, grabbing me by the hair, pulled me to the room where he had a pair of scissors on a table. As I fought and begged him to let me go, he lobbed off a fistful of hair. 'You think I want to waste money on a salon? For this?' He grabbed another bunch and snipped away with the gleeful abandon of a child allowed to use scissors for the first time. 'You are very lucky I did not shave it completely!' I watched my hair fly down, gently, and gather at my feet. When I stopped squirming, Ephraim knew that he had broken me. 'It's a sin to be attached to hair. It is vanity!' I did not care that he saw me cry. For days there were moments I forgot that my hair had gone and it shocked me to touch it only to feel it short and rough under my palm, like a carpet.

I needed to go shopping, buy my own clothes, not these *things* Ephraim bought for me without ever taking me along or asking for my opinion. Long polyester dresses with collars and long sleeves, oversized like boubous but lacking the glamour and vivid colours of boubous. Modesty over fashion, Ephraim's only guide for buying clothes.

'Of course, Nani! Of course!' She sounded jubilant.

The hairdresser Aunty Enuka took me to tried to per-suade me to perm my hair. 'Natural hair is difficult to keep,' she said, touching my hair, feeling the strands between her fingers. 'You have beautiful hair, sister,' she said.

It pleased me that this woman – also in her twenties – recognised that we were close in age. If she had called me 'aunty', it would have meant that Ephraim's damage was permanent, that I had settled well into an age that I was yet to catch up with, that no matter how radically I changed my dress I could not reclaim my age. She trimmed my hair, and after it was washed and conditioned, and combed out, even I was stunned by how I looked.

I had just wanted a haircut but now I was greedy for more. A pedicure. Nail polish. I had not had another human being touch my hands and feet so tenderly for so long. I had neglected myself in Ephraim's house. My fingernails embarrassed me, and I waited for the man who inspected them to say something but he pretended not to notice. He asked if I'd like extensions. Not trusting myself to speak, I nodded. He gently pushed back the cuticles, buffed the nails and worked magic with acrylic powder. 'What colour nail polish would you like?' Bright burgundy on my fingers, red on my toes.

My flip-flops looked like an abomination. I wanted to throw them out right there and then, and ask Aunty Enuka to take me to buy shoes, but I had to be careful with money. I had so many desires, each fulfilled one dragging another. I knew Ugo would send me money should I ask her but if I was refusing Mother's help could I ask Ugo for money knowing Mother was the likely source?

Aunty Enuka said, 'You are so beautiful, Nani.'

No one had told me that in a long time. We drove

267

back to her house, and my vanity drove me again to the mirror. I was restless. Evening morphed into night and I could not sleep. Two more days. Two more days and I would see my children again.

Nani

The next day, at breakfast, my painted nails kept catching me off guard. My fingers looked like they belonged to someone else, like I was just borrowing them. As a child, whenever Mother painted her nails I would beg to be allowed to paint mine too. Sometimes she would send me away. Other times she would oblige me and I would wander around the house the entire day showing off my painted nails. Holy was being taught that make-up was a sin!

'I want my children,' I said, as if I had just come to that conclusion. I took comfort in saying it, as if by repeating it I could conjure up the children. If only there was a way I could get to them without having to face Ephraim. I did not know what it was I feared. Was I afraid of seeing him? Of what he might do to me? Or was I afraid of losing my resolve? Several times I formed the words to tell Aunty Enuka to go by herself, I'd wait for her in her house. But I knew that if I wanted my children I had to be strong enough to keep them. I had to face Ephraim and let him know that I was not the Nani he left at Obiagu Road, let him know that that Nani was dead and I had taken her place. I would have no closure if I did not face this demon. I had to look him in the eye to defeat him. I had to stare him down.

'You will get them. I promise you,' Aunty Enuka said, wetting the tip of the index finger on her right hand to seal her promise. 'Whatever you want to do, I'll be here for you. But you are not going back to that man. Over my dead body. Never!'

Aunty Enuka stood up and drew the curtains. Sunlight streamed in, blinding me temporarily. It seemed as if we had been in darkness and were now suddenly being thrown into the light.

'One more day and you will get to see them,' Aunty Enuka said. 'I promise you that.'

But Aunty Enuka did not know Ephraim. How charming he could be, how he could convince anyone that he was a good man, that I deserved whatever I got. Would Aunty Enuka be immune to his charms? Would she see through that veneer of holiness he coated himself in, quoting Bible passages to suit his case? It was very easy for doubts to start crawling in again. The nail polish on one of my toes was already chipped. I must have hit it against something without noticing. The sight of that nail polish, no longer perfect, magnified the doubts already gnawing at me.

'You don't know him,' I began.

Aunty Enuka raised a palm to stop me. 'I know all I need to know.' Her voice was hard. 'God help me if I set my eyes on him. We will not talk about him any more. I cannot wait to meet Holy and Godsown and PraiseHim.' Her eyes shone as she mentioned the children and I was grateful for that too. 'Trust me, we will get them.'

270

She had got in touch with the Police Commissioner, who was a friend of hers, a woman she had known for years, and she, the Police Commissioner, had promised to send a group of policemen tomorrow. They were to go with us to Ephraim's house. The Police Commissioner had wanted to send her men to Udi immediately to arrest the monster, Aunty Enuka said. That was how outraged she was. And her outrage would match the level of punishment she would order for Ephraim. I never had to worry about him again. I had only to think about my children, whom I'd be seeing soon. And once I got the children, then what? I still had some of the money from Ugo but it could not last forever. When we were young, Ugo, Udodi and I used to fantasise about all the things we could ask a genie for if one were ever to visit us and ask us to make one wish (and only one each). My sisters were specific in their wants: dolls with hair that could grow (Ugo), a house with a swimming pool (Udodi). But one wish to satisfy my own want was not enough for me. What about all the wishes that Doda and Mother and Aunty and all my friends might have had? If I used up my one wish, there would be nothing for them to use, and so I always said that I'd ask the genie for my one wish to be a magic lamp that would grant me an unlimited number of wishes. That way I could carry it along and fulfil every other person's wish.

Now my wishes were specific. I wanted my children. I wanted the means to look after them. I wanted Ephraim permanently out of our lives. I did not know if any genie could grant those.

Aunty Enuka must have noticed the worry lines

beginning to form across my forehead. She said, 'You will not worry about Ephraim today. I have quite a huge collection of Nollywood films. Very good ones. Let's watch some!'

Ephraim always said films lie and Christians should not watch anything that seeks to present the lie as a truth. 'And the way they dress in those films! Not fit for a Christian home.' And so in the years that I had been gone I had not seen a single film. Aunty Enuka asked me to choose. She stood me in front of a cupboard with films stacked from the bottom to the top. I shut my eyes and picked out one at random. There was no need to make a choice when I could not tell the options apart. Aunty Enuka had a smile on her face when I opened my eyes, a film in her hand. 'My favourite!' Aunty Enuka said.

We watched one film after another. I did not once bring my fingers to my mouth to bite my nails, only to be snapped out of it by the bright burgundy on them. I did not even, and this made me sad, think of my three children.

Aunty Enuka and I ate in front of the TV, watched some more films and went to bed. It was like being on holiday and I was aware that after the next day, regardless of what happened, real life would start again. Aunty Enuka would have to go back to work and I . . . I would have to . . . I would have to find something to do. If I stayed in Enugu, would Ephraim not come back for me? I could never escape him, no matter the number of policemen Aunty Enuka knew. Who was I kidding?

I brought out the remainder of the money I had from Ugo. I still had enough to buy myself a ticket to America.

How could I have thought that a change of clothes, a manicure and a pedicure could change the course of my life? Tomorrow, I promised myself, I would ask Aunty Enuka to take me to the travel agency to buy a ticket. That would be my last imposition on her.

PART THREE

The Beginning

Anaghi eni anwuru oku n'ala
You cannot bury smoke

— Igbo proverb

Nani

I fear the man who is my husband.

Finally the doubts have subsided, the tossing and turning in bed has ceased, and in their place is a certain calm at having finally come to a decision. I am at peace. I close my eyes.

Dawn breaks sooner than I expect. As soon as the alarm goes off I get up and run myself a bath. I think how strange the children will find it, filling a tub with water and then stepping into it to bathe. They are used to bucket baths. I would fill a bucket of water for them, first hot, and then cold, and carry it out to the communal shower, which constantly smelt of urine, where I would wash them, sponging their little bodies and scooping water from the bucket with a bowl to wash off the soap.

I have always liked sitting in the bath and at Number 47 I would often read in there too. Ugo said she could never feel clean in a tub and she preferred to take a shower or a bucket bath. I imagine filling the tub with toys so that the children can splash and play. Just thinking of it makes me smile but it also makes me sad because it reminds me again of everything my children have missed.

I towel my body dry and walk back into the room.

On a chair are some clothes I borrowed from Aunty Enuka. I slip on an orange T-shirt and a pair of jeans. My afro is combed out and shiny black. I look like a giant bumble bee. But I also feel like I am pumped up with light and anyone who looks at me can see its glow. For the first time in seven years I do not feel blurred, like an image from a grainy black-and-white TV show. I can finally see myself in high-definition Technicolor. The torpidity that has covered me since that first night with Ephraim is starting to clear and I no longer have lead in my feet. I am at the edge of a precipice and all I have to do is stretch out my arms and jump. I am giddy with excitement but I am also scared. What if there's nothing to catch me when I jump? As a child I tried my best to behave, so as to merit Heaven, because in Heaven I would be an angel with wings to fly. Now, for the first time in my adult life, I feel like I have wings.

Aunty Enuka knocks on the door.

'We have to eat breakfast before you leave.' Her voice does not betray any emotion. 'Whatever you decide to do, I'll support you,' she says. The same thing she has been saying since I arrived. The exact thing I wish I could believe my mother capable of saying.

Aunty Enuka looks more relaxed than I feel. My insides are churning and I am not sure I can stomach anything. I join her at the table she has already laid out. She motions to me to have some fried yam, some fried egg. She is wrapping a piece of yam in egg. 'Eat, Nani.'

'I am not hungry, Aunty.'

Even as a child, whenever I was very excited I could not eat. Excitement sits like a bowl of pounded yam in my stomach and there is no space for more food.

'At least drink something.' She is chewing. Why is she eating so slowly?

I pour out a cup of tea. Excitement fills my mouth so I cannot taste the tea. I do not want Aunty Enuka to think I am rushing her so I try my best not to look at the clock hanging above her head. My palms start to itch and I ignore them.

When did she make all this food? There is enough here for six. Apart from the fried yam and egg, there is toast and jam, leftover stew from last night, Milo and tea. I feel guilty that I did not help.

My heart is thumping so loudly it reminds me of the story Malu at school told once about a neighbour of theirs who died of a heart attack because he was so excited that he got a big promotion. 'The wife was so busy singing and dancing, she didn't see that the man was clutching his heart and dying!' Malu was known for telling lies – 'fabumistress', we called her – but now the story is making me anxious. I try to calm my heart. I pick up my fork and knife and try to concentrate on the food. I try to taste the stew, taste the beef I am eating, but it is impossible. If I die, what will happen to my children? If Ugo and Mother do not want them, will Aunty Enuka, who is only a social aunt?

Aunty Enuka eats and talks. I do not hear a single word she says. Outside, a dog barks. Another dog answers. The barking goes on for a while. The barking dies down and now the only thing I can hear is people laughing. It is now I remember it is Sanitation Day. No car is allowed on the roads until noon so we have time before we leave. Aunty Enuka's neighbourhood, like Umuomam Estate, is always clean. There is a neighbourhood beautification committee who see to it that the roads and the common park are litter-free, so Sanitation Day is just another day to them. On the last Saturday of every month they wait patiently in their homes or stand outside on the car-free streets, catching up on gossip while their children play, until noon when the curfew is lifted and people can go about their business as usual. In Obiagu women and children will be outside, sweeping the front yard, picking up the litter that has been allowed to gather all month, the gutter in front of the house fished for empty cans and plastic bags and whatever rubbish has collected in the preceding weeks. It was only on Sanitation Day that Ephraim and I mingled with the neighbours. 'Mingled' is perhaps not the right term because while everyone else mingled, chatting as they worked, we worked alongside them in silence, the children tailing us. Any neighbourhood that is dirty gets a fine from the sanitation police, to be paid by the owner of the property. Landlords of properties levy their tenants, extracting more than the fine if they fall afoul of the sanitation police. Any household that does not participate in the cleaning gets fined too. Mostly households are represented by women and children. Men help if there is anything particularly heavy to be disposed of, or dangerous. At the end of it they usually gather in the courtyard for drinks to celebrate another successful sanitation, a gathering to which we never went. 'They are sinners drinking beer,' Holy often said, proud of herself, oblivious to my quietly breaking heart. On such days, listening to the neighbours' happy chatter, hearing Holy tell her brothers that 'we do not mix with sinners', I pretended to myself that the pain in my heart was a residual one from the excessive heartburn I suffered far too frequently.

The cavalry arrive just before twelve. It is a van of six gun-toting policemen, and like other essential workers, health workers and fire fighters, law enforcement workers are allowed on the roads before sanitation officially ends. The men look like they have been handpicked for their bulk and frowning faces. They appear agitated, ready to get to work.

They troop into the house, and even though Aunty Enuka is not an officer they salute her and one says, 'Reporting for duty, Ma.'

Aunty Enuka looks at me as if I have to give the order. I nod. 'Let's go.'

It shocks me what a difference a few days away from him is already making to me. My voice is strong. My resolve unshakeable.

We will be escorted by the six policemen to Ephraim's to try to get justice. I do not know what form that justice will take. I told Aunty Enuka that I never want to lay eyes on him again, and she has promised me that it could be done. She has said nothing about lawyers or a court case. They might just beat him up and then ship him off somewhere far away from me. They might lock him up and throw away the key. For once, since Ephraim happened, the scales of justice are tilted in my favour.

Aunty Enuka's feet are tinier than mine, and so even though I am in fashionable jeans and T-shirt I am stuck with the flip-flops with the worn soles which I wore when I left Ephraim's. My toe nails shine bright red. As red as blood. *As red as Jezebel's*, I hear Ephraim say into my ears, and for a second I am so ashamed that I almost want to hide my toes. But the moment passes and a rage takes its place. I am ready to face Ephraim today. Nothing that has happened is my fault. I have silenced the other voice, the contrary one that heaps the blame on me.

The policemen wait in their car for us and when we drive they move after us in the open van. There are two inside the car, the other four sitting in the back, their long guns visible. The one in front beside the driver holds his gun out of the open window. The ones at the back have their guns between their legs. The sight of all the guns makes me a little uneasy but it also gives me faith in our mission. The men look fierce, like people who are immune to any level of charm. Their unsmiling faces console me.

When we drive into the street where Ephraim's house is my heart starts beating so fast again that I fear I will faint. The neighbours are out, pointing and glaring at the police van. Environmental sanitation has just ended, and they are carting off trash in plastic pails. I am sitting beside Aunty Enuka in her own car. She stops in front of the house, kills the engine and looks at me. I smile. It is a weak smile but it fills me with lightness.

We both come out of the car at the same time as Ephraim comes out of the building. At first he does not recognise me and then, when he does, his mouth opens and closes. He is like a puppet with an invisible hand pulling the strings. His mouth opens again to call my name. He calls me like it's a question, like he is not sure that the woman in front of him is actually me. 'Nani? Nani . . . what—'

I stop him. 'I've come for my children.' My red nails are gleaming, spitting fire. I want to strangle him.

Ephraim begins to say something but he notices the policemen jumping down from the van, their guns held out before them, and he starts to run back inside. The policemen run after him. He is shouting but I cannot tell what he is saying. Aunty Enuka and I follow the policemen. I see Philo. She drops her dust bin and her broom on the ground and waves at me. She gives me a thumbs-up and smiles. The yellow of her dress is dazzling like a promise, like a bright future.

Ephraim has run in and is trying to lock the door but one policeman leans on the door until it gives way. Inside, I can hear the children crying. I push my way in, bumping against a policeman and almost falling on top of Ephraim. Two policemen are holding him down and Holy is pulling on one of them, shouting 'Let my papa go! Leave Papa alone!' She looks at me and looks away. She does not recognise me in my strange clothes, red lipstick and eyeshadow. My heart splinters. I call her by name. I spread my arms to gather her to me. She looks at me again, looks away, then she looks back, peers at me and I see the recognition in her eyes. She looks confused. She is crying and thick snot is running from her nose but she does not come to me. Three days of being away from them and already I am a stranger. The change of clothes was perhaps a mistake. Children forget easily, I know, but this knowledge gives me only scant comfort. It splits me open, pulls my heart out and crumbles it.

'Where are your brothers?'

She points to the bedroom with a shaky finger. I go in and I see that Godsown and PraiseHim are on the floor, crying too. At first they do not know who I am but when I call them by name they run to me and hold me around my legs. 'Maman!' they shout then, happily. Dazed. I can smell their fear.

'We are leaving,' I say. I hold their hands and bring them out to the parlour. Ephraim is standing between the two policemen, Holy is in front of him, still crying. She does not come when I call her. 'We are leaving, Holy,' I say.

'Papa?' PraiseHim says and I hush him.

'It's okay,' I say.

Godsown says nothing, just looks at Ephraim, and at me, but he does not loosen his grip on my fingers. I nudge the two of them towards Aunty Enuka, who is waiting outside the door. She smiles brightly at them and holds out a lolly each. They look at me and I nod. They run over to her. I stretch out a hand to Holy. She ignores my hand.

'What of Papa?' she asks. For a child, her tone is defiant. She reminds me of Ugo.

'Nani?' Ephraim says. His voice is cracked. 'What's the meaning of all this?' I am not sure if 'all this' refers to my clothing or to the policemen in his house or to his being held. Whatever it refers to, my response covers them all.

'I am free,' I say. It is the first time I say it loud. There is a sweetness to it. The fear is gone.

He begins to cry. Quiet sobs with tears rolling down from his eyes. Holy looks startled. At first, I am convinced that he is faking it, master of deceit that he is. Then I see a look in his eyes that I have never seen before. He looks bewildered, as if he cannot quite believe what is going on. He is caterwauling in the abandoned, heart-wrenching way that children do. Holy joins him, their voices mingling and rising. I cannot feel sorry for him. I must not feel sorry for him, and so I steel my heart against him. I cannot stand it that, again, Holy chooses him, that even now, when I have come to take her, when she has been away from me for a few days, she is crying for the man she has been with the entire time. I pull Holy away from him. She is wailing and beating me, punching me wherever she can, shouting that she wants her papa, but I hold on tightly as I walk out, amazed at how strong my little girl is. I hear Ephraim's screams, I hear the sound of the handcuffs close around his wrists. Perhaps I imagine that I hear it, for I do not turn back. I shepherd the children into Aunty Enuka's car, Holy fighting me so that I drag her and push her, struggling and wailing for her papa, into the car. 'Papa! Papa!' she screams until I close the door and she beats on the window of the car, asking to be let out to go back to her papa.

I have been holding my breath and now, in the car, I exhale. Aunty Enuka says, 'The Police Commissioner has promised me that he'll stay behind bars for years. He won't have access to anything. No lawyers. No bail. Nothing!'

I want Ephraim punished but like this? My mother used to say that in this country it did not matter what you knew but who you knew. If Aunty Enuka's Police Commissioner friend has promised that Ephraim will never be let out, I can relax. Yet I find that I cannot. Ephraim doesn't deserve to be let off scot-free but everyone deserves recourse to justice, surely? An itch starts between my brows but gives up and recedes almost immediately. I am free of Ephraim. Shouldn't that be enough?

I lean back into the seat. It is as if I have been walking around for the past seven years with a knife stuck into my neck and now that knife is being removed, a little at a time. One day in the future I will not even have the remembrance of this pain. But now Holy is still crying and calling for Ephraim. Each mournful 'Papa' is an arrow that pierces my heart. She is a child, I remind myself. She does not mean to hurt me but it is hard not to feel betrayed. A sensible voice whispers in my ear that this too will pass. I have a lifetime ahead with her to make her forget Ephraim. PraiseHim and Godsown are sucking on their lollies, sticking their tongues out at each other. PraiseHim's yellow and Godsown's blue. They're giggling at something Aunty Enuka is telling them, their laughter ricocheting off the seats of the car already sounding like the future.

Nani

I have been through hellfire and survived. But I cannot rejoice yet, not fully. I did not take anything from Ephraim's house apart from the children: my trifecta of joy. I do not want any reminder from Ephraim's. Nothing to ever remind me that I had once lived there, nothing he may have touched, not even the children's clothes, nothing. The money from Ugo is almost gone. I asked Aunty Enuka to stop at a boutique so I could buy clothes for them. A pair of shoes for me, three pairs of trousers and shirts for Godsown and PraiseHim, and for Holy a pair of jeans with flowers on the bottom, some dresses and a blouse. I have almost nothing left over. When Aunty Enuka brought out her purse to pay for the clothes, I would not let her. 'I want to be the one to buy their first set of new clothes, Aunty. Thank you.'

We have been in the house two hours already and still Holy has refused to touch either Aunty Enuka or me. It is as if we are contagious. When I showed her the hair baubles I bought for her, she knocked the pack out of my hands. She would not try on any of her new clothes, pushing Godsown away when he strutted next to her in his new trousers. She pushed him so hard he almost fell. 'Holy!' I shouted, scooping up Godsown.

She has refused to eat anything, even the pizza Aunty Enuka ordered, and which she has never had before. I had thought once I had them with me I could begin to erase whatever trace Ephraim left of himself on them but Holy is defying me. 'I want Papa,' she says, about to cry. She has kept up this litany since we came in, and I have gone from being heartbroken to anger to irritation.

'Papa is gone. He's not coming back! It's just us now.' My voice can't conceal my irritability. She looks at me out of Udodi's face but her eyes are Ephraim's. They have the malicious glint of his. 'I want Papa,' she says again, stamping her feet. I stoop to her level, hold her wrists a little tightly. 'Holy, Papa is out . . . gone . . . and I am very, very happy!' I am shocked at the little happiness I feel when she winces. 'Come and eat pizza, you'll like it,' I say.

'No. I want Papa!'

Godsown hums his joy at this food with pieces of meat covering every inch of it. 'It's *sweet* food, Holy,' he says through a mouthful, going towards her with a slice in his hands. 'Try it.' He extends the pizza to his sister. He spits food when he talks. She ignores him and moves to another corner of the parlour.

'Go back to the table, my darling,' I say to Godsown.

From where Holy stands she has a view of the pool. I imagine its blueness attracting her like it used to do my sisters and me.

'Would you like to learn to swim?' Aunty Enuka asks, standing behind her.

Holy turns, looks at her and says in a crisp, adult tone, 'Don't talk to me. Mami Wata lives in that water. It is evil!'

Her voice staggers me. 'Holy!' I shout. 'Apologise to Aunty Enuka! This minute.'

I am standing in front of her, blocking her view. I do not know who this person is. I worry that I might not be equal to the task of loving this usurper of my daughter. Holy stares at me, as if she is measuring me up. She says nothing. I lift her, kicking and shouting, and lock her inside my room. I am out of breath and very close to tears when I come back to the sitting room.

'I am sorry,' I say to Aunty Enuka. We can hear Holy pounding on the door. Each thump tears off a piece of my heart.

'She just needs time to thaw,' Aunty Enuka says, and I imagine this child all frozen. How much time is enough? At what temperature? My body is on fire, my head throbbing.

PraiseHim and Godsown run around the parlour touching things. I tell them to be careful, afraid that they will break something, but Aunty Enuka says it is fine. 'Let them touch. There is nothing here that is not replaceable.' PraiseHim runs his hands along the floor lamp, leaving fingerprints on its wide, polished base. Godsown goes to the cupboard with the DVDs. I think uncharitably that they are like wild animals. When they ate the pizza they took huge bites, tearing their pieces apart like feral creatures. PraiseHim licked the knife with which Aunty Enuka sliced his pizza and I told him off immediately. How had I not noticed their manners before? It embarrasses me now. Even though Aunty Enuka's smile never falters, I cannot imagine that she is not disappointed in them. At their age my sisters and I would not have been running around like this in someone else's house. We would have known it was improper behaviour. But of course my children have never visited anyone. Their outings have been limited to Bible school and church.

When the thumping stops I go to talk to Holy. I find her on the floor in the room, worrying an old scab on her knee, muttering under her breath. She looks so small and so like her old self I want to cover her in kisses. At Ephraim's I would have told her to stop but I am finding it difficult to be her mother here. I am not sure I am up to the task so I have lowered the bar. I am aiming for her to like me now.

'Holy,' I say as I slide on the floor beside her. I poke her playfully with my elbow. She eyes me and then she mutters again. It is louder but I do not quite get it. 'What did you say, darling?' I smile at her, sorry for my earlier outburst, willing her to revert to the Holy whose hugs came easy. I reach out and touch her shoulder and she shakes my hand off.

'You are the Whore of Babylon!' she says. She does not sound like a child. Her voice is steady and deliberate. It could have been Ephraim speaking. He has perfected his sanctimony in this little girl. She sneers and says loudly, 'I want Papa! You are not my maman. You are the Devil!'

It takes everything in me, every bit of love in me, to summon up the self-control needed not to hit my own child.

I can hear Godsown and PraiseHim tearing around in Aunty Enuka's back yard. Aunty Enuka is outside with them. I think she is avoiding being in the house with

Holy. If she were not mine, I would not want to be in the same room as her either. I watch her like I'd watch something dangerous.

Yet I love her.

Nani

The children are sleeping, even Holy. Watching her sleep, I see the girl that I wanted to save. She looks so much like Udodi my breath catches. 'I'm sorry,' I whisper to her. I can't believe I came close to hitting her. 'I'm sorry,' I whisper again. It is easier to like her when her features are softened and she is not sounding like her father. I touch her, stroke her cheeks, kiss her forehead without being shaken off. How long does it take for a girl her size to thaw?

My freedom is worth nothing if I spend it stuck in Aunty Enuka's house. Mother will not have all of us in America, and I will not budge. Who would I leave the children with now, even if I wanted to change my mind? Cordelia had cousins who lived with them when we were younger. Twin boys whose widowed mother was working as a teacher in London. Cordelia's father, who was their mother's brother, had taken them on so that their mother could settle and make some money before sending for them. Cordelia said that whenever their mother came on holidays, which was only once every year, it took a few days for the boys to talk to her. They were eight years old when I left the estate, and their mother had been away for four. They called Cordelia's mother 'Mommy' and had to be encouraged to use the same honorific for their mother. 'She has been crying since she arrived,' Cordelia told me once when the woman was visiting. 'She says she isn't going back to London but Daddy told her she has to choose. Missing the children now so she can earn money or coming back and having to beg for money to send them to good schools.' I hadn't thought it a sacrifice then. The twins were being well looked after by Cordelia's family. They ran around the house as if it was theirs. They did not look out of place.

My children look out of place in Aunty Enuka's house, where there are too many shiny things to smudge and too many fragile things to break. And too many opportunities to show me up. I do not want to ask for Mother's help but I cannot ask Aunty Enuka. She has done enough already.

A man who lives by the river does not use spit to wash his hands, and so I tell Ugo I need money, a loan. I need enough, I say, to rent a place. I need to put the children in a school. I need school fees. It pains me to have to ask. I feel like a hypocrite. I remind myself that I am doing this out of love. Love for my children. Doda used to say that one must not swallow phlegm out of shame. Still, there are limits. I cannot bring myself to ask Mother.

Ugo calls back within the hour. Number 47 needs a caretaker. 'Mother says she can give you a monthly salary to act as a live-in caretaker. She says think about it.'

In the silence of the night I do nothing but think. Number 47 is no longer the home of my memories. I can't live there, surrounded by ghosts and bad memories. If I throw this back in Mother's face, what are my options?

I fret all night and by the time I fall asleep it is almost dawn. I am awakened by PraiseHim and Godsown's loud laughter from the parlour. They are sitting on the floor in front of the TV watching a cartoon. Holy is sitting on a couch. I cannot tell if she is watching or not. She looks at me, holds my gaze and looks away. I tickle Godsown and he turns back and sees me and gives me a hug. PraiseHim says, 'Maman, watch!' I sit and he crawls into my lap. Tears blur my vision and I cannot tell what it is I am watching. It is a short while before I realise that it is Tom and Jerry. The cartoon of my childhood. Udodi, Ugo and I spent hours watching it as kids. My childhood is intersecting with my children's the way I had dreamed it would for so long. I place a hand on PraiseHim's head. He does not notice.

If I do not take Mother's money, how would I give them all of this? If I take Mother's money, how would I live with myself?

Ugo

After the phone call with Nani, Mother spends some time pacing. Finally, she turns to Ugo and says, 'I admire your sister, the way she's standing up for her . . . for the . . . for those kids.' Ugo can tell that she is trying not to break down. This is not the mother who said that Nani was dead to her, who swore to Ugo, after Nani left and she discovered that Nani was with a man, that she never wanted to set eyes on her daughter again. Ugo doesn't know how much Nani has told her but Mother looks the oldest she has seen her. The fine lines around her eyes have deepened. Haba! She looks like she went to bed her real age and woke up thirty years older.

Mother pours herself a glass of scotch and sits at the dining table. It's too early to be drinking, not even noon yet, but Ugo says nothing. Mother knocks back the scotch, wipes her mouth with the back of her hand and buries her face in her palms. Ugo thinks of the story of the Prodigal Son and she knows for certain, for the first time, that if Nani were to walk in Mother would give up everything for her. It is a thought that warms Ugo. She gets up and hugs her parent from behind. Ugo takes a glass and pours herself a bit of scotch too and sits opposite her mother. The liquor burns as it travels down her throat; it's as if someone were reaching in and hugging her from inside.

'What I did, with the clinic and everything, it wasn't really bad, you know?'

Ugo nods her head. She knows that Mother believes that she was doing good. If she hadn't taken the women in, they would have ended up on the streets, or dead, their body parts chopped up by ritualists for some get-rich-quick scheme, fa. She's told Ugo this several times. If the government had a way of looking after the women, she never would have intervened. She repeats it as if she's trying to convince Ugo even though this daughter has never faulted her for it.

'You did what you had to do, Mother.'

This is the first time, in a long time, they are actually talking.

'When I left I made sure my nurses, my patients, I left them money. Lots of it. Yet . . . your sister . . . Nani doesn't want my money. She doesn't understand but she needs it.' Ugo nods. 'What's she to do without money? Your father left no will, he never thought . . . everything he had, I own. Nani should have what she needs.'

'I'll try and convince her.'

'No. No. She's stubborn. She won't take it. We don't . . . we don't want to scare her . . . we don't want her to return again to the . . . to him.'

'Never!'

'She . . . she stayed with him for a long time . . . had his children.'

'Maybe I should talk to her again?'

'Never mind. I wish . . . I wish I had found her before

'. . . I should have gone looking for her. Even if she doesn't want to come here . . . we have to . . . she has to be comfortable enough, so she never returns to . . . him.'

'She won't come without the children, Mother, you know it.'

'I am not ready. I don't know . . .'

Mother's voice is breaking again. Ugo wonders if she is thinking of the grandchildren she won't acknowledge. Ugo remembers coming face to face with the children in whose faces she could see pieces of Doda and Mother and her sisters and herself, but who also looked nothing like she'd imagined her parents' grandchildren would. She tries to place them in this house, in the big back yard, in the swimming pool, living the life that she and her sisters would have liked to, but their faces blur into one unrecognisable mess. She should ask Nani to send pictures. She wonders: what would it be like to have them all here? *Am I a bad person for wishing my nieces and nephew don't look like they do?*

'My poor, poor daughter,' Mother says but now she is crying. And for the first time Ugo realises that she knows what happened to Nani. She has guessed it – or maybe Nani told her – but she will not speak of it because it's too dark, too heavy. None of this was what Nani wanted. The vigil to the three children. Ugo doesn't know how Ephraim convinced her to marry him but she does not need to. Mother is crying loudly and messily, like Ugo's never seen her do before, for all that has gone before. Her tears are her way of asking for forgiveness. Ugo holds her and her own tears begin to fall too.

Portrait of a Family

It takes a child five days to thaw. It begins in her legs and then moves up to her throat so that she begins to sound like herself again.

At breakfast on the fifth day Holy asks me if she can grow her hair long enough to hold it in two ponytails like the girl she saw on TV. It is the longest she has spoken to me. It's a gift that I gratefully accept.

'How long do I have to wait, Maman?'

'Not too long,' I say. 'If you let me plait it, it will grow quicker.' I picture her in somegaps like I used to have at her age, baubles around the root of each plait. I am almost breathless with excitement.

'Can we start after breakfast?' she asks, bouncing softly on her chair, her eyes wide and pleading. Please! Please! Please! Please!

Holy. PraiseHim. Godsown. Named by a man whose name I refuse to utter, whose name I have expunged from my system and banished to the underworld where it belongs.

My children start school with new names: Anuli. Ndu. Oku. Joy. Life. Light. A triptych of my flesh and blood. My dream for our family: life bookended by joy and light.

Anuli says she wants to be a teacher when she grows up. She plays school with her brothers when she comes home every afternoon. I tell her she can be anything.

Ndu says he wants to fly. I tell him to dream. To fly, you must dream, I say. People without dreams cannot fly.

Oku says he does not want to be anything, he wants to live at home with me. I tell him that is fine too. You'll always have a home with me, I say.

I am untangling my life, reordering my dream. Number 47 is a tomb. I cannot breathe there, as full as it is of dead and decaying things.

'Tell Mother no. Thanks but no,' I tell Ugo on the phone.

'Are you sure?'

'I am.'

'Your father left you money in his will,' Mother says, coming to the phone, taking over from Ugo. 'If you won't take from me, then take from him.'

Even from beyond the grave Doda is watching out for me, making sure that I am safe.

'At night Mother cries,' Ugo tells me in a whisper. 'Can you imagine it?'

I try to imagine Mother with her solid heart crying but I can't.

'She doesn't know I hear her,' Ugo says.

There is so much I need help with, navigating this new phase. I can't even get a loan by myself. I have no collateral. Aunty Enuka has to co-sign for me but I get a loan to set up my own business, a small restaurant near the house. I call it Nani's.

Some of my favourite memories with Doda are of the times we spent together at restaurants. This is my way of paying tribute to him. My name is emblazoned on its front in shades of red, like tongues of fire. I employ a young woman, not much younger than I am, to do the cooking. Her egusi soup with periwinkles is an immediate hit with the civil servants and university students who come in every afternoon for lunch. These are the days of small beginnings. But I am already dreaming big and I am ready to soar.

Money from Doda's will rents me a house on a street with lots of trees. In every room there are flowers in vases. In the back yard there is a rooster the children have named Wacko. Ndu says Wacko cannot tell time because it never crows at dawn. Sometimes at night its crowing keeps me awake. Anuli wants a swing in the back yard. One day, I tell her. And will they meet my sister? And their grandmother? One day, I say again. 'One day you will.' I am not surprised that I mean it, that excitement flutters near my belly button and spreads outwards like a wing when I say it. Mother and Ugo have been calling daily. 'Just to ask how you all are.' I do not mind it as much as I had thought I would. Perhaps not having to rely on Mother for money makes it easier to accept her attempts at reconciliation.

One day she calls and Holy gets to my phone before me.

'Hello? This is Holy. Sorry, Anuli.'

I stand by the door and watch my daughter drape herself in her new name. The joy on her face when she shouts 'Oh! My grandma?' pulls at my heart and I gasp. When she gives the phone to me Mother does not hide that she is crying. I cannot hear what she's saying through the sputtering but it does not matter. My heart can make out the things my ears cannot decipher, and it is full. It is overflowing.

Udodi, the Chorus

Whosoever's voice is heard is not dead:

Once upon a time, a girl was wandering the bushes. She had no parents, no family, no one looking for her. Her life had been one of drought. O di ndu onwu ka mma. One who's alive but who'd rather be dead. What joy it'd be to fall asleep and to never wake up, she said to herself often. Once, she ate a plant she believed to be poisonous. It cramped her stomach and gave her watery stool for days but she did not die. She lay beside trees and hoped a wild animal would kill her. She prayed for her death to be swift and painless and clean. The wild boar and the lion and the tiger and the hyena and the cheetah and the wild dog all sniffed her and went their way.

One morning, a magical bird attached to a ball of yarn came to her and said, 'If you unravel this yarn, I'll turn into a genie and I'll grant you whatever you wish. But be careful not to break the yarn or both our lives will be ruined. Oh, and you cannot ask for death, for I cannot grant that.'

The girl who had nothing to lose thought about this for three minutes. She said to herself, I'm o di ndu onwu ka mma. If he cannot give me death and I succeed, maybe I'll live a life worth living. If I fail, well, I can't go any lower when I'm already at rock bottom. So she accepted the challenge. She worked all day and all night. She worked carefully and quickly. She unravelled the yarn and a genie appeared to grant her her wish: a light within her to give her hope; flowers that bloom all year round, purple and pink and red and yellow – a riot of colours to fill her days, the sweet fragrance of roses to make her head spin; freedom and a new life.

There are days that girl won't be able to breathe for happiness; there will come a day she will forget that all these – the joy and the flowers and the colours – were once new and she will want more because to forget and to want is human.

Acknowledgements

First of all, Baba God, thank you, Ekene dili onye nwe anyi.

It takes a village to birth a book, and I am incredibly grateful for mine. Thanks to the SYLT Residency for African writers in Germany, where the first draft of this novel was written many years ago, and my employer, Georgia College & State University, Milledgeville, for the Faculty Research Grant that enabled me to travel to Nigeria to research baby factories.

And to the two friends who wouldn't want public gratitude, for providing me space in Lagos to work on the edits. I'm so glad you're in my life.

And to Dr Ezechinemelu Eloka Umeh for the Igbo creation story with which Udodi begins the book. I ga-adi.

And to Sandra of the Red Cross and the young women who shall remain unnamed, who spoke to me of their experiences;

And to my early readers, Shulie Son and Brian Chikwava; Ada Onwudiwe and Ike Ilegbune. Also Shulie's cakes are the best!

And to Anja Sebunya and Rose Sackeyfio too;

And to Chikodili Emeleumadu who's been waiting for this book.

And to Kate Johnson, my agent, for walking this path with me.

And to Ellah Wakatama, my editor, who has the best eyes in the industry, who'll never grasp the magnitude of my adoration for her.

And to Michelle Dotter for providing a wonderful US home at Dzanc for this baby;

And to Lorraine McCann, my copy-editor, and Rali Chorbadzhiyska for your notes and line edits and queries.

And to Oby Omenka, who shared the story – and most likely has forgotten – of a former FGGC Benin girl who fell into a 'one-chance' relationship with a man much like Nani does. I'm still rooting for her.

And to every single member of my team at Dzanc and Canongate.

And to Mrs Weruche Emeruem for being my 'Number One fan' ☺

And to her daughter, my sis, Dr Ebere Okereke for letting me know;

And to Amaka Omenka and Ndidi Obele, BFFs from UNN;

And to Daria Tunca and Liesbeth Bekers for the paprika chips, the Antwerpse handjes and everything else;

And to Enyi Omeruah for cheering on every single thing I write;

And to Obiageli Anozie Aniagoh aka Virtuous (☺) for the long phone calls;

And to Uwem Akpan and Samuel Kolawole for letting me rant when I've needed to;

And to Chikere Ezeh for the online games of Scrabble (go play your turn!);

And to Chioma Offodile; Ben Egbuka (cosmic twin); Frances Ogamba (sorry the title changed, but I'm still going to rock that T-shirt); Kasimma Okani; Uka Olisakwe; Diane Tanger; Nkem Umeh; Kelechi Ohaegbu;

And to the other friends I haven't mentioned here, but you know you, because a girl is nothing without friends.

And to my nieces and my nephews, Songoli and Bo Nnawubas (and BJ); Duka and Maya Nwosu; Ayanna and Bianna Unigwe; Stephanie, Debbie and Cindy Okeke (and Dominic); Odera, Kosi, Dumebi, Kamso and Zite Unigwe for expanding our family and bringing us so much happiness.

And to my nieces and nephew across the pond, Heline, Sarah and Marijke Jaf; Koen, Leen and Inne Vandenhoudt for being so magical.

And to Jane, Winnie, Vic, Maureen, Okey and BG, for being the best siblings ever, and my loudest drum-beaters.

And to my mother-in-law, José Branders, who (together with my father-in-law, Rene Vandenhoudt, of Blessed memory) carried a lot of the burden of raising our boys when they were young(er) when Jan couldn't, so that I could write and go on residencies.

And to my parents, Ochiagha Fred Unigwe and Afuluenu Winifred Teresa Unigwe, for never doubting, for their unconditional love.

And to Stefaan Nkeazi, Ralueke, Tomike and Jefeechi: suppliers of great hugs, givers of thoughtful gifts. My pride and joy. I love you kids to the moon and back. Jan and I are blessed to have you.

In Jan's native Flemish, an alternative translation for 'I love you' is 'Ik zie je graag', which literally means 'I like to see you'. In my native Igbo, it is 'afu m gi n'anya' (I see you with (my eyes)). Isn't it beautiful that both phrases have 'see' as the operative word? We cannot begin to love if we cannot see (the other).

And so, to Jan – who sees me fully and therefore supports me fully and therefore completes me fully. And who still brings me coffee every day.

And finally to you, Dear Reader, because a writer is nothing without readers. You are appreciated.